THE REVELATION OF EARTH

THE REVELATION OF EARTH

◄◄◄◄  ►►►►

First Contact

As penned by
Frank Sims
Chief Archivist of Haven Tower
Year 2323 on the Pre-Cataclysm Calendar

iUniverse, Inc.
Bloomington

The Revelation of Earth
First Contact

iUniverse books may be ordered through booksellers or by contacting:

iUniverse
1663 Liberty Drive
Bloomington, IN 47403
www.iuniverse.com
1-800-Authors (1-800-288-4677)

ISBN: 978-1-4759-3506-6 (sc)
ISBN: 978-1-4759-3507-3 (hc)
ISBN: 978-1-4759-3508-0 (e)

Library of Congress Control Number: 2012912061

Printed in the United States of America

iUniverse rev. date: 07/18/2012

TABLE OF CONTENTS

PROLOGUE

This is the first episode in the event known as the *Revelation of Earth*. I am Frank Sims, chief archivist of Haven Tower. Both my boss and my benefactor have tasked me to produce a narrative of the Revelation Event to make the historical records more appealing to read. The event will be added to the <u>Chronicles of the Talon</u>, a collection of stories detailing my benefactor's life. I am an eyewitness for much of this event and this is the reason for which I have been chosen for this task.

The year is 285 on the Post Cataclysm Calendar. My benefactor and my boss have requested that I use the old Christian calendar format in order to maintain continuity with previous archival entries. All dates are hereafter given in said format. The year, then, is 2323AD. Thankfully we still use the same twelve month calendar system.

I will also use the galactic date system where appropriate. Thanks to an apparent fact about life, what produces and sustains it, most planets naturally able to support life have a day and year that is not too dissimilar from that of Earth's. The galactic community uses an average of these numbers to create the Galactic Standard Time, or GST. Most local star systems only use their local time formats. Star system governments use the galactic calendar when necessary. The Iksus, whom I introduce later, are one of the instigators of this system and use it on a regular basis.

All instances of Iksus records contained herein are in the galactic format. Months and days are given in local time and the Iksus have an extensive library of date formats. Months and days in systems which they have no data on are given in a simple progressive number format starting with zero.

1

This is galactic year 8719, or eight-thousand seven hundred and nineteen, years since the last Ikar'ys invasion. I include with all Iksus dates those of Earth time. Some entries overlap with others and I found it difficult to keep track of who was where when. I expect this will also aid the reader in maintaining a proper timeframe.

It is important to keep in mind that any military keeps a full twenty-four hour day and so do their records. I do not include the exact times at which events happen. So, "Early Moring" is after "Mid-Night", and "Mid-Morning" is half way between "Early Morning" and "Mid-Day", and so on. I say this in order for the reader to make sense of any apparent discrepancy in timing. It would be a tediously boring read if I kept the original formats.

I must at this point emphasize that this is a historical narrative work. I have condensed all journal entries and military records and turned them to narrative with the exception of those of Mr. Artus and the Iksus Admiral. The information provided is correct. I have met with and interviewed the persons involved. I've only included that which they allowed. Each individual has been given a copy of the final draft for review and are accepting of my portrayal of events. Bear in mind that this is an archive entry, and the focus is only on that which was deemed most important.

I have been instructed that a brief introduction of certain information be given to inform the reader of some history. The following is my understanding of the particular archive entries my benefactor wished me to reference:

The Cataclysm that I have already mentioned occurred in or about the year 2039. It has been learned that it was initially caused by the rogue asteroid Apophis, which many believed had a very high improbability of impacting Earth, but a margin for error did exist. To make the situation worse, the asteroid hit a place in North America known as Yellowstone.

Yellowstone was a National Park of the old United States and was also a super volcano. The asteroid impact caused the already weak surface crust over this volcano to give. The resulting eruption was not as violent as was feared. It was a slow eruption that lasted for nine days and covered much of the Earth's surface with an ash cloud.

The temperature plummeted and sheets of ash and ice up to a mile thick formed and covered much of the northern and southern latitudes to nearly 45 degrees on both hemispheres. The ice has receded to between 65 and 70 degrees. A thick layer of ash and debris still covers much of the northern hemisphere up to one half mile in some places and a full mile in others. This layer of ash has settled and compacted, making archeological study difficult.

It is known that there had been a world war not too long before the Apophis impact, but the extent of the conflict few have ever known. Much of the information was destroyed and lost in the Cataclysm. At the request of my benefactor I do not include much of that war and its details due to his involvement, which he considers a dark moment in his life. There are archive entries of the war that I have read and will make reference to those things that are necessary where allowed.

Particular mention will be made of the Greenland family due to their involvement with the centuries past war and the Revelation Event. They are not the focus of this work and are merely side characters. When my work with this particular archive entry is complete, I may produce a comprehensive collection of the Greenland family involvement.

The Federal Government of Earth and its Colonies is the current governing body of the Sol star system. Earth has colonies on Luna, Mars, and Mercury. There are colonies, mining operations, and industrial centers among many of Saturn's and Jupiter's moons.

Mars remains a wasteland despite repeated terraforming operations. Some subsurface habitations are successful. For the most part, Mars is a military reservation. All manner of training and weapons testing occur both on the surface and in orbit. Phobos and Deimos are popular haunts for training and thrill seekers alike. Mars is home of the Federal Navy, and a large shipwright orbits at a distance further than Deimos.

Luna, Earth's moon, is home to the largest single colony and is under Earth's direct control. It is home to Moon Base Armstrong, a major starship dry-dock and naval station. Titan, in particular, is home to

Capellan Armaments. Ganymede is home to the Hephaestus Naval Yard. The industrial base of both Titan and Ganymede produce and provide most of the heavy equipment and ships for the Federation.

Earth's relationship with Ganymede and Titan is the reason for the only war in space that Earth has ever known until the Revelation Event. The Capellan Armaments employees did not feel as though they were being treated fairly, which has been considered odd by many given the amount of pay and benefits they received. On April 16, 2308, the workers used their products to mount a violent coup against their employers.

This revolution succeeded early on. The Federal Government stepped in with two Marine combat landings and an army ten thousand strong. The war ended with the rebels laying down their arms en mass after a gas attack on the Capellan Arms H.Q. orbiting Titan. All aboard the station were killed.

I begin the story with an ex-army corporal, now commander in the Earth Federal Navy, Vergilius Arétus who is better known as Vergil Artus. He will be referenced as such per his request. He is 29 at the beginning of this story and the youngest naval commander, soon to be captain, in the history of the Federal Navy.

Please note that parental discretion is advised. My benefactor wished me to keep source material as natural as possible in order to provide a proper frame of mind for the reader. I have toned it down and, in direct quotes and journal entries, have opted to black out certain rude or inappropriate words, comments, and references.

An appendix has been provided at the end of this work. It contains notes, terms, definitions, a list of important persons, and other information the reader might find useful. Enjoy.

ASTAROTH, GODDESS OF FERTILITY

Journal of Commander Vergil Artus
Entry #1
July 11, 2319

*P*romotion! I can't wait. I'm writing this journal to catalog the key events in my life as a new captain. I've been given the brand new CC-6 battle cruiser named <u>Bismarck</u>. She is the only ship of her class. I've only seen it in pictures and vids. In all seriousness, I must question: Why me? I didn't realize that I had impressed anyone and there are definitely more experienced commanders out there.

There is, of course, no current conflict. There hasn't been since the Capellan Incident at Titan. There was no space combat, which is the main reason why I left the army for the navy after the conflict was ended. I still have nightmares of my time on Titan's surface, though not of the fighting. It's a harsh environment, Titan, and one to which I hope never to return.

I'm also concerned about the ship's name. I may be young and relatively inexperienced, but I'm not ignorant of history. The original was hunted and gunned down just as it made its way into open seas. That was nearly three-hundred and eighty years ago.

It's been a family tradition that I had ancestors on both the <u>Hood</u> and the <u>Bismarck</u>. At least the <u>Bismarck</u> went down fighting. The <u>Hood</u> never stood a chance. That's how the story is told anyway. I suppose I should look on the bright side: when a ship as big as the <u>Bismarck</u> goes down, everyone knows it.

5

Entry #1 Additional

It's not that I'm complaining, but the red tape on my transfer is insane. My new security clearance is not activated yet and no one informed me until I arrived at Moon Base Armstrong. They denied me port. I'm stuck in orbit until things get cleared up. It wouldn't be so bad if the shuttle was more comfortable or if I could see my new ship from up here.

Entry #3
July 14, 2319

It's been almost two days and nothing spectacular has happened except that I'm finally on Armstrong. I've given my taxi pilot, Boris, a large bonus for putting up with me and the situation. He was happy to be of service and said that if I needed a ride to give him a call.

Entry #10
July 24, 2319

This is getting ridiculous! I know I'm new, the ship is new, the crew is new, but I've been hanging out in this sleazy dive bar for a week. The Captain's Lounge refuses to believe that I'm a real captain. I don't blame them. I'm young, probably the youngest in private, commercial or military service for decades. My brother was hoping for some of the decorative gift plates they sell, but he'll have to wait.

At least I've picked up some information in this place. It seems that some political upheaval may be the cause of my delay. There's been a scandal in the House and Senate and some people have resigned. One of them was the senator, Mr. Whitney, who supported me and is probably the reason I went up for this promotion.

It did strike me as odd that he showed so much interest in me for no particular reason. I'll probably be implicated in something, which is why my superiors are holding me back. I think they agree with Senator Whitney about me for some reason and are trying to keep me from the spotlight in order to protect me. And by me, I mean them.

Entry #11
July 25, 2319

I could be on to something with my theory. I've just been arrested. So much for my faith in my superiors; or whatever is going on is out of their control. At least they let me keep my journal.

The Master-at-Arms read my few entries. He laughed, handed it back to me and said, "Man, that sucks." I don't know if he meant anything by it, but he came across as though he knew a lot more than he was going to tell; almost scared in a way. He refused to answer most of my questions. Looks like I won't get to see my ship for some time, if at all.

Entry #12…?

As for my current state, I have no idea how long it's been since my last entry. I'm being held for no apparent reason. I was sitting in my favorite dive when four very heavily armed men and the Master-at-Arms came up and drug me away, kicking and screaming like a stuck pig. It seemed like a good idea at the time. Talk about adding insult to injury.

It would've been a lot worse if there had been any other witnesses. Come to think of it, this whole affair is like a very strange dream. There are so many things that don't add up; the Master-at-Arms, the lack of an audience at my arrest, the amount of fear the guards have when I ask why I'm being held. This does not ring of political scandal. I'm beginning to think there is something else going on. Perhaps this is the military way of protecting me or maybe it has to do with my promotion. It could even be someone's sick joke to haze the new boy. I apparently have plenty of time to figure it out.

Entry #13…?

Yet another day in my cell and I've been trying to remember something my philosophy and ethics professor told me my first year at the academy, something about destiny. It served me well during those hard days and I told myself that I would never forget it. I'm sure it will come to me in time.

Now if my cell were made of stone I could count...

At that moment a man with silver hair and green eyes burst in, gave Artus a look over, and motioned for the guards. Artus could hear the Master-at-Arms yelling about holding an innocent man without a warrant. Artus thought it was nice of the MA to argue on his behalf, albeit only to the extent the law required. He noted that at the exact same moment he thought of this, the silver haired man said the exact same thing to the MA.

The guards gave him the sensory deprivation treatment. He was chained, gagged, blindfolded, gloved, and ear plugged; the works. Artus had no sense of anything. He contemplated many things; family, old girlfriends, the dive bar he decided he liked. He had come to the conclusion that this was truly a nightmare.

When he was finally released he found himself in a dimly lit room with two chairs, a table with an odd little device sitting in its middle, and the silver haired man. "Well, this is stereotypical," Artus thought as the man motioned him to sit. Again the man openly agreed with him. "Is he psychic?"

Now that he could get a good clear look at this guy, he realized that his hair and eyes were real, well... real enough. It was possible that a good make-up artist could pull off a convincing fake. The man stood six feet tall at the least and was hard as a coffin nail.

He wore an odd uniform that bore two insignia that Artus recognized. The one on his shoulder was a military insignia, but not one that had been used for over two and a half centuries. It was an eagle with wings spread wide on a blue field. In its talons it carried a cluster of arrows. The bottom half was surrounded by olive branches and the top half by stars. The only letters spelled: Department of Defense.

The other insignia was on the man's hat. Artus had seen it once before. He didn't know what it meant. It had never been spoken of by anybody or described in any book. He'd only seen it in a picture. Artus surmised that this insignia had been what caused such great fear in the guards.

He had seen it on the cover of an old, leather-bound, book in a glass display case in his philosophy professor's chambers. He thought the title was, *Konat Marna*, but it was old and worn and appeared to be a language he was not familiar with. When he asked about it, she told him to mind his own business.

Every time Artus had described it to anyone he thought might know what it meant, they shut him up or ignored him altogether. Once, he was drawing it on a napkin in the dive he liked so much. The old bartender saw him, snatched it away, and burned it. Artus came to the conclusion that his arrest was more to do with his curiosity and not the politics he wished were the cause of his terrible sinking feeling.

This insignia was never the talk of conspiracy forums or on the net, even though he was certain they knew something about it. If these four white talons on a red shield could keep the most radical conspiracy nuts quiet, then the fear that began to wash over him was well earned. He gained a new respect for the MA that had stood up for him; a lesser man would have kept his mouth shut and probably hid in the restroom trying not to wet himself.

Artus and the Silver-Haired-Man sat in silence for an interminable amount of time. Artus thought that he would die of old age before the matter was settled. The man had zero expression. It would've been a champion poker face if he played poker at all.

"This isn't a dream; it's me sitting next to you, sharpening an ax," said the man as he heaved a very real ax onto the table. Artus had a sudden urge to do some things best left unmentioned.

The man's voice was cold, harsh, and completely devoid of any emotion whatsoever. He then proceeded with his interrogation. It began with a series of control questions.

"What color is your hair?"

"Blonde."

"Your eyes?"

"Grey."

"Height?"

"Five foot, eleven inches."

Artus went along with the questioning. What else could he do? The rest of the questions consisted of the usual: who are you, why are you here, how long have you known this person? The questioning went on for some time. Artus learned nothing about his situation from the questions asked. When the interrogation was over, there was more silence.

After a short stare the man cocked his head and squinted an eye as if he were trying to figure something out about Artus that he couldn't get from asking questions. Artus thought it might be safe to ask a question of his own.

"Why have I been arrested?" asked Artus.

"You're being transferred," replied the man. "There's a bit more to it than that, but that is all I'm allowed to say."

"So I'm getting my ship?" Artus felt a glimmer of hope returning.

"That's not for me to say, though I don't know why not. My bosses have done their best to put you on it."

"What?"

"You see, I've said too much already. I have a bad habit of that, so I'm told. I'm also told it's a product of my breeding; which is a nice way of saying that I'm a ▇▇" The man suddenly looked sullen as if he'd just depressed himself.

Artus thought that whole conversation was a bit strange. The man recovered and seemed more relaxed. He leaned back in his chair and propped his feet on the table.

Artus felt as if he had hit an all-time low. He was no longer afraid, but he was still anxious. He tried feeling good about his situation; nothing positive came to mind.

If the purpose of this episode was to break him, then it had probably worked. Artus now wondered what they were doing here since the inquisition was obviously over. The instrument of doom and despair sitting across from him seemed as if he was just as anxious for this to be over. He seemed to be waiting on something. Artus couldn't think of anything to say or do.

Eventually, projecting from the device on the table, a hologram of a hooded figure appeared. "Is this him?" the hooded figure asked in a feminine voice that Artus thought he recognized. The Silver-Haired-Man rolled his eyes and sighed.

"No, this is not him, it doesn't even look like him, stop asking," argued the Silver-Haired-Man, who sat forward.

"But, brother Astaroth, you of all should know the prophecy. This man fits the description perfectly and..."

"Um," interjected Artus, "I don't suppose you'd mind including me in this conversation about myself?"

"Yes," they blurted. Artus jumped at the outburst and sat back once again.

"Now look, flesh pile!" yelled the silver haired Astaroth. "I am first and foremost not your brother. Neither is this poor soul sitting across from me the man you are looking for. I know Aetonyx personally. Might I also remind you that this stupid religion of yours is a waste of your pathetic existence?"

Astaroth stood and glared at the little hooded woman. "He didn't create the Legion, or this 'Order' you call yourselves, for the purpose of chasing down fantasy and whim. He created it for the defense of Earth. It was never meant to become a cult and it wasn't a prophecy. You are taking his words out of context. I honestly don't know why I'm having this conversation. I've told you I know exactly where he is, but do you listen, do any of you listen..."

"I do, master Astaroth," chimed another voice. This one was masculine. Another tiny figure had appeared on the table. Artus thought how confused he'd be if it hadn't been for his recent treatment. This voice Artus certainly recognized. It sparked a memory from the academy and a face, but the man's name eluded him.

"Sorry, Legate, your time has run out," said Astaroth. The little woman began to interject but was cut off and disappeared. As soon as the woman had gone Artus sensed a flood of anger emanating from the new figure. The emotion was so strong Artus swore he felt the air move.

"You should show more restraint to your superiors, child!" growled the man. The comment struck home on Astaroth, who looked genuinely ashamed. "She may be a puppet to keep the real powers that be safe," returned the man, "but she is still in charge and you still report to her like the rest and no, this is not a cult or religion." The man sighed and the tension subsided. "I must admit most of them think so. I've been around far longer than you and I have seen the desire such authority can bring and the trouble it can cause. I have been busy, but that is no excuse to let their behavior get out of control. I will deal with the attitude of the Order at my earliest convenience." Astaroth showed signs of relief.

"You can also expect another lecture about keeping your mouth shut," continued the figure. "I know that information you are often privileged to puts you at odds with the Order. It's difficult enough keeping the sanctioned conspiracies straight and under control without your input, especially those that involve the Imperial Magistrate. It's as much for the Order's protection as ours." The little hooded man regained his composure. "Now then, Mr. Arétus has met with my personal approval. Has he passed security?"

"Artus," growled Artus. He was ignored.

"Yes," said a frustrated Astaroth.

"Then get him to his ship. Have Hudson downplay Mr. Arétus' involvement with Senator Whitney. The last thing we need is for the court to find a jester. I also need you to go with him. Carpathian is investigating a Mustering of the Armada." Astaroth went pale. "I have sent an alert to the Magistrate. Carpathian should be back with plenty of time to awaken the defenses should it prove necessary, but I need you there also. I will contact you with more information later. I'm sending Hudson along as well. She has been overworked with the Whitney business and deserves a break. Now get to work."

"A Mustering of the Armada," Astaroth said to himself. "Such a thing has not happened since…"

"… I know," replied the man in an equally forlorn tone. "It's best not to think about it."

"Care to inform me what this is all about?" asked Artus of anyone who'd listen.

The little man made a gesture towards Artus. "In fact, it would be a good idea if Mr. Arétus didn't think about it much either. Inform him of his rights and what the Order expects of him. Then do whatever it is you do that makes your victims think they're dreaming." With that, the little hooded man signed off.

Artus gulped and decided that he was already asleep and this was truly just a nightmare. He ventured a question on the only thing he thought he understood, "Isn't Astaroth a God...?"

"... A Canaanite goddess of fertility, yes," interrupted Astaroth with a roll of his eyes and a sigh. He looked at Artus and said, "Sorry for the mix up, yadda, yadda, yadda. I've been authorized to give you your clearance, your ship, and you are now a member of the Order. The last is non-negotiable, but you can ignore them. I do. You'll be more useful to me and my masters if you tell them to shove it. If they give you any beef, call me. However, if you should choose to recognize their authority, then you are bound by their rules and the only one who can do anything about it is Tavion."

"The Order?" Artus ventured. "Isn't that a bit cliché?"

Astaroth chuckled and nodded. "Glad you understand my problems. It does, however, help convince people they've been having a dream or nightmare. If you think that's clever, hang on for the next bit." He handed Artus a card with his name on it and a coded transmission frequency. "You also get a neat little insignia to put on your uniform. It comes with an easy to read uniform guide. You have your choice of the color grey or this dull silver color."

Artus just stared in shock at the two identical grey patches and the bad joke. Then, recognition slapped him in the face. Tavion was the name of the man on the table. Artus was about to ask a more useful question, but the guard injected something into his arm. He quickly slumped into unconsciousness.

Artus awoke on a shuttle that was eerily similar to the one he'd spent two days on waiting to land at Armstrong. His ordeal rushed back into his memory quickly and unpleasantly. He moaned as loudly and as obnoxiously as possible, and then ran to the restroom to throw up. When he returned, he noticed his journal was lying in the seat next to him. He decided he should write down what had happened.

In it he found a brief message from his mentor at the academy wishing him well. He placed the voice of the woman on the table, Lieutenant Commander April Fisher. She had spoken of fate and destiny. He couldn't remember the exact quote. Maybe what happened to him and what she'd said at the academy about fate was no coincidence.

He thought about her for a while, surprisingly young and attractive for a professor and lieutenant commander at a military academy. He knew she was smart and didn't get the job from her good looks, although he was certain that they helped. Then again, she could have gotten the job the same way he'd apparently received his captaincy.

The man on the table, Tavion, was obviously calling the shots. A memory of this man had stuck with Artus more strongly than his mentor. Tavion had been with Artus at the Academy and was notorious for the often brutal manner at which he conducted war games. Tavion had been expelled. Why was Tavion calling the shots, and just how old was he?

There was also the matter of Carpathian, the Armada, and the Imperial Magistrate. Of these, only Carpathian stuck out. Artus thought that he remembered the name from a history of space travel lesson at the Academy. The Carpathian in the lesson was the only successful space pirate in history. Artus hadn't taken the lesson as serious as he should have, because that was all he knew.

As for the latter two subjects of interest, there was nothing to go on. They suggested to Artus that there was more going on in the galaxy, perhaps the universe, than anyone realized. Then again, there was whatever Astaroth had drugged him with. The whole episode felt like a dream, but he didn't want to take any chances. He planned to research what he could.

He admitted to himself that he would actually prefer to deal with Astaroth than this 'Order' group. Astaroth, he realized, wasn't just the cold figure he'd thought. The silver haired man had actually given him a lot of information, even though it got him in trouble. The information was a bit more obvious than what most spies and black-ops types gave out. The information given may have been unintentional.

He began writing it all down under entry #14, date unknown. Along with his ordeal he made note that he was actually going to be a captain of the CC-6 Battle Cruiser *Bismarck* after all. For the rest of the flight from wherever, back to Armstrong, which gave him no problems upon arrival, he contemplated what the coming days would be like. He was certain that he'd not seen the last of this Astaroth fellow.

THE BISMARCK

Journal of Commander Vergil Artus
Entry #15
August 1, 2319

*T*he christening and commissioning of a new ship is always hectic, and horror stories of every nature exist, from the champaign bottle not breaking to gremlins. The actual truth is that a christening and a commissioning are two different things. A ship being christened doesn't mean it is ready for front line service or even a test drive. Crews are missing, paperwork has to be done, bugs have to be fixed, the elevators don't work, and the food won't be hot, etc. It would be a nightmare for anyone, but me. I've missed that.

The commissioning, which is where I take command, means the ship is ready for duty and will be entered into the official navy books as an operational ship-of-the-line. Compared to my run in with Astaroth, this is nothing and I'm glad for it. I still haven't been able to see her but today's the day.

As for the politics involved around the Bismarck's existence I have little opinion. I will note that the lack of conflict has often brought forth the argument of why have such large naval forces. The base reality of this argument comes down to the preference to have it and not need it than need it and not have it. Plus, it is an excellent way for the young and inexperienced to get cheap, effective training, discipline, and a vote.

The Bismarck will be ready to cruise soon enough and to "Boldly go where *no one has gone before."¹ I don't know where the phrase originated. This was my academy class motto, and the motto of so many others. It often sounded trite and thrown around more as a joke, but it is somehow fitting.*

I'm on my way to Alameda Naval from Moon Base Armstrong and of all things I am using the same shuttle I was on days ago when I first began my journey to the moon. After all the time I've spent on it, it is almost home. I sleep in it sometimes instead of the quarters I've been given on Armstrong. There is probably some psychological nonsense about becoming attached to something in the midst of stress, but I don't care.

I call it the Phoenix and have made many homey touches. I have requested it as my personal transport for service on the Bismarck. The quartermasters laughed at me, but signed the paperwork anyway. The owner and pilot, Boris, doesn't mind and is looking forward to it. I can't imagine why beyond the steady pay I've offered. The engineers and mechanics on the Bismarck are supposed to be top notch. I figure Boris can get them to teach him some things to make this old shuttle a pretty snazzy piece of work...

"This is *Alameda Naval*. We have you on our screens now. Please identify." Artus could hear everything in the cockpit. Boris, the pilot, responded with the appropriate data and a confirmation came back, followed by more codes. Artus was pleased to note that *Alameda* would allow him a fly-by of his ship and to walk its deck before the four months of simulations, pre-voyage briefings, and the commissioning ceremonies. Artus would also need to meet and test his crew. Meeting his officers was one of his objectives during this pre-mature visit.

This was the first time Artus had been aboard and it was not standard procedure, especially since he hadn't reported for duty yet. Someone must know something more about his ordeal than they'd let on and felt sorry for him. After all the pomp and briefings, he would get to go back aboard the *Bismarck* for the actual show.

He had been appalled to find out that his promotion from commander to captain wasn't official until the commissioning. It was going to be one of the ceremonies held dock-side. They weren't even going to *frock* him.

He couldn't help looking on the bright side: at least he wasn't in that dank hole with that demon Astaroth.

A few minutes later and there she was. Not the size of a modern battleship, but still pretty amazingly big. The *Bismarck* was the size of three old world battleships.

Being a battle cruiser, the *Bismarck* and other ships of her class were designed as a balance of speed, armor, and firepower. The battle cruiser concept was ages old and often didn't last. They were designed as a middle ground between the basic cruiser and battleship weight classes.

Cruisers were smaller than battleships and thus faster. They had less armor protection and less firepower. They were cheaper and easier to produce. Most of the frontline ships in the Earth Federal Navy fit into the cruiser weight class. They served many roles, from fire-support to interdictors, and could even serve as command and control vessels. Along with the smaller destroyers, cruisers were one of the few navy ships that were purpose built. They were designated with a 'C' and whatever other letter that designated their role. Few had any form of warp drive. Once they were on station, they often stayed there for the duration of their lifespan.

The battleship was built as pure engineered destruction and the survivability of said destruction. They were not fast enough to keep up with anything other than a ship of the same weight class or bigger, such as some older designs with the conspicuous nick name of 'battle wagon'. Most battleships were refits of large colony or freight vessels. It was rare to find two battleships that looked alike. Armor and weapons were stuck on wherever they could fit. As a result, one battleship might be better for a task than another because of the weapons and systems that could, or could not, be made to fit. They were designated as 'BB'.

The battleship fleet had recently been equipped with a relatively new, and large, drive system that allowed them to warp space at one point and then travel to another at relativistic speeds without having to go through warp gates, which were still in early stages of operation. Most battleships and battle wagons had a slow-to-charge operational version of this technology in their drive system.

Fleet carriers were in a class of their own. They were usually between the sizes of cruisers and battleships, but they were the largest purpose built navy vessels until the battle cruiser program was initiated. These vessels were the modern, space-faring, version of the old world aircraft carriers. They could carry up to two air wings of fighter-bombers and interceptors. They could be outfitted to carry and support almost an entire army or Marine combat division. The modern fleet carrier was a logistical wonder. They had warp drives. A fighter sized vessel that was close enough could piggy-back a carrier's warp field. Procedures were in place for this operation, but no one wanted to test it.

For Artus, it was a battle cruiser. The battle cruiser initiative for the E.F.N. was fairly new. Only five other ships with the designation of C.C. existed. The initiative was meant as a test-bed for new ship designs.

The problem with the battleships was that they were too big and inefficient due to their lack of purpose built design. The problem with cruisers was that they couldn't pack the same firepower nor absorb damage like a battleship could. The battle cruiser was designed to provide a happy medium. So far the program had not produced a viable solution.

The *Bismarck*, however, was breathtaking. Its design would likely meet full scale production. It was even speculated that the entire E.F.N. would be refitted or scrapped in favor for the new design concept. Rumors suggested that Capellan Armaments were already working on fresh concepts for ships of all weight classes using the *Bismarck's* design. If and when that happened, it was likely that the weight class designations would be rescaled. The modern battle cruiser would die as a weight class, like its predecessors.

The *Bismarck* was different due to advances in power plant efficiency; namely an efficient fusion reactor and miniaturization. There was enough power and space left for more than the usual number of large guns and a Class 3 defense field which protected her from a good majority of energy based attacks. All these improvements aside, it was her communications system that could prove to be her biggest asset.

Through more complicated technical jargon, the *Bismarck* could, theoretically, communicate at a distance of a light-year or better almost instantly. You didn't need line of sight. This meant that she could send messages through stellar bodies without having to maneuver into open space.

The problem with this system, as Artus saw it, was that he couldn't actually talk to anybody with it. The only other entities that had the system were the Alpha Centauri colony and fleet headquarters. The gates used a similar system to communicate with each other. No other ship in service had this ability and he himself could only send short, coded, and to the point messages which had to be typed into the system. It was good if you didn't want anyone to know where you were. Artus was getting the idea that this ship was designed for cloak and dagger type stuff.

Since there was no enemy beyond the one his psyche had conjured up in that nightmare with Astaroth, he expected that he would be used as a scout, interdiction, and policing vessel like most other battle cruisers of the fleet. He might possibly be used to patrol the outskirts of known space. Given the range of his communications and the furthest away humanity had traveled, it was a good bet the ship's posting would be Alpha Centauri.

The *Bismarck's* shape was not quite what Artus had expected. He had been told it was to lessen weight, increase internal space, and maximize his firing arc. The *Bismarck* was large, somewhat elongated, and hollow, resembling a modular, hexagonal tube consisting of three sections which nestled into each other. The bow and stern sections fit inside the middle section.

The first, bow, section housed sensors, three of the main guns with some smaller ones, and reverse thrusters. The nose could open, allowing access to a hollow, open cavity that extended through the length of the middle section. This was to allow for easy access when refitting the modular internal compartments and loading cargo. This allowed the *Bismarck* to be refitted, re-tasked, and resupplied in record speed. At present much of the inner workings were not installed due to the need to carry supplies and equipment.

The second section held primary operations and was designed for command and control. It was the everyday life section. It was also the most heavily armored section for that purpose. It held the hangars, crew quarters, the bridge, and the majority of the weapons. The nine main guns of this section, similar to those on the first section, were arrayed around it.

With cargo being the major concern at the moment, this section had a large void at the center accessed by the front section. The empty space allowed for viewing of the fusion reactor and the light gave an eerie purple hue, casting shadows across the interior. The outer, surrounding layers were very thick armored plating. With the shield, it made the *Bismarck* almost invulnerable to broadside battle tactics by anything short of a battleship.

The third, stern, section held the drive systems. The primary helm control system and its crews were stationed in a heavily armored bunker at the interior extreme of this section near the core. The engines surrounded the end of this section and were housed in armored vents. The overall effect of the design made the section look like a large beehive.

The vents covering the engines could be opened and closed in increments. This was not so much to control speed, though such operation was possible. This ability was mostly concerned with both maneuvering and protecting the engines. This also allowed the energy emitted by the engines to be absorbed and reduced. This practice allowed the *Bismarck* to operate with a much smaller energy print on sensors. This was known as running silent.

To help in this, the *Bismarck* was coated in a black and grey substance that worked much like stealth material from ages past. It deflected or absorbed scans, energy, and light. This helped to make the ship difficult to find or identify, visually or otherwise, against the cold blackness of space.

Artus' biggest combat worry was that the shield only kept out energy based attacks. Projectiles and smaller craft, such as fighters or perhaps an ambitious transport, could still get in. Thankfully the designers had realized this and given the *Bismarck's* close in defenses and exposed superstructure more than adequate anti-fighter weapons and some slightly larger guns for the more ambitious support craft. It also had an armored curtain system that could open or close the nose and the points where the three sections met to prevent access.

Artus found that the *Bismarck* was only a battle cruiser in performance. She was larger than normal, much more like a streamlined battleship. He discovered that the better than standard fighter force was due to the way the ship was designed. The primary hangar extended the entire length of the middle section from the front to the back and opened at each end. The hangar, a secondary hangar, and some smaller access points could be secured against attack by heavy doors and the armored curtain.

Half of the large, domed, main gun-turrets held massive, twenty-inch, double hyper-velocity guns. The ammunition came in two types. There were large metallic spheres which could explode if necessary. There were also large, elongated, slugs that looked very much like magnetic train rails. The latter was designed for armor piercing.

The other main guns were single ion cannons. These were excellent energy based weapons. They were perfect for draining shields and the disabling of electronic systems. One had to be careful with ion cannons. They were meant to disable a ship, not kill her, which they could still do. The amount of energy needed could, if not controlled, become a concentrated death pulse or ray, causing damage in a way the hypervelocity guns didn't. It was best to use ion cannons first to beat down any shield and then re-task them on ship components such as weapons or engines. If you used them in a slugging match, you could cause serious damage to the other ship and crew, which was not always desired.

The rest of the armaments were smaller projectile and energy based batteries. These were mostly for short and medium ranged engagements. Point defense weapons were the smallest and ranged from precise to spray-and-pray accuracy.

3
Artus Makes a Pit Stop

Journal of Commander Vergil Artus
Entry #15
August 1, 2319; Additional

I'm surprised to find out that I've already been to the Bismarck, but no one has actually seen me. Apparently someone has been gallivanting around as me and done all the paperwork, making plausible excuses for my reclusiveness. One, in particular, is that I seem to have eaten something bad in order to explain my disheveled appearance. What I have just found out is that the ship's doctor has been informed and has prepared special medication and food for me per prescription.

It would appear that some of what I experienced wasn't a nightmare or imagined. I know there is nothing wrong with me and I guess that this is Astaroth's idea of a joke. I know that a man with his talents could have said anything he wanted. People would have done what he told them out of fear, or because they actually believed him. He could've told them anything, but he had to tell them I was sick, was to be put on medication, and a special diet.

Boris has been cleared for final approach. He's an odd Slavic man. How he keeps this shuttle, which is older than I am, running is amazing...

As Artus disembarked the beleaguered shuttlecraft in the *Bismarck's* large primary hangar, he came to the realization that he had a fighter squadron under his command. Not just any fighters; these were new, brand new, and not even on the shelf yet. They were the new Capellan Armaments' *Joint Strike 18* craft with some kind of multi-directional vectoring thrust. They could be used as interceptors, bombers, and just about anything short of actual dog-fighting, depending on the need. Artus walked up to one to touch it and look inside.

As he walked over he could see and hear the mechanics gawking and joking about the *Phoenix*. The crew was obviously not expecting his arrival and must have assumed it was a lowly transfer or spare parts. Only one person had noticed him walk over to the fighter. As Artus reached up to touch it, he noticed a grimy woman in her mid-twenties walk up and raise her hand to knock his away. He had plenty of time to react, but realized he wasn't in uniform. He decided to let her hit him and see how things played out.

"Get your hands off my plane!" she yelled as her hand swatted Artus'. She began to give him a chewing out, which drew a crowd. She was kind of attractive under all that grease. The chewing out consisted of insults mixed with rules, regulations, and more insults.

Artus noticed that she bore the rank of lieutenant commander and had a wing commander's insignia where her epaulets would be if jumpsuits had them. This surprised Artus. Just how many fighters did he have? A battleship carried twelve to fifteen bomber escorts, which were five to seven short of a bomber wing. A fleet carrier had almost two air wings outfitted for various missions. Anything less than a full wing usually only had flight commanders and tactical officers to coordinate their operations, reporting to the duty officer or the captain.

This wing commander was in the middle of telling Artus he could be shot on the spot for spying when a security team and a group of officers pushed their way through the crowd. Among them was his first officer, who he'd met only a few times and not long enough to get to know her. He noticed that a good portion of the officers who'd appeared were female. He wasn't sexist by any means, but it could be a problem. The deployment would be long and he didn't want to have to deal with any relationship issues that might arise. He had two sisters and they practically controlled his life even after he left for service. He also recognized the fact that these officers were in dress uniform.

He quickly picked out respective branches of the military; navy and Marines, an air force liaison officer, and oddly an army colonel. The colonel was the only one outranking Artus and Artus knew him. Colonel Allen Richards was Artus' commanding officer in the army and they had seen much together. He was pleasantly surprised to see the man.

This situation puzzled Artus. This whole affair was navy. The air force man he guessed was here for the fighters, but an army line officer didn't make any sense. Col. Richards was definitely the oldest in the group and was dressed in fatigues. He looked as though he'd earned his rank and the only medal he wore.

Hanging from his neck was a Medal of Honor. Such a medal had been in existence in one form or another for hundreds of years. It demanded respect and higher ranks were advised to salute the lowest ranks if they wore such a medal. It was rare to find a medal winner alive. Artus immediately snapped to attention, called the deck to order with, "Medal on deck," and saluted the man who, in good disciplined order, returned his salute.

The very irate wing commander was becoming agitated that Artus was no longer paying her any attention. She was shocked at the crowd, the officers, and the fact that Artus, a man who wasn't in uniform, was saluting an army colonel who was saluting back. She became quiet, dumb-founded by what she saw.

The wing commander came to some of her senses and saluted the colonel as well, who at this point, despite his discipline, was doing everything he could to keep from laughing as he returned the salute rather more haphazardly than he did for Artus. When he was finished, he laughed outright, which quickly quieted the hangar.

He shook his head and said, "██ Carmen! I've been in bad spots before, but you've gone and jumped in a fox-whole with a bunch of poisonous snakes. No General in the universe would dare hit and then berate the Captain of the Boat… Good to see you again, Arty." Artus didn't let just anyone call him Arty. Richards shook Artus' hand. He turned and walked out of the hangar, chuckling maniacally all the way.

Artus was as blank as Carmen at the reaction. When the colonel left the hangar, the crowd of pilots and mechanics that had gathered to watch some punk get killed by their commanding officer shrank away in as much fear as he had felt when he'd met Astaroth. It felt good to have that kind of power. He was beginning to see why Astaroth was the way he was. A man could get a lot of pleasure out of such reactions.

Artus and Carmen both looked at the other assembled officers who were still standing at attention and were doing everything they could to keep their respective feelings from exploding and maintain good order. Artus couldn't stand it. His sides busted with laughter and he began to cry.

Everyone was still very confused and didn't dare do anything, though Artus' laughter had definitely relieved some of the junior officers of their fear of reprisal. A couple of lieutenant commanders and the air force man began to laugh too. Artus told the rest to stand easy. Some began to laugh, some still stood at attention, and others just wiped their brow and went back to work. Artus turned to Carmen. "I'm Commander Vergil Artus and I don't think we've been properly introduced," he said in in his smoothest voice in an attempt to sound charming.

"I'm Carmen... lieutenant commander," she managed to squeak.

"What's your last name?"

"That is my last name."

"Oh, well what's your first name?"

"I'd rather not say... sir." She tried making a salute.

"Put your hand down. There'll be time enough for that later. Now what's your first name?"

"George," she squeaked even quieter than her last name.

Without pause or show of surprise about her name, Artus motioned her toward his shuttle. "Step into my office, George. Please, excuse my lack of uniform. Oh, and don't forget to pick your jaw up off the deck. You don't want it to get stepped on."

Artus had, over the past few days, been able to somewhat compartmentalize the *Phoenix* into an office and sleeping quarters. Boris didn't seem to mind too much, as he'd lived in it with three different wives. Change and rearrangement were both something he was used to. However, he had no romantic intentions toward Artus, and Artus had none toward him. The only reason Boris allowed it was because of the steady pay Artus had promised if he stayed around. It was cramped, but Artus saw it as home away from home.

"So Lieutenant Commander, I'm new around here and I'm a bit curious. Just what is a wing commander doing aboard ship without a full wing of fighters? You're also pretty young to be at rank."

"The rest will be delivered in a show at the commissioning." The woman had regained some of her composure and was standing at attention.

"So unlike any other ship this size, I'm going to have a full wing of fighters?"

"That's correct, sir. As for my age, I don't see where it's a problem. Your own reputation for being young has shocked many."

Artus nodded his agreement.

"Sir?" questioned the lieutenant commander.

"Yes?"

"You won't report what happened back there, will you?"

"For what, discipline?" Artus gave a slight chuckle. "Lieutenant Commander, you've done more damage to yourself by that spectacle than any punishment that I or the fleet could dish out. However, something like this will spread like wild fire. You certainly haven't heard the last of it." Artus paused for thought. "I'm going to meet with the command crew in individual interviews before the ceremonies start. I'll tell them, order if necessary, to keep their mouths shut and enforce respect among the crew. I made a fool out of myself not but a few days ago. Only difference is that I didn't have an audience that big." Artus stared off into nothing as he remembered his arrest in the Armstrong bar and visibly cringed.

"Sir?" questioned the lieutenant commander.

"Nothing, I'll tell you the story some other time. I'll let you try and get back to work or whatever it was you were doing. I'll send someone for you when I'm ready for your interview. Oh, and I'm not captain yet. So stand easy until then."

"You still out rank me, sir."

"Oh, yes… Well, I'm not in uniform and I'm on this junk heap." Carmen looked taken aback. "Oh, uh, not the *Bismarck*, this little shuttle."

"Shall I throw it into space for you?"

"No, no. That won't be necessary."

"Shall I go, sir?" Artus nodded and Carmen left.

When Artus finally arrived at his quarters he found that he had an office, two stewards, a waiting room, a conference room, and briefing room. Next to his quarters were those of Commander Greenland and Command Master Chief Billings. Cmdr. Greenland had her own office opposite of his. CMC Billing's desk was in the waiting room with those of the stewards.

The waiting room was not empty. The command crew, minus Lt. Cmdr. Carmen, and some junior officers filled the space. It was standing room only. What bothered him was that they all tried to salute at the same time only to make themselves look foolish in the cramped space. Most of them must be new, young, and eager to please, Artus thought. He couldn't help but notice that many of them were indeed women. He saw Col. Richards, Cmdr. Greenland, and CMC Billings. He motioned for them to enter his office.

"Mr. Billings," started Artus.

"Sir," responded the well-disciplined chief. Artus had served with the elder Englishman before and had requested him for this assignment.

"Mr. Billings, is the briefing room large enough to hold all those assembled out there?" asked Artus.

"Yes, sir," snapped Mr. Billings.

"See to it then."

"Sir!" with a quick salute, Mr. Billings returned to the waiting room.

Artus sat down and motioned for the other two to follow suit. "No offense meant and I'm sure that they are more than capable, but what's with all the women?" This seemed to catch his first officer off guard, but the colonel grunted amusement.

"They've heard about your looks and charm," mused Richards with obvious roguishness. Greenland turned on the colonel and was about to say something when Artus stopped her.

"Now, now, Commander Greenland, there's no need to get defensive about it. As for you, Colonel, I think our friendship should be downplayed. I would prefer a more official answer to my question. I'm also curious as to why there is an army line officer on my ship?" That seemed to make Greenland change her attitude and she smirked at the colonel. Then a shocking realization hit them both.

"Sir?" they questioned in tandem. They obviously expected him to know more than he did.

Artus could see confusion. "Look," he said, "I've had my nose in paperwork just getting transferred before being kidnapped on Armstrong." The two officers were taken aback by that statement. "Don't ask, I'll explain later if I'm allowed to talk about it at all. I've been given very little information about what's going on and what this ship can do. I'm also not due to be promoted until the commissioning. They won't frock me either. What I have learned of the situation and this ship, I figured out just from looking around. Due to the sick sense of humor of one man in particular, I now have to take medication for which I have no need and a rather boring diet. I know you're as confused as I am, but please just tell me what information you have."

Richards sighed. "I've been assigned to the *Bismarck* with an engineering battalion for the Alpha Centauri colonists."

"So our mission is Alpha Centauri. I didn't know there were any inhabitable planets," said Artus.

"There's apparently one, just. My mission is to go there and secure areas habitable for colonization. Once established, if I don't have enough men, then they'll send more. Until then, my men and I are at your disposal."

"As for the ship, sir," Greenland chimed in, "the *Bismarck* has been at full combat operational status for almost three months." That was one more shock Artus wasn't ready for on a rapidly increasing list. If a ship was commissioned then it should have been ready, but reality never lived up. "We have a partial wing of the new Capellan Armaments' *JS-18's* commanded by Lieutenant Commander Carmen, newest warp drive, and as for the women, many of them did get where they are because they are women. You understand academy politics. Influential people want their children to be with the best or they give their brats everything they ask for. Some are here, like many of the men, only to say they served with you. If you succeed, they succeed. They can do their jobs. If there are any problems most of the traditional discipline techniques should work. Thankfully, many of those in the hangar when you arrived are merely support personnel and won't be going with us."

"Good, please continue."

"As for those who've earned the right to be here, all will serve well; although, they are very green, and that's not just the women. Most are straight from the academy and eager to please. We've got the highest percentage of honor graduates in the fleet."

Artus stood and went to get a drink, motioning to the others if they wanted anything and asked Greenland to continue.

"As for all those in the briefing room, among them are your senior officers for weapons, engineering, quartermasters, helm, sensors, bridge crew, and Marines. We are supposed to have a psychologist and her team, but they haven't arrived. It's an obvious cover. I've run into them before. They act funny."

Artus raised an eyebrow. "I assume that's Hudson?"

"Uh, yes sir, one Lieutenant Commander Reyla Hudson. Do you know her?"

"Only by reputation. I learned she would be joining us a day or two ago. I can't say that I'm looking forward to meeting her. If you've met her or her team, you know more than most people I've met." Artus leaned against a wall and sighed. "Nothing I can do about it. Please, continue Ms. Greenland."

"Sir… The rest are junior officers who have papers that need your signature and some are here because someone promised them a chance to meet you." At that Artus began to hit his head on the wall he was leaning against. When he went to prop himself against the wall with his hand, he fell through it.

Artus found himself on the floor of his room, his drink spilt, and at a complete loss for words. His doorbell chimed emphatically. Greenland and Richards had obviously noticed his absence. Since his room was the only thing on the other side of that wall he had just come through it made sense that they were trying to enter.

His rooms were locked, and he didn't have the code yet. Mr. Billings would have it, but the security system probably wouldn't let him use it. The room had to be activated by using Artus' personal codes for it to work. He wondered if his falling through the wall counted. He pushed himself off the floor and began examining the wall he'd just come through when he heard a voice he'd hoped to never hear again.

"It's an escape route for late nights or unwanted visitors," said Astaroth.

"I gathered, too bad it doesn't work," said Artus shaking.

"Calm down, Mr. Arétus."

"It's Artus, and I don't see how being calm is possible after what you've put me through."

Astaroth ignored him. "I'll teach you how to use it, but don't ask for the details of how it works. You wouldn't like them." He walked over to the wall. "I made certain that it was put there; you may need it, especially with that Legion, Order, harpy, spy."

Artus took a guess. "It wouldn't happen to be the psychologist would it, Lieutenant Commander Hudson?"

"So you've meet her then?"

"No, the junk you shot me full of didn't erase my memory, just made it foggy. Plus Greenland mentioned something about her. I assume she is the one Tavion mentioned?"

"You've recovered better after that than expected. Yes, she is the one Tavion mentioned. He can't get on to me about using his name now since you've obviously figured it out."

"We were at the academy together. He's difficult to forget."

Astaroth let out a chuckle that became a laugh. "And he gets upset with me for mentioning the slightest thing. I am thankful that I don't have his job. Now then, back to business.

"The Order, as I'm sure you've guessed, is militaristic. Don't ask me where they got their start because the two men who would know don't tell. They are often left to operate independently. Tavion fears that, if they get wind that I'm here, they may very well guess why."

"Why are you here?"

"That is a good question and one I'm not at liberty to discuss. What you heard in that interrogation room stays between us. My bosses don't want the Order involved for the very reason I'm here. They believe, and I agree, that the Order has been compromised and can no longer be trusted. An investigation is already underway, starting with Senator Whitney. A purge may also be necessary."

"Purge?" Artus questioned.

"Yes, it is as ominous as it sounds. I'm certain that more will be revealed to you, if needs be. I can guarantee that you won't like it. Your adventure was merely to make certain that all of the proper paperwork had been done. I'm sorry if it gave you a scare, but that is partly its intent. I would have known from the first moment your hood came off in that room if you were going to be honest."

"It seems a bit overboard."

"Overboard is me shooting you on sight because you had anything to do with Senator Whitney. Now, a word of warning about Lieutenant Commander Hudson. She is officially part of the Order, and high up, but I don't know how high. I do work for her on occasion. Her inclusion in this mission is intended to give her a rest, but she will do the job she has been officially sent for. She will be conducting psych evaluations on the Alpha Centauri colonists as well as the crew, and you in particular.

"Be aware, though, that she does not have clearance for any sensitive information; she is not on the need to know list for this mission. I have not been briefed about her orders beyond this, but experience has taught me to be cautious when the bosses send someone out of the way. She may have an ulterior motive. The bosses may be getting her out of the way because she's in danger, or she really needs a break. They may also believe that she is the leak and are hoping to catch her in the act. Keep your eyes peeled for trouble."

"Is she dangerous?"

"Very, but in this situation, I cannot tell how much danger she could be to you or the ship. Even if she is the bad apple, I don't think she would do anything to jeopardize her ride. Only confront her if you think you have to and, then, only on work. If there's a danger, my bosses will take care of it."

Astaroth moved over to the wall and knocked on it. "It's a pass through Nano-wall. Any amount of tapping or banging will make it work, but it only recognizes you and anything you are directly touching. I suggest you go let them in before they begin to worry. I also enjoyed watching your spectacle on the hangar deck."

"What about you, where are you going?"

"I'll leave after I've met the others. I'll be back before the ceremonies."

"Right," said Artus indignantly, "the mustering."

"I'll have to check the expiration date on my knock out drugs," said Astaroth as Artus walked through the wall.

Artus entered the waiting room where Greenland and Mr. Billings were trying in vain to open the door to his room. Richards was sitting back, relaxing and smoking a cigarette. Artus walked up to the colonel and snatched his cigarette. "No smoking," said Artus. The colonel jumped in surprise, then turned to Greenland and Billings.

"See, I told you he'd be back," said the colonel.

"Sir, what happened," cried Greenland.

"I have been authorized, somewhat, to let you in on some information." Billings turned to leave. "No, Mr. Billings you should probably see this too."

"Very well sir."

"Now get me my codes so I can open the door and try not to freak."

Artus opened the door and the four of them entered his living quarters. Astaroth stood on the mezzanine from the living room to the bedroom looking out the window at the lunar landscape beyond. He was wearing his unusual black uniform. He turned and approached.

Artus could hear Greenland gasp in amazement, Richards cursed, and Billings stayed quiet. Either Billings was very well trained or he had no idea what the fuss was about. Artus turned to see that Greenland was more interested in the man himself. Richards was covering his eyes and muttering to himself something about not knowing anything in a fake German accent.[2] Artus knew that the colonel had recognized the insignias on Astaroth's uniform or the man himself. Billings remained the model of discipline.

Astaroth approached and introduced himself. "Hello again, colonel."

OPERATIONS

From the personal notes of Commander Artus

Primary operations for the *Bismarck* were separated into seven divisions. Medical was in charge of the obvious: the physical and mental well-being of the crew. Helm consisted of the engine control and steerage. The engineering division was in charge of the engines themselves and other maintenance operations. The sensor division consisted of several sensor stations throughout the ship, but the primary sensor control battery was housed deep in the ship. The communications division was in charge of all internal and external communication. Weapons were in charge of fire control for all of the *Bismarck's* guns. Marines policed the ship and defended it should there be a boarding operation. They could also perform landings or provide escort for any excursion.

The *Bismarck* senior bridge staff included two helmsmen, two sensor officers, two communication officers, and two weapons officers. Each position on the bridge was headed by one junior officer and two to three enlisted crewmen or specialist technicians. The system was designed for three, eight hour shifts, but the *Bismarck* would be sailing under crewed. This meant twelve hour shifts. This was tiring, but in periods of low activity many systems could be operated by a senior NCO and a handful of crewmen. Mostly they just watched for anything to happen, at which point the NCO in charge of the station would alert the Officer of the Deck or

CMC Billings and they would alert the next appropriate command, even if it meant dragging them out of bed or out of the head.

The chief medical officers were Lieutenant Commander Evaline Burns and Lieutenant Thomas Briggs. Lt. Cmdr. Burns was the ships trauma surgeon and in overall command of the medical division. She could also override the captain in certain situations. Lieutenant Briggs was a general practitioner and an able surgeon on his internship. While both doctors were available for whatever might ail a person, most everyday problems went to Dr. Briggs. Both had their own nursing crews and corpsmen to aid them.

The medical bay was located between the primary hangar and the secondary. This was to allow swift treatment of any arriving casualties. There were a few senior nurses that had stations located around the ship in case of emergencies.

Lieutenant Commander Carmen had a flight surgeon available that accompanied her fighter-bomber wing. Lieutenant Gregory Marshal was a trained flight operations doctor and already up to speed on the flight crew's medical history. He had worked with them for a few months. They were his primary responsibility. All flight crews were supposed to report to him for treatments. He had no problem consulting either Dr. Burns or Dr. Briggs. He would, on occasion, defer to Dr. Burns due to her experience.

All of the doctors had access to a state of the art medical lab. The doctors' first use of the lab was to perform pregnancy tests on all of the female members of the crew and the Press Corps. Many objected, but the fact of the matter was that the *Bismarck* would be on station for some time and sending a prospective mother back was an unacceptable risk and expense. Plus, a warship was no place for a baby.

The helm team consisted of Lieutenant Michelle Collins, Lieutenant junior grade Timothy Kern, an Ensign Apprentice, two Chiefs and four

Petty Officers of first or second rate depending on shift. Lt. Collins was senior and was the ships navigator. All movement commands from Captain Artus, Commander Greenland, or the Officer of the Deck would pass through her or her second, Lt. j.g. Kern. Kern was next on the helm pecking order and he ran the night shift. Ensign Apprentice Rachelle Landry ran the evening shift with the senior NCO. Her shift was the longest of the three. She would wake early and take instruction from Collins and bunk late after a class with Kern. Both lieutenants were qualified navigators and pilots. All of the other helm personnel were the primary pilots or aided in the route of information.

The wheelhouse was located in a heavily armored and shielded box deep in the bowels of the ship.[3] Whatever happened, if the ship still had engine power, then it needed to be controlled. It had its own backup power, air filtration, and pantry. It had its own sensor station with just enough incoming information for navigation. If more information was needed, it was routed through the Combat Information Center or patched in directly to the helm sensor station. There were always two Marines on guard outside the helm and two inside. If anything happened Collins, upon losing communications from the command crew, would be in active command of the ship with the sole purpose of escape and evade until communications were restored or safety reached. Back up procedures were in place in case standard communications failed; which had happened in the past for things as simple as flicking the wrong switch on a communication consol.

Most of the actual piloting was done by computer. The pilots would input speed, direction, and a multitude of other numbers and then computers would send control signals to the engines, thrusters, and maneuvering vents. It came across as point and click and that's how it was described to most people despite the reality.

Manual control could be used to pilot the ship, but only in emergency or time of war. It was far too expensive to go joy riding. Should manual control be needed, both wheels and manual engine control systems were locked until the two lieutenants, or another ranking officer with clearance, overrode the system.

The sensor battery was also housed in an armored box with much the same setup in personnel and security as the wheelhouse. The major difference was that it held most of the incoming and outgoing information on the ship. It was tied directly to each sensor node throughout the ship. It handled everything from astronomical data to whether or not the head was clogged. They never bothered with the latter due to the fact that whoever did the clogging was responsible for the unclogging.

If there was a problem aboard, the Sensor Box, as it was known, was the place to ask. It had the most personnel in one spot. The information was diverse and communication from sensor cubicles within the box was strictly controlled by a Senior Chief Petty Officer and two Chief Petty Officers. The computers were top notch and could analyze, project, and interpret data, but they could not make decisions. They could and did make mistakes. They also needed a constant eye on their calibrations.

After the base sensor information was collected and sifted, it was sent to a second computer system. The second system was a database which formed a single cohesive picture. The officers in charge could manually sift the information and isolate pertinent data. This was routed to the Combat Information Center on the bridge. The captain could request specifics and the officers in charge would find them.

Lieutenants Samuel Cole and Gregory Simons were brilliant, consistent, swift, worked well together, and, most importantly, were correct in their communication of data. They viewed the primary sensor display simultaneously and worked in tandem to identify and classify all targets, bogeys, and anomalies. Lt. Cole operated on another plane of existence. Lt. Simons interpreted and communicated on Cole's behalf.

Cole could speak for himself, but couldn't communicate on a level that anyone else understood without knowing the language. Simons was junior to Cole, but was the designated communicant to anyone else on the ship. He didn't always know what was going on in Cole's head, but could figure it out quickly and correctly. Most of the time, Cole typed his communication to Simons at the same time as doing two or three other things. Cole would speak up if Simons got it wrong. Capt. Artus, Cmdr. Greenland, and Lt. Cmdr. Carmen would sometimes insist on

Cole's personal vocal comments. Simons was also in charge of two junior lieutenants and two ensign apprentices.

Lt. Cole needed help just to live at times. He often had to be forced to eat and be pulled away from his work to use the head. He took medication to function on his own, but it slowed him and disrupted his usual brilliance. His senior crew members did their best to look after him. He had been promoted for two reasons. First, he was exceptional at his job. Second, the only other thing he appeared to care about as much or more than his job was his uniform. In full dress, he looked good and seemed to take an almost inhuman pleasure in snapping to attention and saluting. Capt. Artus greatly respected the man and did his best to return each salute with as much vigor and crispness as it was offered.

Lieutenant Nguyen Yuan and Lieutenant junior grade Patrick O'Hara were in charge of communications. They and their subordinates handled internal communications, communications with other ships, stations, and traffic control, both civil and military. The lieutenants handled the most sensitive communications and anything to be reported to the captain or Officer of the Deck. Lt. Nguyen was the fleet officer in charge of coordinating with fleet command as well as most military ship to ship communications. Lt. j.g. O'Hara was the ship officer in charge of communications within the ship.

Communications crew members were responsible for handling whatever specifics were given to them. This mostly consisted of communicating with other space faring entities such as coordinating with a specific ship or telling operational zone infiltrators, both identified and unidentified, to get out or be fired upon. The entire communications crew operated from the bridge and the CIC.

The communications crew comprised the bulk of the CIC personnel and laid claim to the most personnel across the entire ship. There were representatives from every shipboard system. Other than communications crew, weapons and sensor control filled the majority of the bridge and CIC.

Weapons were probably the simplest system on the bridge. The weapons themselves were another story, especially the lasers and hyper-velocity guns. Gun crews lived near their weapons. They loaded, operated, and maintained them. Computers, however, did all the aiming. The weapon consoles received target data from the sensors. All that Lieutenants Jenna Carver or Ishmael Amari needed to do was select the desired target, then the desired weapon, and confirm the order to fire. It wasn't as easy as it sounded.

Some of the larger guns took time to reload or recharge. Some guns, such as the hyper-velocity guns, needed constant servicing and might need cleaning during a fight. The weapon controllers had to be constantly aware of the readiness of the guns they were preparing to fire. They also had to remain in constant communication with the helm so that the ship could keep the best line of fire available.

This meant that the *Bismarck* would need to rotate along its long axis so that as one gun fired the previous gun could recharge. The helm had to keep a constant speed of rotation in order to make the most efficient use of weapon recharge times. It was the weapon controller's job to communicate which weapons were ready to fire and often needed to input tactical navigational data. The captain could make directions, corrections, and 'push the button' all from his personal console.

The Combat Information Center was directly behind the conn and the captain's chair. All ship and fleet information could be routed to it. The captain could receive and direct all the information from it to control his battle space. Senior NCOs operated, sifted, and controlled whatever information the captain needed at the moment. It was led by the most senior lieutenant on the bridge, Chester Whitfield.

When Artus and Greenland were not at conn, it was Mr. Whitfield who took over. He was due to be promoted to lieutenant commander just before launch like Artus. He would be on the bridge and in charge during the official commissioning.

At the CIC Artus could read each individual communiqué, target contact, and direct navigational information. The CIC was mostly a live, streaming database that did its best to supply the captain with real time combat information, hence its name. It was a place where the bridge representatives of ship operations could co-ordinate. If there was a lot going on, the captain was usually in the CIC There was a captain's chair, but it didn't get much use.

When Greenland or CMC Billings were on duty, Artus could sit in his chair and think. Greenland would often station herself in the CIC and micromanage. Micromanaging was discouraged in the navy, especially since Mr. Whitfield was already stationed there for this purpose, but it was often unavoidable. Mr. Whitfield's primary purpose was the control of the thoroughfare of information. He would communicate the captain's orders to the appropriate station, which would then relay to the necessary division, or he would flag the information the captain wanted and put it on the main bridge view screen.

Greenland was often poking about for specific information as well as taking pressure off of Mr. Whitfield. People who'd never done Mr. Whitfield's job before thought it was easy and often unnecessary. However, CIC controllers had a very high mental breakdown rate trying to bring order to chaos.

CMC Billings would listen to internal communications and respond to situations, in person if need be, in order to rectify the problem or to be Artus' eyes and ears on location. He would often go to the location on the ship to view the situation with his own eyes and be ready to report before Artus realized that there was a problem. Whoever was acting first lieutenant, usually Lt.'s Nguyen or Carver, would also provide similar aid.

The bridge chatter that Artus listened to was not that of conversation. The everyday hustle and bustle is what Artus listened to. For the most part he simply enjoyed the way it sounded, an ordered chaos, like some bizarre symphony. From his first command it was something he loved. He would hear tidbits of seemingly meaningless information coming in and then something would stick out at him. These tidbits often proved to be useless, but now and again they turned out to be items of significant importance.

Artus had tried to explain it to others, but the best he could do was call it a gut feeling or sixth sense.

One thing he liked about Greenland was that she appeared to have the same sense. If it was not as adept as Artus', then it was geared to the information Artus usually forgot or thought irrelevant. She would often compile a list of information she thought important and present it to him without his asking. It was usually the information he wanted to know.

The information Greenland brought to his attention was not always useful, but sometimes having the information in front of his face instead of in his head or on the viewer made all the difference. The lieutenants weren't that good. Mr. Whitfield probably was, but his job was that of a traffic warden, not command and control.

After one simulation, he asked Greenland about it. She told him that he had mumbled something or asked a direct question that she then pursued. This had caught Artus off guard because he was unaware that he'd even spoken. Apparently, during one simulation, they'd had a full conference and Artus had thought it was his imaginings. She gave herself the compliment, which Artus seconded, that he had not had the privilege of such fine and able officers and crew to allow him to utilize the full might of his brain until he came to the *Bismarck*.

After Greenland had revealed to him his habit of talking to himself, he did his best to make his requests for information more vocal and authoritative when something caught his attention. He was in charge of a brand new ship. He needed to look like he was giving orders to please the cameras and investors.

5 SENIOR OFFICERS

From the personal notes of Commander Artus

Commander Melanie Greenland was Artus' second in command. She was two years his senior both in rank and age. She did not appear to be upset that she was being passed over for what would have surely been her command if Artus hadn't been there. She was a very capable officer and had captained a destroyer before being appointed to the *Bismarck*. Unlike Artus, she had ascended through the ranks by doing her duty, being patient, and playing the game. She was no fool. Greenland had been doing her best to study Artus, an officer she considered to be better than herself, and looked forward to serving with him even as his junior in rank.

Cmdr. Greenland was a bookworm. She had forgotten more about military history than Artus knew existed. In Artus, she saw the chance to learn about war from someone who'd actually been there.

The commander's father was a frigate captain. He and his ship had gone missing while on assignment out past the Kuiper Belt beyond Pluto. Admiral Fleming said that both her attitude and personality were exact matches of her father's. The Admiral also believed that this, plus the loss of her father, held her back.

It was the Admiral's opinion that this lead to an over cautious approach to many situations. The commander would study more and worry about making the mistakes her father made instead of making a decision. Admiral

Fleming had pushed for the commander to be Artus' second because it might bring the real Cmdr. Greenland out and produce an excellent fleet officer.

Despite this flaw, or perhaps because of it, Greenland was a superb strategist. She did her best to think ahead and have multiple back up plans. She admired Artus because it came naturally to him. Greenland had to work hard to reach what she considered an acceptable skill level.

She made decisions based on what the books told her was the correct way to do things. A problem that stemmed from this was that, with her encyclopedic knowledge, she spent too much time searching for the most correct answers. This reflected poorly on her tactical ability. She would often react instead of act. She was slow to seize initiative.

Artus was happy to have her because of one incredible skill that he often had trouble with or found boring. Greenland was a logistical wiz. What she lacked in combat she made up for by having an uncanny knack for predicting most things both mundane and unlikely. These things would turn out to be pivotal. Her paperwork was clean and efficient. Artus agreed with Admiral Fleming that Commander Greenland was destined for a fleet command.

Lieutenant Commander George Carmen wasn't a fan of her first name. Others had difficulty pronouncing her last name. In fact, most people had trouble comprehending the full length and breadth of her name.

Lt. Cmdr. Carmen's father was a traditionalist. Although their family hadn't been religious for a century or more, long names with one or more Catholic Saints mixed in were the norms. Her first name was actually Jorgina, but she had been called George from an early age and never escaped it. Carmen was her grandmother's name and, other than her first name, it was the only one that wasn't a saint or difficult to pronounce. Only the relatives she liked ever got away with calling her George. This small cadre of individuals consisted of her father, her eldest sister, and only brother.

Other than name, and what Artus considered an attractive physique and an excellent natural tan to go with it, the only thing of her Hispanic background that showed was her ability to ramble off curses incoherently using her family's native tongue. A combination of name and linguistic ability made her a legendary verbal opponent. You did not dare to use her unwanted nickname or insult it.

Lt. Cmdr. Carmen had a tendency to lash out at what many would consider slight offenses. Although superiors frowned on this, as well as her subordinates, she ran a clean and disciplined unit. For the most part she'd kept her record near spotless. There were a few incidents that found some jokers in hospital recovering from well-deserved punishment for offenses ranging from attempted groping to laughing at the name that must not be spoken.

Carmen's attitude was what many thought a fighter pilot's would be. The lieutenant commander proved to be not just a fighter in spirit, but an exceptional pilot also. When she was flying, she was a cool, calculating, death-defying acrobat. It was unlikely that a dogfight in space would ever emerge in modern warfare, but if it did, Artus would bet on Carmen.

She learned quickly and broke records at the Navy's Top Gun School. She excelled in all environments, with or without gravity. The air force had better planetary pilots, but when it came to space combat they didn't transfer as well as history would have anticipated. Only one who had spent at least half of one's life in space could cope with no ups, downs, lefts, or rights. Her father had been a racer in both planetary and zero-g environments and taught his children everything he knew. Carmen was the youngest daughter and the only one who took to it.

When a new joint strike fighter-bomber was developed that could operate in zero-g, Carmen was at the top of the test pilot list. The plane itself was originally billed to the air force, but its new thrust vector system showed potential for space that had not previously been seen. She and her pilots had been training with the new plane for a year and a half before being assigned to the *Bismarck* for operational command trials. It was rumored that, upon completion of the trials, a new joint forces strike wing would be activated with Carmen at its head.

The pilots were a motley crew. Some were navy and some were air force. Some of the pilots were standard for logistical support purposes, such as ferrying supplies and transporting personnel. One such pilot was renowned for having a few solo distance records, although Artus had never heard of her. Sadly, trouble seemed to follow this particular pilot wherever she went. She had been only a junior lieutenant up until a few months ago when she was busted for improper maintenance of her plane. She was now an ensign. She needed a major shot or she would be retired. This voyage would either make her or break her.

Carmen had an odd, older sister, attitude to this young pilot which showed that the lieutenant commander could be nice and loving when not laying a beat down on her pilots and crew. The young pilot was new to the command, but had been made a welcome addition quickly. Artus respected Carmen for being a professional that could be approached on a personal level by subordinates. She had formed her pilots and flight crews into a family.

Artus' personal opinion of Lt. Cmdr. Carmen was private. It was also against regulations. He hoped that she received the inevitable promotion quickly so that she would be transferred to another command where Artus hoped navy regulations would allow the relationship he wanted. This plan hinged on whether or not Carmen accepted him.

Captain Samuel Mitchel was the *Bismarck's* Marine Commandant and chief of security under Cmdr. Greenland. He wasn't as ignorant or fool hardy as the stereotypical Marine was perceived to be, few Marines were, but it was difficult to tell sometimes. He was a well-educated man, but often misinterpreted or misunderstood history. Like countless Marines before him, Captain Mitchel was full of himself.

Artus held the Naval Corps of Marines in high regard. He was impressed by and applauded their ability and saluted their history. The problem Artus had with them was that they often interpreted deeds long past as though they were deeds of the present. Marine lineage was something the Marines held highly and rightly so. However, they hadn't been involved in conflict since Titan, and then only for the initial landings. Before that they had not seen action for the one hundred and fifty years they had been trained for space duty. Nonetheless, the individual Marine tended to have an overinflated sense of self that culminated at a collective level.

The modern Federal Space Marine was a well-trained blunt instrument and all that implied. The primary purpose of Marines back through history was that of naval infantry. They protected the ship at port, conducted boarding operations both offensive and defensive, and performed amphibious landings or the likes thereof. They were shock troops and police. Marines were never intended to conduct prolonged land based operations.

The modern Marine was too expensive and specialized to be used where a transport load of draftees could serve. Artus had witnessed this first hand during his army service on Titan. It was no secret that the best Marines were often recruited because they had a certain mentality. Many misunderstood this mentality as brutish. Most were quite capable in the brain department, but there was something in the way they thought about and approached situations before they were recruited or trained, that made them good Marines.

If ever the Marines were called upon for their combat prowess, they needed every bit of the confidence they exuded to perform assaults, landings, and ship security. Thus they often believed that they did all the work belittling other branches. This didn't mean Artus hated or even disliked them. His life had been saved by a Marine on Titan and he would gladly have one at his side if ever there was a fight. He simply wished that they would only speak when spoken to.

Marines, like any military force, needed a clear chain of command. The Naval Corps of Marines, or more popularly the Marine Corps, was a corps of the navy and had always been. They were infantry at sea and thus used an infantry ranking system.

The uninformed observer, and some who really should know better, often got confused about the difference between Marine and navy ranks. Although Mitchel was a captain, he was two ranks inferior to Artus. Most of the civilian population did not know there was a difference. It often made things needlessly complicated.

Marines were soldiers, not sailors, and the best Marines, in Artus' opinion, were those who followed orders and kept their mouths shut. This was easily trained, but Captain Mitchel missed those classes. He followed orders, some more reluctantly than others, and had similar trouble in keeping control of his mouth. There was one such moment that stuck in Artus' mind.

Artus and Colonel Richards walked onto the secondary flight deck where the army was to bunk. They caught Captain Mitchel giving a lecture on how to look presentable to a freshly arrived, and rather disheveled looking, army squad. Artus had served with their master sergeant on Titan. The others had at least one combat star on their rifles. The sergeant and his fellows stood at attention and took the lecture well. The sergeant announced command on deck and he and his fellows saluted the commander and the colonel. Captain Mitchel wheeled around and saluted.

"Good day Master Sergeant McNamara," said Artus who returned the collective salute along with Richards.

"Sir," responded Sergeant McNamara smartly as he clicked his heels.

"Get yourself and your men cleaned up, Sergeant," ordered the colonel, "and get some rest. Report for duty tomorrow on the flight deck at 0500."

"Sir," saluted McNamara and his fellows. They snap turned and were about to leave when Artus spoke up.

"Sergeant McNamara," said Artus.

"Sir?"

"Please report to my office for a meeting at 1900 this evening in casual dress, with the colonel's permission of course."

"Certainly," said Richards, "as long as I'm invited."

Artus nodded. "That's all. Thank you Sergeant." The group marched smartly off the flight deck. Artus turned to Captain Mitchel. "Come with me Captain Mitchel. Colonel, do you want in on this?"

"He's your man, Commander. I need to check and make certain my babies didn't get their feelings hurt." As he left, he barked, "Lieutenant Steiger, leave that Ensign alone!"

"At ease Captain Mitchel," ordered Artus once they had found a suitably remote location. "In future, Captain Mitchel, you will refrain from lecturing your betters."

"Sir?" questioned Mitchel.

"Master Sergeant McNamara has twenty years in the uniform and three combat stars on his rifles. I served with him on Titan. He, the Colonel, and I fought on Titan together. Sergeant McNamara also has two Bronze Stars and a Distinguished Service Cross. The others all had at least one combat star and all wore the Distinguished Unit Citation. I also saw a silver star, did you? I grant that their appearance was not what it should have been, but they are all recalled from retirement for this mission and know a hell of a lot more about fighting than you. You would do well to exercise better judgment before you open your mouth next time." Mitchel looked taken aback. Artus sighed. "This is not an official reprimand. Dismissed!"

Artus couldn't understand how Captain Mitchel earned his post on the *Bismarck*. His record was nothing special. He did not have friends in high places or any other connections. He seemed an agitated and bitter individual. Artus guessed that he held some grudge and someone was trying get rid of him for a time.

Of the senior officers assigned to the *Bismarck* only one remained to be seen. Artus didn't know where Lieutenant Commander Hudson was. She was assigned as the ship's counselor. Artus had never met her and her file was heavily censored. However, she had two reputations; one naughty and one terrifying, both career ending.

Admiral Fleming had confided that Hudson was everything she claimed to be and more. She was the eyes and ears of some powerful people in the government and military. It was the Admiral's opinion that she was going along to ensure that everything was being done according to the book and policy, as well as reporting to the appropriate investors.

Lt. Cmdr. Hudson's reputations, as far as Artus could tell, were legend. This meant that they were built on rumor and speculation, and therefore not to be believed, at least not fully. Most rumors had some basis in truth. Events were often misheard, misunderstood, or fallen from the grapevine and thus figments of imagination or taken out of context.

Artus had heard enough reliable reports, Colonel Richards' being one, in order to be nervous. Hudson could make or break a career. Artus was curious how a lieutenant commander had such power. Even with high level officials backing her, certain procedures remained in place to prevent or slow what she was reported to be capable of. He found it hard to believe that so few seemed to have firsthand knowledge of her or her exploits.

Her other reputation, the naughty one, added a whole different level of anxiety to Artus' expectations. One report about Hudson that was the only constant among them all was that she was a babe beyond reckoning. It was universally understood that her looks were the basis of most of the rumors. Those rumors were the most outlandish and unbelievable. There were no pictures of her anywhere, official or otherwise. Lt. Cmdr. Carmen had some form of firsthand information, so Artus went to see her.

"**I** haven't met her," said Lt. Cmdr. Carmen when Artus asked about Hudson. "One of my pilots is here on a special assignment that I don't have clearance for. Ensign Heinz might be able to help you."

"She is the distance flyer, correct?" asked Artus.

"Yes. I requested her transfer here because she is an excellent distance pilot and can go solo if need be. Trouble seems to follow her, however, and I thought she could do with a proper chance. If the stories of Hudson are true, and Ms. Heinz does know something, then please, be careful what you ask and how. Ms. Heinz is missing six months on her record and I don't want a pilot of her experience transferred out just as soon as I got her."

"Noted," replied Artus. He requested a meeting with Ensign Heinz to talk about improvements and maintenance for the *Phoenix*. The pre-text of the meeting being that her years as a distance pilot would have taught her how to make a ship a home away from home. It was to be a casual, off the books, meeting since the *Phoenix* was not navy property.

ENSIGN HEINZ

**From interviews with Commander Artus and Ensign Heinz
Conducted by Frank Sims**

Space travel had many benefits. It also had many negatives, especially on the human body. Not all vessels had facility to produce artificial gravity. Such technology, while simple, was large and expensive. People who lived on other planets, such as Mercury, Mars, or Earth's moon, where there was less gravity, could never again walk on Earth. The same could be said for anyone who was born and raised in space.

Ensign Valerie Heinz was a smallish figure, standing at 5'3", with light brown hair and hazel eyes. She had never stepped foot on any planetary body. Upon joining the navy, she had been given several treatments to rebuild her muscle mass and endurance. Without these treatments, she would not be able to serve on many ships or ports. Her treatments had recently been given a major increase for her service on the *Bismarck* due to its near-Earth gravity. She had progressed far enough in the treatments to be able to wear an exoskeleton suit, which helped her stand and walk.

She was understandably nervous being one-on-one with Commander Artus. They spoke briefly and looked the *Phoenix* over. Her knowledge of older craft was excellent. She had many ideas for cheap, effective upgrades and renovations. After a time, Artus realized a lingering anxiety in the young woman that the love of mechanics didn't cure.

"What's bothering you, Ms. Heinz?" asked Artus.

"Permission to speak freely, sir?" she asked.

"We're off duty, and this isn't navy business, so speak your piece."

"Well, sir, other than age, it seems to me the *Phoenix* is well-kept. Boris does a good job. As far as homey touches, it's a matter of personal preference. It's your ship. Anything I suggest may not work for you or Boris. If I may say, sir, you don't need me to tell you how to fix up your own ship."

Artus barely concealed his shock. Ensign Heinz's file was full of misdemeanors and suspect comments about her skills as a mechanic with a poor intellect to match. However, it sounded as though she was calling his bluff.

"I've also heard that you already half live in the *Phoenix*," she continued. "You've already settled in."

"You are very observant," replied Artus, "but that's not what's bothering you, is it? Your face lit up and zeroed in when I lifted the hood for a look at the engine. You like the *Phoenix* and what's more, you like engines."

"Well, to be more blunt, sir, I'm nobody and have always been nobody. Every time I think I'm getting ahead some guy wants to... you know... take liberties. I'm a good pilot and mechanic, but every time I'm up for promotion... or a superior says he'll help me if I help him..."

Artus choked. He was completely off guard. This was not what he expected.

"Oh! No, sorry," gasped Artus. "I didn't... I wasn't... sorry if I made you uncomfortable. My intentions, while ulterior I admit, are completely honorable. I didn't even realize I might be sending the wrong message."

"In that case," said Ensign Heinz, "there's only one thing you want from me." This realization seemed to make her nervous and shifty. "You want to know about 'She who must not be named'."

"What?"

"...A certain officer who is coming with us, but has yet to show her face. I transport a lot of people. I hear a lot of things. I also received new orders for a special assignment to be revealed to me at a later date."

"Was I that obvious?"

"No, but if you didn't want me, then you want what I know. There is only one thing I could know that most everyone doesn't." Ensign Heinz stared off into nothing for a moment and her lips shook. Artus recognized the fear of a flashback and was afraid she may lose control.

"Ms. Heinz," said Artus, "please take a seat and have a drink. If anyone asks, tell them I pressured you for information. It should put blame on me and I will insist that you are left alone."

"Thank you, sir." She sat for a while and sipped her drink. Then her mood changed and she brightened up as if coming to a certain realization. She gave him a wink. "There's nothing you can say or do to protect me from her. In fact, I don't think congress or the President could do anything to protect me from her." She winked again.

Artus caught her change in mood and the winks. If he understood correctly, she was trying to communicate what he wanted to know without actually saying it. His opinion of the Ensign's mental ability went up dramatically. He hadn't played this kind of word game since Titan. He wasn't certain that he had enough practice to make it work.

"Congress... Hmm..." Artus thought hard and carefully about his response. "Congress, as a whole, can't do anything without a vote. Individuals, however, are often more powerful than their peers. They can sway votes by dealing under the table. Representatives are elected from local regions. It's uncommon for all from the same state to agree with each other on anything, or to be elected for consecutive terms. This makes it hard for them to consolidate any real personal power. No, there is no dangerous information in the House except for payroll. Any real danger would have to come from higher up."

Ensign Heinz nodded her eyes. Artus fought back a smile. "So far so good," he thought. Ms. Heinz took a long swig of her drink and sat back much more relaxed.

"If any one person wanted real power," continued Artus, "they'd have to be a senator, the President, or a member of Cabinet." Artus realized that he had not worded that simply enough.

"I suppose I'd have to agree, sir, but then YOU know better than I. I am nobody. You're not a politician, but YOU do have to have a nomination for the academy. I wager you know more about the dangers of government than I. I have figured out that the more power one has, the more one has to lose. It's usually a spectacle."

Artus nodded. "Well put."

The Ensign sat forward. "Anyone who could cause extensive damage to someone so powerful would have no problem stomping little old me." She sighed. "I'm a simple person with simple wants and needs. The last thing I need is to be drug off to some backwater outpost and killed in a riot. As far as spectacles are concerned, I like them simple too. Have you ever heard of Stormy, the albino bear?"

Artus responded without pause. "My sisters took me to see her at the Miami Zoo. She's the white six footer with the strawberry patch on her head, right?"

"That's the one," replied Heinz with a wink.

"She seemed kind of runty," said Artus, "but I've heard that all the other bears leave her alone."

"That's because she's WAY stronger than she looks. I reckon she had to fight the others a lot. She had big claws too…" Heinz put her fists together as she spoke and then pulled them apart in an exaggerated motion. Then she began to wave an invisible object around as she continued. "Big claws they are, sharp and pointy. I reckon you'd have to use the biggest gun you could get your hands on if you were going to take Stormy on." Heinz turned her right hand into a gun and made to holster it.

"Well," said Artus, "I can think of a few, high caliber hunting rifles that could do the job." Artus thought that with Hudson's identity established as a bear that it would be safe enough to ask more direct questions. "I've never been hunting. What do you think?" It was certain that Heinz had no informed opinions on hunting growing up in space, but then Stormy the albino bear was fictitious also.

Heinz scratched her chin in thought. "I wouldn't think that you would have time to set up a decent shot with a rifle. I mean, as far as Stormy is concerned, you would probably be better off with a pistol of remarkable size. Probably one designed for piercing armor, just to be on the safe side."

Artus nodded. "Well, in that case, my first choice would be the Federal Enforcer. I've seen what that .50 caliber weapon can do against most things."

Heinz shook her head and pointed up and mouthed, "Bigger."

"Bigger," mouthed Artus in shock. "The Devastator needs all manner of bracing and assistance," he gasped.

"Not if you have a custom job and know what you're doing. In fact if you were going to go up against Stormy you might want two, one for each hand."

"One per hand?" questioned Artus. "That's not possible!"

"One in each hand might be a stretch, but if you had a good set up and the strength to match, you could use one single-handed easy. If you got a shot at Stormy, you'd have to make it count or she'd get you with the claw." Heinz made the drawing and swinging motion she'd made earlier.

Artus gulped. "Thank you for your time, Ms. Heinz. I enjoyed our chat about politics, bears, and hunting. I also thank you for the pointers with the *Phoenix*. I'll talk it over with Boris and, if he doesn't mind, you're more than welcome to help him tinker on it when you've got some free time. Not while on duty. I'll inform Lieutenant Commander Carmen so she won't yell at you for being around it. Also, on a personal note, I am impressed with your knowledge. You are aces in my book. Keep it up."

"Thank you, Commander. I think that you should also know that my meeting with Stormy was terrifying, but afterward..." Heinz gave a big smile. "...being near her gave me a sense of calm and security that I've not had from anyone except my parents. The *Bismarck* and its crew are quickly becoming my home and friends. I believe that they would do what they could to keep me safe and happy. However, I would put my life in her hands before anyone else's, even yours, sir. Well, except for, maybe..." Heinz bit her lip and looked across the deck where the army was exercising.

"Lieutenant Steiger?"

"How did you know?"

"It's my job to know what happens on this ship. Plus, Colonel Richards can bellow the best drill masters into the ground."

"You heard that?!"

"Everyone on the flight deck heard that. It may please you to know that regulations regarding relationships with different branches of the military are not as strict as they are for the same branch. Both Lieutenant Commander Carmen and I wish you the best of luck with Lieutenant Steiger, but this will be a long deployment so don't get too close. Work comes first and keep it professional while on duty, understood?"

"Yes sir."

"If you'll take my advice, Steiger seems a good fellow, but make him work for it. Any self-respecting woman should never be easy."

"Yes sir. Thank you, sir."

"That's all Ms. Heinz. Don't forget your drink."

Artus analyzed all that he might have learned from Ensign Heinz back in his room. He gave the Ensign high marks, not just for using a clever word game to communicate, but also for having the guts to even try such a thing. She could have easily told him she didn't know anything, claimed it as top secret, or worse, accused him of harassment. He was glad that she trusted him. She might have told him everything he wanted to know.

He had been curious why his senatorial sponsor, Mr. Whitney, was under investigation. Ms. Heinz's comment about Artus needing a congressional nomination to the academy was plain enough. This confirmed more of what he'd heard in his nightmare with Astaroth. It seemed that Senator Whitney had something to do with whatever Heinz knew. Her comments about only getting ahead in her career through back-alley physical favors may have been all Artus cared to know about the specifics of the event.

It was not uncommon for politicians, male or female, to have bits of fluff on the side.[4] However, if Lt. Cmdr. Hudson was as dangerous as rumors suggested, then the offense would have to be bigger than the senator having a mistress or being accused of harassment. As far as Artus knew, his senator had not been charged with either of those. Such a scandal would have been damaging, but not as ruinous as the media made it out to be.

Mr. Whitney's son, however, was a different story. He'd served on Artus' first command as a favor for Mr. Whitney. Artus despised the son with a passion. It was more likely that Heinz was involved through him, but that still didn't explain Hudson's involvement. Whatever had happened must have been worse than fooling around, and Heinz must have had some idea.

Ensign Heinz's particular mention of a backwater outpost could be a direct reference to where she'd spent the missing six months in question. The specific mention of a riot meant that it must have been a prison facility. He would look into recent prison riots, as well as read up on Senator Whitney's son to see what he came up with.

Everything about Stormy, the fictional albino bear, was in direct reference to Hudson herself. It confirmed reports of her being about six foot tall and a strawberry blonde. This made Hudson taller than Artus by an inch at least. Artus had correctly guessed her hair color based on rumor. Of course, it could be dyed.

The rest had to be about Hudson's physical strength and the application thereof. Heinz's description was clear. Hudson looked frail, but could quite easily handle herself. Perhaps frail was not the correct word. Artus wouldn't be able to quantify that aspect until he saw for himself. Artus was reminded of something his academy boxing instructor had told him:

"There is training and then there's talent. If you have both then you'll beat any opponent. Then, there are primates. A trained, talented, two-hundred pound prize fighter against a two hundred pound primate is no contest. The primate will rip the fighter's arms off and then use them to beat out whatever life the fighter has left. If you ever find yourself up against such an opponent, you'd better hope it's stupid or slow, preferably both."

Artus believed the ensign. It was one thing to hear a story from someone who heard it from someone else, but you could never find the person who claimed to have been there and witnessed it. The ensign's emotional flashback and use of deliberately vague communication was proof enough for Artus. The fear that she displayed could not have been faked. It was also plain to see that she believed it herself with the eyes of someone who had watched it happen first hand. Artus hoped that he never gave Hudson a reason to make a professional visit.

The last thing Ms. Heinz said about Hudson was that she was terrifying, yet calming. Artus didn't quite understand what she'd meant and decided that he would probably find out. He was impressed by the statement Heinz made about whose hands she would put her life in. This meant that there was a level of trust, real or imagined, between the two that was without equal. This in and of itself was the final piece that convinced him that Heinz's story was to be believed.

Artus tried to put these thoughts aside, but couldn't. It was time for him to go off duty so he went to the officer's mess where he found Colonel Richards and Commander Greenland had just finished a game of chess. Carmen watched as she ate her evening meal. Greenland challenged Artus to a game.

CHESS

"How did you get so good at chess?" questioned Greenland.

"Practice," answered Artus. "The key to getting better is by playing against someone who's better than you."

"Who's better than you?" asked Carmen.

"Well, my father for one. He's got trophies."

"Wow," exclaimed Carmen.

"The colonel here can beat me."

"Only just," grunted Richards. "I've only won eight of our last twenty matches. Of course, I might do better if we played more often."

"You keep track?" questioned Artus.

"As you said Arty, the key to getting better is by playing against someone who's better. If I want to get better then I've got to keep track. I've been keeping track since the first time we've played."

"That was back on Titan," Artus responded.

"Yes. I've got a few trophies myself you know. I was more competitive back then and I was very upset by being thoroughly trounced by a young upstart corporal. I'd say I've improved."

"I agree that you have improved," replied Artus. "You almost got me yesterday, and you don't throw tantrums anymore when you lose." They all laughed.

"Hang on now," started Greenland when she'd caught her breath. "I used his defense just now and came nowhere close to winning."

"Old age and guile Ms. Greenland," said Richards, "old age and guile. Plus Arty and I have played hundreds of games against each other. We're familiar with each other's games."

"If it helps to understand," returned Artus, "I attempt, most times, to win as soon as possible. Unless the other player makes certain moves in the opening two turns the fastest way is checkmate in four moves. This can be easily defended against."

"But I did block by pushing my pawn up two and filling in behind with my knight," argued Greenland.

"All that did was slow him down," said Richards. "Ok, it's not mate in four moves, but the basic attack is the same. He led you on in other places while setting it up. You left your knight there, where it can't do anything, thinking that the approach was defended. Then you ignored it until it was too late."

"Oh." Greenland sighed. "So how do I beat you?"

Richards laughed. "That's a good question. Tell us Arty. We're all dying to know."

"The best defense is a good offense," stated Artus. "Instead of trying to remove a power piece from line of attack or moving something to block for it, make a counter attack. If you do that, then I have to decide whether or not to continue my attack or defend. If I defend then I give you turn advantage. If I attack, that leaves you free to do damage with your counter attack.

"Don't put your knight behind a pawn to slow down an attack. Put it to use. Find a place to put it that will threaten. With mate in four, place it where it can threaten my queen's or bishop's approaches. This will force me to do something else. Force the situation to your advantage. Once you have the advantage you have to keep it by maintaining your attack within reason. Don't overextend yourself. Let your attack form slowly enough that it can be backed up, but not so slow that the advantage gets away from you. The proper use of pawns helps. It's not too difficult, but it does take practice."

Greenland analyzed the board. "Hmm… Well, I've got work to do. I do expect a rematch." Greenland excused herself.

"I'll play you, but I'm not much good," said Carmen.

"I'll take it easy."

"Don't you dare! I'm in like mind with the colonel here. I'm competitive and intend to get better."

"Ok." Artus reset the board and Carmen took her place across from him. She opened by moving her Queen's Knight.

Artus opened with his King's Pawn by advancing it two spaces.

"Now then," resumed Carmen. She moved her King's Knight. "I'm interested to know what you learned from Ensign Heinz."

"The ensign didn't give me many details," started Artus, "but the two of them have a prior history." Artus moved his King's Bishop.

"Who has a prior history?" questioned Richards.

"Well Ensign Heinz is a transport pilot," answered Carmen. Carmen's knight took Artus' pawn. "She's the one your Lieutenant Steiger hangs around."

"I've told that boy to be working not flirting," groaned Richards.

"Oh, he works. He volunteers to help her load or unload her transport. Don't worry; she makes certain he sweats. He's showing off, of course, but the work does get done faster. As long as the work gets done, they keep personal comments to themselves, don't touch each other, or do or say anything in which I have to enforce policy then I'm ok with it." Artus moved his queen to threaten Carmen's knight. She pulled her knight back. Artus advanced his Queen's Pawn by one space.

"Anyway," continued Carmen, "she's become the usual pilot for that silver-haired spook. He made a comment about Lieutenant Commander Hudson coming with us. The poor girl went white as a ghost. I've heard the gossip surrounding the lieutenant commander before, but Ms. Heinz's reaction was unique. When Captain Artus came by to ask about Lieutenant Commander Hudson, I took a guess and sent him to Ms. Heinz." Carmen advanced her Queen's Pawn by two spaces.

"Hudson is dangerous territory," said Richards. "It's not a good idea to go digging for answers you don't want."

"Sounds like you have a past history with her as well," said Artus as he moved his King's Bishop to check. Carmen scowled. She moved her King's Knight to block.

"I do, and the demon Astaroth. He's her enforcer and he has no qualms about killing in order to keep secrets. If that girl knows something and Astaroth is using her as his pilot, then it's probably a threat."

"A threat to who?" asked Artus. He advanced his King's Knight.

"To both of you. A threat for you to stop asking questions and a threat for her to stop answering questions."

Carmen glared at Artus. "You were careful how you questioned her, right," she hissed.

"Yes," replied Artus. "In fact, she brought it up. She thought I was coming on to her. When I freaked she said that the only other thing I could want was information about 'she who must not be named'. "

Carmen gave Artus a disapproving look. She advanced her King's Pawn two spaces.

"So," urged Richards, "what does the ensign know?"

"I'll not betray her confidence," replied Artus. Artus moved his Queen's Bishop to threaten her queen. "Suffice it to say that the ensign's encounter must have been memorable. I did some research into the information I think I learned. It involved the son of my Senator Whitney."

"That little twerp who can't keep it to himself," growled Carmen. She responded to Artus' threat by advancing her King's Bishop and smashing it down to check Artus. "Check," she growled.

Artus jumped. "You know him?" He castled short.

"He thought because he was the son of a senator I'd do whatever he wanted or whatever he told me to when he first joined up," said Carmen who fought to keep her emotions in check.

"Bad move," said Richards. Carmen nodded in agreement. She captured Artus' bishop with her queen.

"All I know for certain is this…" Artus took her queen with his knight. Carmen grimaced. "…our young ensign has six months missing from her record. Not the kind of six months that special forces and black-ops get. They usually get a mention at some embassy or as a cook someplace. Our ensign just up and disappeared for six months. I tracked her movements to Far Reach Gamma where she was waiting to make a supply run. Then she showed up on Moon Base Armstrong six months later assigned to the

Bismarck with a free pass and special orders to be revealed en route. There is no record of her arrival either. She disappears in one place and then appears in another months later, as if by magic."

"That's a cover up if I ever heard of one," said Richards.

"Let me guess," said Carmen, "she went to prison and got caught in the riot?" She moved her bishop back to cover her king and threaten Artus' knight.

"What," questioned Richards?

"Far Reach Gamma is a deep space supply station for some civilian mining operations on the edge of the Kuiper Belt," said Artus as he advanced his knight to take her King Bishop's Pawn. She rubbed her temples in frustration. Artus continued, "There's nothing out there of military significance except *Outpost Lima*, a high security federal penitentiary where many of the prisoners are kept in cryogenic stasis. The son of Senator Whitney was at Far Reach Gamma for transfer at about the same time as Ensign Heinz. He was killed in a riot on *Outpost Lima*. He wasn't the only one. The prison warden, several guards, the son's lackey, and the senator's top legal counsel were also killed in that riot. A short time later, Senator Whitney is arrested along with some ranking naval officers."

Both Richards and Carmen stared in disbelief.

Carmen recovered and advanced her Queen's Knight to her left. "I heard about the riot, but I didn't think there was much to it. It's a prison and a riot. They go hand in hand."

"Exactly," replied Artus. He advanced his Queen Knight's Pawn two spaces. "I also deduced, from a conversation about an albino bear and how to hunt one that, 'she who must not be named' is a trained fencer and uses a Devastator one handed with no assistance." Both officers' jaws dropped.

"You can't be serious," argued Richards, "you need an APA just to pick it up!"

"It was suggested that the weapon was modified," continued Artus.

"You can't modify a Devastator! The best you could do is a custom job from the ground up. It uses a .75 caliber round. The force of the round itself is tremendous and if it is a custom job…" Richards fell silent, shook his head, and rubbed his face. He sighed and sat back in his chair.

Carmen responded to Artus' pawn by taking it with hers.

"I don't know enough about it to make any kind of informed opinion," returned Artus. He took her pawn with his bishop. "Ensign Heinz probably doesn't either. She could have made a mistake and thought it was an Enforcer, but I asked her about it and she seemed to be certain that it was larger than that. The only other thing it could be is a Devastator."

"I'd be more willing to believe an Enforcer," said Richards. "It's a big gun, but I've seen some who could handle it without assistance, Master Chief Billings for one."

Carmen castled short.

"That's something we're not going to know until we see it. Regardless of the size of the weapon I do not believe Ms. Heinz is making it up. She claims eye-witness knowledge, she's missing six months, and the manner in which she communicated to me was meant to prevent anyone who overheard it from understanding what we were really talking about. When she realized what I was wanting from her she almost had a panic attack. She actually wished that I had been coming on to her. She did not fake that fear. I don't know what happened at that prison or how she is involved, but it was bad and she saw it." Artus moved his rook one space to his left.

Richards decided he was done with the conversation and excused himself.

"If you've made life difficult for that girl, I won't be happy." Carmen gave Artus the universal 'look'. Carmen's rook took his knight.

"Well, if it makes you feel better, I don't think she is in any danger. Astaroth is a scary individual and he does come across like Colonel Richards described, but I've talked with him enough to know that if he'd had orders to threaten Ms. Heinz or myself, he would have just done it. He's the one who kidnapped me on Moon Base Armstrong. I also don't think Lieutenant Commander Hudson will do anything either for the same reason. Ms. Heinz also said that, although the woman was terrifying, she would put her life in Hudson's hands before anyone else's. Well, Lieutenant Steiger's maybe, but there may have been a whole different meaning to that particular statement." His bishop advanced to take her rook. "Check."

Carmen squirmed. "She has been a bit more open about her feelings toward him since your talk with her. Did you tell her we decided it was ok?" She moved her king left into the corner.

"As long as the work gets done, they keep it professional while on duty, and don't get too close during this long voyage. I wished her the best of luck. Of course, I haven't talked it over with Colonel Richards yet, but it's not against policy as long they don't get caught anywhere and there's no pregnancy. I did tell her to play hard to get." He advanced his Queen's Pawn up to threaten her knight.

"Good. I will keep an out, just in case. As far as her danger goes, I'm not going to take any chances." She took his pawn with hers. "Next time I see that Astaroth fellow I'm going to tell him to behave himself around my people and on the flight deck in general. He hasn't been a problem, but this whole conversation has made me a bit paranoid."

Artus' rook advanced to take her bishop. "Sorry about that. It wasn't my intent to bother you, but I decided that it would be a good idea to tell the truth."

"I'm glad you felt that I was worth the truth," she said with a satisfied smile. She advanced her King's Knight to threaten his queen.

Artus advanced his rook one more space. "Checkmate."

"What?!" Carmen searched the board for moves. She slumped in defeat. "You were just toying with me weren't you?"

"A little."

"You distracted me."

"It was not my intention. I assume you would like a rematch?"

"Yes, but not right now and only if you don't distract me."

Artus chuckled and began to put the pieces up. "I will try and keep my mouth shut next time, but I expect distractions will be unavoidable."

Carmen looked him over, bit her lip, and sighed. "That's probably true." She excused herself before he looked up.

Heinz has a Flashback

From an interview with Ensign Heinz
Conducted by Frank Sims

Ensign Valerie Heinz was new to the navy but not to flying. Her father was a long range cargo hauler. She had spent her childhood in the shipping lanes on the move. What education she received was from her mother and father.

Valerie knew a lot about transporting cargo, flying, long distance flying, and maintenance. She didn't have a proper education by navy standards. It took her some time to prove she was navy pilot material. She was a trained fighter pilot and did well enough, but she excelled at long distance solo flights. Due to her cargo hauling experience, she understood the paperwork and the language.

Lieutenant Commander Carmen asked for Valerie to be transferred to the *Bismarck* because of the mission. The *Bismarck* was going to be a long way from home and it needed a pilot who was "broke in" to distance flying and dealing with passengers. Lt. Cmdr. Carmen wanted someone who could go the distance between the colony station and the planet the army would be surveying. Resupplying the colonists and transporting the army would be a big task and the ability to work multiple shifts was a must.

Valerie was also well known for being able to make and keep things flying. One would think she would have been promoted for the amount of unwanted work she did. Sadly, she couldn't keep the repairs within guidelines. Her fixes were cheap, but efficient and effective.

Her work outperformed most, but she had a bad habit of trying to improve and subsequently breaking things. Carmen wanted someone who could maintain and improvise. If Valerie could control her curiosity and desire for improvement, then Carmen would look after her.

On board the *Bismarck* Valerie met Boris, the Commander Artus' personal pilot. He was thrilled to have her around and they both worked on the *Phoenix*. He admitted to her that he'd always wanted a daughter and that she fit his ideal. She took some time to adjust to that idea, but she decided that it suited her.

The *Phoenix* was almost as old as Valerie. It had so many fixes and patches she could hardly believe it flew. She had thought her knowledge was great, but Boris' was immense beyond her reckoning. He taught her a lot. Valerie was griped at by her lieutenant and Lt. Cmdr. Carmen for talking to Boris instead of doing her work. She was in awe of Boris.

Valerie had never been officially reprimanded on the *Bismarck*. She thought that her lieutenant wanted to cite her more than once. Carmen sat Valerie down one day and told her that she had potential, but potential could be bad or good. Carmen said that this voyage could make or break her career. Valerie took everything Lt. Cmdr. Carmen said as law. Obeying that law was something she tried her best at. It wasn't easy.

Carmen was an exceptional pilot who had started young like Valerie. Although there were no battles to Carmen's name, she was considered to be the best in the fleet and second in brilliance only to Commander Artus, or maybe even Commander Greenland. At least, that was what Valerie thought. She was in awe of them all. Even her crewmates were amazing.

Valerie didn't have friends growing up. She didn't have siblings. Her parents were all she had. In Valerie's third year at the Academy her parents were killed in a hijacking. Her parents death left a void she didn't think could ever be filled. The *Bismarck* was doing its best to fill that void.

Valerie didn't know how to deal with it. She wasn't very social and her parents were dead. Boris reminded her of her dad, but Russian. Carmen, though young, reminded her of her mother. She wasn't sure where Commander Artus or Commander Greenland fit yet. She didn't know them very well. They were, perhaps, heroes. Valerie had friends on the *Bismarck*. She had also met an army lieutenant named William Steiger who'd had an equally bleak career in the army. They were together as much as possible and they were yelled at a lot to get back to work. A bleak, lonely world had begun to shine brightly in Valerie's eyes.

Valerie had been flying support for the *Bismarck* during its trials. Six months before her transfer to the *Bismarck*, Valerie was stationed on a deep space outpost in the Kuiper Belt past Pluto. Valerie was on her third supply run from Earth with top secret equipment and two lieutenants. The lieutenants were not as good as they thought they were. The senior lieutenant was the son of a senator. He and his friend had only signed up for the uniforms, and with a senator for a father, they got away with a lot. They were being transferred to the station as guards for the prison. This seemed to please the senator's son who saw it as an opportunity to get an eye into the criminal mind and then use his experience to work in politics. He and his friend were there because fleet was tired of looking at them. Valerie was the only person who told them how it was.

Valerie would have kept her mouth shut, but the two men got frisky on the long trip, and she'd had enough taunts and grabs. The only reason she put up with it on the prison station was because she didn't stay long. When the two lieutenants made their advance by force, she stabbed the junior one in the arm with a screw driver and wasted no time in drawing her sidearm. The senior lieutenant decided she didn't have the guts to shoot and was extremely surprised when he found out that she did.

Valerie forced the junior lieutenant to drag the senior lieutenant to the cargo bay. She threw them some rations and med kits, then locked the door. The navy had a habit of recording everything that happened on a ship and the data was on Valerie's side. Even so, she didn't think her odds were good against a senator. She reported the incident, sending copies to the station and back to fleet headquarters on Mars.

Valerie was arrested on the station. None of the lonely men who usually flirted with her opened their mouths or touched her. The two lieutenants were taken for medical treatment. Every officer on the station showed up to reprimand Valerie. Then, Lieutenant Commander Hudson arrived.

Lt. Cmdr. Hudson was on the station for separate business, the transfer of an exceptionally dangerous prisoner into her care. She had presented herself to Valerie alone, in full dress uniform, with a very large sidearm and, oddly, an officer's double edged sword. When Valerie first saw her, it was evident that both men and many women would do whatever she told them to for various reasons, most of which were obvious. Valerie remembered being stunned at Hudson's beauty. She had no identifying marks other than rank and name. She had the look of someone who could handle herself in a fight. She was ice cold.

The warden of the prison station was a full captain. He kept trying to give Hudson orders and rules. She ignored most and threw the rest back in his face with all manner of legal codes and procedures. After speaking to some of the prisoners and the few respectable personnel, Hudson intervened in Valerie's case.

The warden said that the court-martial was going to be held on Mars and there was no reason to send a guilty woman, Valerie, back for a trial only to spend the time and money to have her brought back to prison. Hudson made a call to an Admiral who then told the captain that a prosecutor was on his way from Earth via a warp transport. The court-martial would take place on the station. Until the prosecutor arrived, Hudson was in charge of the investigation. Each party involved was to be held in separate cells.

Valerie had been in trouble before, but never this bad. When Hudson made her way to Valerie, she was certain that the cold blank look was not a good sign. Hudson read Valerie's record aloud. Then she read the charges. The records of the event had gone missing. Another phone call later and copies were sent from Mars. Those responsible for losing the data were quickly arrested for interfering with an investigation, tampering, and many other vague charges, all of which stuck. Valerie verified that the audio and video were accurate.

Hudson made one of her visits to Valerie with fresh blood splattered on her immaculate uniform. Valerie asked if she needed assistance. Hudson replied, "During beatings it is very difficult to keep one's person clean." This was said in the trademark coldness Valerie had come to expect. The fact that the Hudson was so open about using violence suggested that she didn't care about any person's status, rank, or backlash. This gave Valerie a slight glimmer of hope.

Once the prosecutor arrived, he conducted his own inquiries. He was particularly interested in the broken nose and black-eye of the son's friend. Security footage of the "face breaking" existed. The fool had tried to get his hands on the lieutenant commander. When the prosecutor was ready, the court-martial began.

The prosecutor was somehow connected with the senator. He was highly experienced and expensive. He was certain of his ability to win the case. He looked down his nose at the Hudson and joked about the gun and sword.

The court-martial took place on the cell block floor. The ranking officers for the court-martial were displayed on the cell block's large view screen on the wall. They would decide Valerie's fate. The warden insisted that the Hudson's weapons be removed, but she replied that they were within military dress code. The prosecutor didn't object and neither did the five senior officers who made up the Court.

The Admiral who resided as chief justice of the court asked if the special counsel was ready. Everyone but the Admiral and Hudson were confused by this. Another monitor was wheeled in and it revealed nothing but a shadowy figure. The prosecutor asked what it was all about. Hudson replied in legal code.

The prosecutor was taken aback and looked through his legal papers. He'd never heard of such a thing. Hudson commented that he should've been more prepared for a military tribunal. The other four officers of the court looked nervous but confirmed the rule as obnoxiously obscure, but entirely legal.

The court-martial proceeded with the prosecutor's opening remarks. They were lengthy. Hudson stated matter-of-factly that there was no need for show in such an open and shut case. She asked the prosecutor if he would mind getting on with the trial. The prosecutor made a courteous comment in reply, which Hudson ignored. Valerie smiled when his look of confidence switched to confusion when his comment failed to illicit a response. Valerie was confused also, but anything that put the prosecutor off his game made her feel good.

The trial continued for a time with both lawyer's hurling legal code at each other. They eventually got to the business at hand. The charges against Valerie were presented: harassment, assault with a deadly weapon, and attempted murder were the primary charges. The evidence was presented. The prisoners who witnessed the trial from their cells became quite upset with the prosecutor. Everyone, except the prosecutor and the presiding officers, seemed to think that the two lieutenants should hang.

A recess was called while order in the cell block was restored. Valerie was actually cheered as she was escorted out. She smiled. There was no way she could lose.

When the trial resumed, the parties involved gave their testimonies. Then they were examined. The prosecutor slandered Valerie hard, citing her infractions of navy policy, failed attempts at seducing senior officers, suggesting hormonal and emotional issues. Valerie argued and was scolded by the Admiral.

Hudson examined the lieutenants and used their records against them. The prosecutor argued that their records weren't relevant due to the fact that the lieutenants had never been officially cited or convicted. When asked to cite relevance by the court, Hudson's response was well put.

First, Ensign Valerie had never had a criminal charge, but the two lieutenants, regardless of outcome, had thirty-three between them. The second reason was because the prosecutor had used Valerie's record against her for the very purpose to which he was now opposed. The Admiral allowed it. The prosecutor still seemed confident of victory, and Hudson noticed.

She studied him and the court officers keenly as the trial progressed. The court recessed for the night. Valerie couldn't see how she could lose. Hudson didn't seem so sure, but said that Valerie would be okay regardless.

The next morning, Hudson was late. The Court was not willing to wait. They had come to a verdict. Valerie was nervous. It didn't look good. Three of the four captains declared Valerie guilty of the most severe charges. The fourth captain only gave guilty verdict on the weaker charges of safety violations and the like. He seemed disgusted by his fellows. The ultimate verdict in this case, luckily, was the Admiral. The Admiral deliberated as long as possible. Just when he was about to speak, the cell block doors slammed open.

Hudson stormed in, dragging behind her two guards with severe wounds. They were both very aware of their surroundings. The warden looked nervous.

Hudson claimed that three men had broken into her quarters and attacked her. One had a broken arm and leg. One had a bandaged stub where his left hand had been. The third was lying on the floor of her room with a letter opener in his head. The two survivors had informed her that the warden had put them up to it. Knowing that their testimony wouldn't be enough, Hudson invaded the security office. The video and audio to her room had been switched off; something only the warden had authority to do. Records showed that his access code had been used. Hudson then quickly found audio and video evidence of the warden soliciting the three men to murder her. The evidence was produced and the warden looked as though he was going to cry.

The Admiral demanded that the warden share all he knew. He admitted the prosecutor told him that the senator would make it worth his time. He told the Court the time and place of this meeting with the prosecutor and the security information was retrieved. All of the guards distanced themselves from the warden now that they knew who'd won. The warden, the prosecutor, and the lieutenants were detained.

The special guest who sat in the shadows of his own view screen leaned forward. He thanked the Admiral for his service and ordered him to arrest the three officers of the court that had pronounced guilty all across the board and for the fourth to be held for questioning. Ms. Hudson would return to investigate their dealings with the senator. The officers in question had disappeared from their screens. The man said he was issuing a warrant for the senator's arrest. He told Ms. Hudson that she had done a good job discovering links and leads to the senator's misdeeds, but she should now get back to her primary objective.

Hudson asked what to do with the prosecutor, warden, lieutenants, and guards. The man replied that he did not know who she was talking about. She then asked about Valerie. He asked if there was an issue of security. Hudson didn't think so. The shadowy figure then suggested that Valerie be read her rights, given some vacation time, and a new posting with an appropriate story for cover up. Once his monitor switched off, Hudson drew her sword and easily sliced off the heads of the two guards kneeling in front of her. She then drew her large sidearm.

This was the first time Valerie had a good look at it. She could tell it was big. The gun was a Colt Devastator. It was a mighty big number for the tall, relatively dainty and pretty figure of Hudson. All of the prisoners saw what was coming and hit the ground.

Everything happened so fast the guards were caught completely by surprise. Hudson's Devastator hand cannon boomed three times. The warden and lieutenants died instantly with expressions of shock on their faces and holes in their chests large enough to put an arm through. She walked up to the prosecutor and told him that a federal prosecutor should have a better sense of justice and loyalty. Then she cut his belly open and let him bleed to death in agony.

Hudson addressed the entire cell block. She told the prisoners to behave themselves or she would come back for them. She told the guards to behave themselves, also, until their relief arrived. She made it clear to everyone that there would be consequences to their actions. She ordered the guards to clean the place and throw the bodies out an airlock. All of the paperwork would be taken care of for them. Hudson told the senior guard she wanted the letter opener back once she had collected the prisoner she'd originally come for.

The prisoner was in a cryogenic chamber that was loaded onto Hudson's ship. Valerie was given an hour to clean up and collect her things. Then Hudson, Valerie, and the unknown prisoner went back to Earth. On the way to Earth, Hudson said that the incident would be wiped from Valerie's records. It wasn't classified, but no one needed to know. Valerie would also receive increased physical therapy and conditioning to build muscle and endurance so that she could survive at her next posting, the *Bismarck*.

The incident was a chance encounter that involved an ongoing investigation. It was an opportunity too good to pass up. Hudson was sorry that Valerie got involved at all and was kept out of the loop in case the warden wanted to interrogate her. Given the high level nature of the investigation, if Valerie told anyone, then Hudson couldn't protect her. Valerie never wanted to see Lieutenant Commander Hudson again. Valerie Heinz lived in fear of Hudson.

Before the *Bismarck* had set sail, Valerie learned from a shadowy figure called Astaroth that Hudson would be coming along. Valerie had also learned that the senator had been arrested, tried, and found guilty of numerous crimes. This particular senator had also been the force behind Captain Artus and his promotions. There were rumors that Captain Artus had been arrested and held for three days.

HISTORY OF CARPATHIAN

Journal of Commander Artus
Entry #29
September 5, 2319

I have researched the man known as Carpathian based on what I overheard during that nightmare episode with Astaroth. I must say that I am impressed, if it can be believed. The fascinating thing is that, there is plenty of credible information in easy reach. There isn't even a cover-up, as far as I can tell.

I checked out a copy of <u>The Navy's History of Extraterrestrial Warfare</u> from the library here on Moon Base Armstrong. It contains all of the credible reports of Carpathian's operations, all one-hundred and fifty years of them. Of course, those are only the sightings of the very large, dreadnaught weight ship, <u>Black Jack</u>. Whether or not Carpathian is still alive and in charge of the ship is another story left to theories. What follows is a brief summary of what I've learned:

The <u>Black Jack</u> is not the original name of the ship in question. It was commissioned as, <u>Sol Defensor</u>, or <u>Defender of Sol</u> in Latin. It was commissioned by a cult called, The Guardians of Sol. They were an early leader in space technologies after the Cataclysm.

The Guardians of Sol derived their name from that of our home star and the idea that there were other beings in the universe who wished to cause us harm. They were often made fun of and treated like many of the passing religious fads before and after the Cataclysm. They even had the same type of followers: actors, artists, musicians, politicians, and business persons. As a result they were well funded.

They built the Sol Defensor for the purpose of protecting Earth while it recovered from the Cataclysm. So influential were the people involved, that they quickly established a financial and industrial following around the world. This ended much of the strife seen before and after the Cataclysm. It began what is agreed to be a reconstructive golden age.

The technology involved in the ship was incredible even by today's standards. First and foremost, it was large. It had a design unlike anything we would expect. It was elongated and had articulating joints. It was described as a short worm or snake. It had a maw at the front that was designed to grab hold of objects in space and consume them. The intent was to mine asteroids for materials and then bring them to a depository orbiting Earth for processing. The original processing facility is apparently still in use, but has been upgraded and added onto. This facility is no longer recognizable.

Another technological feature of the Black Jack was its weapons. It had large hyper-velocity guns which had been developed a few decades before the Third World War and the Cataclysm. It also had two revolutionary developments, the ion cannon and disruptors. These weapons were overpowered by today's standards. The ion cannon was known as, 'Planet Cracker'. It was theorized to have enough power to break planetary defenses and shields, which hadn't been invented yet, with one or two shots. The disruptors could cause damage to just about anything, even if it was protected by a shield. After witnessing what a disruptor could do, they were outlawed in the Federation and the Sol Defensor is the only known vessel to have any.

It has also been argued that the ship had a functioning warp drive. This is unconfirmed. Also unconfirmed is its source of power. It supposedly had a fusion core not unlike that of the Bismarck's and was fueled by an anti-matter reaction.

As for Carpathian, little is known. It is agreed that his is a taken name. What skills he had, or by what reasons the Guardians of Sol had to appoint him captain, is still a mystery. What is known is that the ship was launched prematurely. There had been a falling out between Carpathian, the Guardians, and several other benefactors.

On January 18, 2169, Carpathian stole the ship. It was a very humiliating experience for the Guardians of Sol. The ship, which cost the world its life savings, was stolen! They lost all trust and respect in the eyes of the world community. They dissolved and went their separate ways.

That episode in and of itself says a lot about the situation and the man. It is the most expensive and ballsy theft in the history of... ever. I find it interesting that it is the only major theft Carpathian or the Black Jack have ever committed. The few sightings since that day focused on freight and supplies. There are very few casualties reported. The space pirate reputation is earned, but only just.

I also think it interesting, that even though the ship was stolen, it still performed much of its intended purpose. It delivered trillions of tons of raw materials to the processing station. The golden age that started is never accredited to Carpathian, the Sol Defensor, or the Guardians of Sol. Not even the naval archives accredit them, though it is obvious that we would not enjoy our current space faring lifestyle without them.

As for the ship's current name, Black Jack, there is no information on where it came from. The only thing I can surmise is that it was created from the very real fear felt at the time of having such a powerful ship in the hands of anybody, let alone an ill-tempered and not altogether sane man like Carpathian. It may be a reference to the man himself. It could be that Jack is Carpathian's real name and this was his blackest moment.

No one has seen anything from the Black Jack, and less of Carpathian, for well over eighty years.

I now harbor a nervous curiousness about the mention of Carpathian by Tavion and Astaroth. Is he still alive, or is the ship only attributed to him? If he is still around, I wonder what he could be doing. Why has no one seen the ship?

I am also realizing that this 'Order', and its apparent power, may be the remnant of the Guardians of Sol. What little I know about the Order I learned from that brief moment in captivity. From what I've read, both groups seem to have a common purpose and it is conceivable that not all of those involved with the Guardians gave up their beliefs or their purposes. With such influential and paranoid people involved, it is possible that they kept a lot of the power they had gained despite what the world was led to believe.

Seeing as how the <u>Sol Defensor</u> still performed its duty even after being stolen, one could make the assumption that the theft was merely a perpetration of some of the more paranoid and in control individuals, Carpathian chief among them. I have no idea where Tavion or Astaroth fit in the scheme of things. I can guess why they keep Astaroth around, and I'd probably be right. Lieutenant Commander Hudson sounds like trouble despite what they said about her needing a vacation.

I have no leads on this mysterious Aetonyx either, but I have done some research and the name is Greek. It means Eagle Talon. This would explain the emblem I was doodling and the patch on Astaroth's uniform. It sounds more like a title than a name. That's all I've got and it's not much to go on, especially since people avoid it when I ask about it. If my memory is correct, Aetonyx sounded as though he was the power behind a great many things. It sounded as though Tavion and Astaroth both took orders from him.

Regardless of what the future holds, someone has a lot of explaining to do.

WARP 10

The warp gate from the Sol system to Alpha Centauri needed power and a lot of it. So did its counterpart in Alpha Centauri. Earth's home star, Sol, was very capable of providing the needed power. The Sol gate was located below the star on the Y axis to keep it out of the way of the space lanes and so that any radical extremists, if there were any these days, couldn't get to it. Civilian ships could get there, but it was so far out of the way traffic control was easy.

The Alpha Centauri gate was located near the Alpha Star. It didn't need to worry about traffic control. Also, since the two stars of Alpha Centauri orbited each other every seventy-nine years or so, it would be necessary to reposition it from time to time in order to maintain a connection with the Sol gate.

Artus couldn't wrap his brain around the math involved behind warp travel. His navigator and engineers had to pass classes in the top five percent at the academy to be allowed into the training program where only one or two from each class graduated. Artus understood speed, direction, coordinates, and the basic principles of warp theory, but the mathematics involved were truly astronomical. His senior lieutenant in charge of sensor operations, Lt. Cole, could probably calculate warp mathematics in his head, on the fly, while doing two other jobs.

In as close to laymen's terms as Artus could put it, the warp-drive of the *Bismarck* operated through a system of contraction and expansion. It contracted space in front of a bubble of dense gravity created by the ship's warp drive and then allowed that space to expand behind pushing the ship along. This system allowed time within the bubble to pass normally and avoided the infinite mass issue altogether, which hurt to think about.[5]

Although the *Bismarck* wouldn't actually be traveling very far or very fast, the space around it would. The scientists said that the process was more like folding a piece of paper in half and traveling from edge to edge. The computer-rendered demonstration they used looked more like the operations of an old jet engine. Artus passed his necessary classes because he memorized the information, not because he understood it. He would often lapse into a coma when someone tried to explain it in detail.

In practical application, the *Bismarck* could travel at many speeds using warp. When it moved around in populated, traffic rich areas, it used what was known as slow warp. Essentially, this was warping space for travel at sub-light speeds. This would allow for better early warning and maneuvering at speed. It was also less costly on the engines, fuel supplies, and the human body. When in less traffic rich zones, the *Bismarck* could reach relativistic speeds, i.e. light speed or better.

The ship's drive was a revolution in science, industry, and mechanics. The *Bismarck* was powered by a stable, self-sufficient, fusion core fueled by an anti-matter reaction. This tiny star was dense enough to provide some gravity on the ship as well as create the gravity bubble necessary for warp speed. Other, larger, ships had a similar system, but they had to carry massive amounts of fuel to maintain the reaction. Artus, and many of the ship's engineers, were not allowed in on the secret of how and why this core was different from the others.

The warp gate functioned by warping space also, but to an extreme which few believed possible. Their concept was elementary school simple, but the math was beyond such education and far more complex than the common description. This process really was in line with theoretical worm holes and much more like the scientists' explanation of folding a piece of paper. The gates made the actual relative distance one had to travel only a short walk to the post office instead of a walk around the world.

Many of the principle mathematics were the same for both systems.

The major difference between them besides layman's descriptions was that, with the contraction system, the *Bismarck* could change direction and relative speed in flight. You still had to travel a good distance and number of hours to go anywhere in the Solar System, but it was far faster than most commercial and even military traffic.

The gate made interstellar travel practical by allowing a vessel to transit light years almost instantaneously. The catch with the gate system was that you couldn't navigate or change course if something got in the way. A few were concerned about the flotsam and jetsam of space floating across the path. Most were certain that a rogue asteroid or comet was an unlikely problem, but regardless of math they couldn't be psychologically certain that a moon or planet sized object would not be an issue. Operational tests had already proved successful.

Artus knew that line of site communication was not needed and so did the scientists, but the colony ship deployed sensor and communication beacons during its journey. As long as the extremely classified communication system between the gates stayed functioning loss of a ship in transit shouldn't happen. The beacons were not wholly necessary either. They remained as a backup for the guidance computers just in case something went wrong. The system had been tested many times and supplies had already been sent through remotely, but the *Bismarck's* voyage would be the first time anything that large and with living organisms had gone through.

The warp gates were an amazing piece of technical magnificence that completely escaped Artus' perception of reality. The gates finer functional details were top secret or better. They were rumored to have been found, not invented or developed by humans. The argument being that the tech had somehow been reverse engineered and was primitive in comparison to the original, but that was mostly conspiracy theory.

COLONY EMERGENCY

Journal of Captain Artus
Entry #48
October 4, 2319

It's been two months since I first stepped foot on the Bismarck. I am now heading back as her official captain. It's about time.

I was getting bored of meetings and briefings. One was simply to discuss how to reference the Alpha Centauri binary star system in all communications. It was decided that Rigil Kentaurus would be used to avoid the confusion one found in saying, "Alpha Centauri Alpha or Beta," respectively. Any abbreviations, such as RKA and RKB or RK Alpha and RK Beta, are also acceptable. I don't know why I even had to be there for that one. I'll use whatever I'm told to use.

We are going to take the maiden voyage out to Rigil Kentaurus to drop off Colonel Richards and his battalion. Our route was a long and winding, out of the way course. Our launch date was scheduled for two months from now, but it's been pushed forward dramatically. I've been told that the colony has had an emergency and is in need of assistance as soon as possible. We are now going straight to Titan in order to refit the army for war games. Freighters supplied for the colony emergency, whatever it is, are going to meet us at the gate.

Total travel time to the warp gate is now only about a month. It would be faster, but we've got testing to do that I am insisting on and my superiors agree. Although the Bismarck is supposed to be fully operational, I'm not about to go to the far reaches of explored space without being certain. It is a new ship and a new crew. Things need to be checked and understood before we traverse the gate.

Even with the pre-launch simulations, which the crews needed in order to get used to each other, there is still much to do. The command crew especially needs practice since none of us have served together. Most operations are standardized and well learned, but there is much more to being able to communicate than simply saying something. Learning each other's voice and body language is important. I've learned all I can of the ship's operations without putting to sea, in a manner of speaking.

Our course puts us in the shipping lanes so we'll be using slow warp. Total time to Titan will be approximately three weeks with a non-warp section through the asteroid belt where we will conduct some weapons testing. Time from Titan back to the belt will be one week with more testing in the belt. From the belt to the gate we'll use fast warp; travel time will be approximately thirteen minutes.

The original course came across as a pleasure cruise for the media. The Bismarck would've first headed through the asteroid belt to Jupiter's moon, Ganymede, then proceed to Saturn's moon, Titan. We would then return through the asteroid belt on course to pass Mars, Earth, and Venus before making the run for the gate. Thankfully, that has all been cut out.

We do have right of way through the shipping lanes. They are being cleared as we speak. I, for one, am glad to be skipping all of the in-between political showing off at Mars, Mercury, and the various industrial moons.

The speed restrictions will be lifted on the Rigil Kentaurus side so we should be able to make good time. We'll sit for a few hours after the warp gate travel to ensure there are no problems.

The voyage to the gate should be mostly uneventful. There will be some war games and drills. The major difference between these drills and the regular kind are the addition of civilians. All of the civilians aboard the Bismarck are *being issued action stations. They will learn firsthand what it will be like on a modern, the most modern, ship-of-war.*

The shipboard drills are not going to be any easier because of civilians. They might be slower and there will be plenty of problems to sort out, but that should be no trouble. All civilians have had to go through an extensive screening process and sign the appropriate legal releases before they were allowed aboard.

While operational trials will be underway the entire length of the trip, I was told not to be too forgiving of the Press Corps. It has been, and will be, a circus and most people know it. It is made worse by the need to show the various political, special interest, and investor groups what their money has bought in person. At least I don't have to make any speeches, and I do have a strict schedule that I'm not allowed to deviate from. This should deal with any cumbersome local authorities.

From what I understand, the real purpose of the army's war games is to provide them with something to do while the colony gets fixed. Then, their primary objective will be resumed. We will serve as the primary transportation and communications relay for Colonel Richards' battalion and the colonists. After the colonel is settled, we will make several more trips with more colonists in a convoy and a full regiment of the Army Engineering Corps who have the means to build an established settlement.

The colonists arrived to find a barely livable planet around the Beta star almost five years ago. They don't know much about it. They set up shop quickly but were not equipped for planetary exploration or habitation. They only finished constructing the gate system on their side a few months ago and so have been unable to receive the necessary materials or expertise until now.

It was decided not to send any transports with said materials or expertise because they would arrive after the gate was already up and being used. Communication also takes a very long time. I've been given new transmitters and receivers to deploy for the colony's use as well as some prefabricated warp gate parts and supplies. I have been given three top of the line machine shops as well as two laboratories. The colony must be in need of some serious work.

We are also being issued with Emergency Medical Pressure Pods. These pods are designed to carry wounded in case there is a loss of pressure or exposure to vacuum. They come in pallets of ten that can be quickly loaded onto a support craft. Once on site, they can be unloaded and used. They have hooks and rings so that they can be tied down in flight. We've been given forty.

This concerns me. The army on maneuvers can only get proper medical help, if needed, by coming back to the ship. This is the only explanation I can think of that makes any sense. Even then we have brand new everything, so there shouldn't be such a problem with our transports. Still, such accidents are better not tempted, especially with the amount of Press coverage we're going to have.

I've learned that the last member of my command crew will be picked up along the way. Lieutenant Commander Hudson is on Titan and was the primary reason for going so far out of the way until this emergency came up. I asked why she couldn't be transferred closer, but many do not know why and those that might, Admiral Fleming for one, said that her work could not be rushed.

I find this hard to believe for a psychologist. I don't think matters of mental health should be rushed, but there are plenty of psychologists. I don't see why whoever is on Titan couldn't just get another one. Well… considering her reputation, whatever she is doing probably has nothing to do with psychology.

I must also consider my nightmare with Astaroth. She was mentioned in a way that seemed to have nothing to do with psychology. It may be her schooling and training, but it's not what she does.

Then there is Carpathian and this Armada. If Carpathian and his demon of a ship are still around, then they could be trouble despite what Tavion or Astaroth said. At least he's a known quantity, sort of.

As far as the Armada is concerned, I don't know what to make of it. The change up for the army and the rush to get to the colony would suggest that there is a real threat. Of course, I base that on my experience. The official reasons for rushing make perfect sense.

I admit that, however unlikely, extraterrestrial life could and likely does exist in some form. The galaxy and universe are too big. I'm not the first to dream about meeting other sentient life, but the use of the word "Armada" sends chills down my spine. If there is anything about my nightmare that was a dream, I hope it was that.

In other news, Lieutenant Commander George Carmen, or just Carmen as she prefers, cleans up attractively. I've always enjoyed a good dress uniform, but Carmen in one makes it a pleasure. If I weren't her commanding officer, I might try and get a date with her. Right now I will settle for our weekly chess matches.

As for Astaroth, he's nowhere to be seen, but I know he's lurking about somewhere. None of the officers, except for Commander Greenland and Colonel Richards, claim to have heard of him or seen him. There was Mr. Billings and the stewards, but they understood keeping their mouths shut was best for them. Colonel Richards refuses to believe in the encounter; I can't say that I blame him, and Commander Greenland is in awe for some reason.

Greenland couldn't keep her eyes off of the blue D.O.D. patch on Astaroth's left arm. When it was all over she told me it was authentic. I'm not sure if that was some womanly intuition or an exceptional eye for detail. I know I'll be glad to have that brain of hers...

12 MAIDEN VOYAGE OF THE BISMARCK

October 4, 2319

Artus stepped out of the far fancier shuttle the Brass had ordered him to use. His command crew and many of the junior officers and NCO ranks were there too. The Marines and the army battalion were all present. Artus felt more like an emperor going to war than a ship captain going to improve the lives of some colonists. Artus was sure that's what some who had called themselves emperor thought.

It was definitely a media circus. Artus walked down toward his officers and when he reached an unseen line in front of them everyone in uniform snapped to attention and saluted.

The ages old whistle alerted the boat to the presence of "captain on deck". Artus walked to each of his command crew and did the prescribed greetings, thanks, and all he was supposed to for the show. When he made it to Commander Greenland he said, "Thank God for the end of the line. Now let's get this peanut operation under way, shall we?"

"With all due haste, sir," replied Greenland with a smile. "Make ready the ship for sail," Greenland bellowed and continued to bark sailing orders.

Most of the commands she gave had been in use since Earth's oceans were the frontier. The entire hangar came alive. More orders barked by other officers and NCO's to their teams. Artus loved the navy most because he loved the sound of a ship taking orders. As captain he gave the orders and then his senior officers repeated them, then the junior officers, and so on down the chain of command. Every man and woman knew what to do. Even the army had been given action stations.

It was Artus who had the upper hand on the Press now. They were running every which way trying not to get run over. He was certain that the Brass was thoroughly enjoying the spectacle and had probably helped in the planning, hoping to have this very thing happen.

Artus and his command crew formed two lines with Marine escorts in front and behind, clearing a hole for them on the way to the bridge where his bridge crew, headed by Lieutenant Commander Whitfield, were already waiting. Artus was eager to get underway, but the Marines were setting the pace and he could only go as fast as they could. They were not wasting time.

The Marines were pushing the Press out of the way and bellowing, "Command crew, make a hole." This seemed to please them. Artus realized that everyone on the ship was eager to have this over with and get the civilians off so they could do their jobs.

Some of the journalists were appalled by their treatment. There had been press briefings, warning them of this sort of thing. Once the orders were given, it was first and foremost a navy ship of the line and for anyone who got in the way there would be no inward or outward sympathy. If you didn't want to get run over, you'd better get out of the way. Artus loved it, as did most of the crew.

The Marines in front of him certainly seemed to be enjoying themselves more than they ought to. After a few corridors, Artus noticed that the two Marines were making a game out of it. They were taking turns bellowing in a round robin sort of way. One would call, "Command crew," and the other would continue with, "Make a hole." There were a few times some exceptionally nosy or slow witted reporters didn't get the message and the marines had to push.

If the first two got bogged down, the next two in line would move up to the front to keep the line moving. He would take the names of his escorts and congratulate them harshly for the lack of respect they were offering to the civilians. These Marines were under strict orders to not salute or address anyone until they were safely on the bridge. He would make sure that all the men in this detail would get a chance to be the two in front.

Unknown to the other officers, some of the admiralty had bet him a year of captain's pay that he could not get out of space dock by the scheduled time. He let the Marines know this and offered them half a year's pay if they could assist him in a timely manner. It seemed as if nothing would stop them.

Artus was not surprised that much of the Press Corps, both civilian and military, would be aboard for the duration of the Kentaurus mission. This, of course, was public relations trying to appease public actions and special interest groups. Artus didn't have much of a choice, but forbade any except the most experienced correspondents on the bridge or in any other sensitive area that would be observed or viewed by the public.[6] This included engineering and labs for the science buffs, some of the less sensitive weapons areas and machine shops; really anyplace not marked restricted.

Even if they didn't mean to be there, plenty of warning signs existed guiding them away, so there wasn't much they could do to argue their case. They'd been told they would be put in the brig until the next stop, where they would be investigated by the local authorities and then be left to make their own way. Ten had already been put off the ship before the ceremonies had even begun. It had been explained to the crew that the same would happen to them if they allowed anyone without clearance where they didn't belong.

When Artus and his troop arrived on the bridge, there was a vocal command to announce "Captain on deck." Everything went silent. Artus surveyed the bridge, all eyes were on him.

"Helm, control; prepare to weigh anchor and put to sea," ordered Artus. This was not where they were going, but it was the ceremonial thing to say. It was a standard order, though not used very often, if at all. In most circumstances, the order was a combination of colorful expletives and "out of here".

"Prepare to weigh anchor and put to sea; helm, aye," replied Lt. Collins from the wheelhouse.

"Alert all crew to launch order."

"Aye, sir," chimed Greenland. Her voice echoed over the ships intercom calling the ship to order.

"Communications, control; signal space dock and request launch clearance," called Artus.

"Signal space dock and request launch clearance; comms, aye; wait. Conn, comms; launch clearance granted," replied Lt. Nguyen.

"Launch clearance granted; conn, aye."

"Conn, comms; moorings and umbilicals disengaged. We are given the all clear," said Lt. O'Hara.

"All clear; conn, aye," acknowledged Artus. "Ms. Collins, take her out."

"Take her out; helm, aye." The *Bismarck* began to move slowly.

It was later described as, "A leviathan awaking from slumber." The space dock had sold tickets to transportation companies and private ventures to watch the show in shelters and private vehicles out on the lunar surface. Artus' sisters were out there capturing it on video. His sisters had some of the best seats in the house. They weren't with the military shelters, but they were still in an excellent position to watch the *Bismarck* fly overhead. They were going to send him a copy of the vid when they had a chance.

They later told him that it was like a demon screaming a war cry as it passed over them. He was going to joke about there being no sound in space, but realized that the building his sisters were in had an atmosphere. Since physics still worked and the energy coming from the *Bismarck's* engines was focused and intense; the building would have vibrated violently and the people inside would have had a good time.

The *Bismarck* roared away from the space dock a lot faster than it looked. It then performed a rolling, upward maneuver known as an "Immelman Turn," and then made a flyby. In less than two minutes they were in a high orbit over the moon and making their run to Titan. Artus had won his bet and the Marines would be pleased. He had to remember their punishment though, completely unacceptable to push people around like that. Something unspeakably easy and fun should do nicely. The other Marines had been informed that they too would get a chance at such punishment.

Since the route had changed, the *Bismarck* would now come close enough to Mars on the first pass for people to have a look. Then he would move on to the asteroid belt to conduct weapons testing. After that, they would travel to Saturn's moon, Titan, and then to the warp gate. Although the voyage now had a rushed feel, he would not allow the ship to leave the home star system without some operational testing. Admiral Fleming agreed and her bosses ensured that the Press and politics didn't get in the way.

He also planned training sessions for his Marines on the guns, and fighter pilots would have lessons on piloting the *Bismarck* herself. There would be other various cross training procedures as well. He wanted his crew to be well versed not only in their own jobs, but have back up jobs just in case.

The Marines and pilots would have fun learning their jobs, but he wasn't so sure about everyone else. Even the accompanying Press Corps would be drilled. Artus made the announcement shortly after passing Mars. Almost all the civilian media made complaints. "While you are on this ship you are my responsibility and so a member of this crew. You'll do as you're told," ordered Artus. That shut most of them up. The rest would be put in the brig and left at Titan. That quieted any remaining complaints.

"**B**attle stations!" barked Artus out of nowhere. The bridge crew, as well as the rest, were probably wondering what was going on as he had failed to mention the weapons test to anyone but his command crew. The *Bismarck* had reached the asteroid belt.

"You heard the Captain," snapped Greenland. "Battle stations!" Claxons began sounding all across the ship. Lieutenant Commander Whitfield repeated the order over the ships speakers. Most of the civilians were caught off guard by the rush of personnel. Gunners went to their guns, pilots to their briefing rooms while their flight crews began to warm up their planes, Marines posting guards at key points on the ship, medical teams, engineers, everybody went to their assigned station.

Most of the civilians were assigned as medical support groups such as stretcher bearers and assistants. Some that had experience, such as the military press teams, were given loading positions and placed at ammunition stations for the gunnery teams, in support, of course. Some were confined to common areas like one of the three mess halls or the gym.

Someone must have sent a message out on open channels, because the tactical officer reported a lot of civilian traffic approaching. They'd come to watch the show. Artus didn't mind as long as no one got hurt and no such transmissions were ever made again.

"Batten down the hatches..."

"Beginning activation of armored curtain, aye!" answered the defensive coordinator Lt. Amari.

"Weapons, conn; lock on asteroid located direct forward. I want a three kilometer by three kilometer barrage. Fire one salvo from each of the main guns at my command. All other batteries fire until ordered to cease."

"Lock asteroid direct forward, three kilometer by three kilometer barrage, one salvo from main guns on command, all other batteries fire until cease order; weapons, aye," called the fire controller, Lt. Carver.

"Helm, conn; began maneuvers for broadside port. Prepare to roll the ship giving both port and starboard alternating fire."

"Begin maneuvers for broadside port, prepare to roll ship for alternating fire; helm, aye."

The *Bismarck* turned to starboard to present its port side parallel to the asteroid. "Broadside... fire." ordered Artus. The ship shook as every gun on her port side fired simultaneously. "Roll maneuvers. Starboard guns make ready. Port guns reload"

"Roll maneuvers, aye."

"Starboard guns make ready, port guns reload, aye."

When the *Bismarck* rolled into position everyone had to hold on despite being strapped to their seats. The starboard side guns fired. Artus allowed this for two more broadsides each, and then ordered the helm to stabilize.

"Volley fire."

"Volley fire, aye," acknowledged Lt. Carver.

The guns began to fire from the front to the rear of the ship like a wave and repeated two more times. Then Artus had the ship roll so that the starboard side could do the same. When all was said and done, the asteroid had been reduced in mass by several tons and its surface features had been severely changed.

"Helm, return to original bearing."

"Return to bearing, aye."

"All sections; prepare rolling advance, weapons ready to fire by batteries, on my mark.

"All sections, prepare for rolling advance," Lt. Cmdr. Whitfield called over the intercom.

"Helm, conn; make your course one, five, zero degrees relative, ahead full."

"Course one, five, zero degrees relative, ahead full; helm, aye."

When the *Bismarck* had entered the field from head to tail Artus gave the order: "Rolling Thunder!" The ship began to roll, still moving forward, and the guns opened up. "Independent, fire at will," Artus ordered about five minutes in. Every gun fired on the nearest asteroid or lump of rock. After another five minutes, Artus ordered a cease fire.

Few aboard had ever performed such a maneuver. The Press Corps in particular enjoyed the experience likening it to a roller coaster. Some of the civilian space traffic that had shown up to watch had recorded the spectacle. Soon images of "the pin-wheel of death", as someone had called it, were all over the system.

Another drill was scheduled on the return journey through the field. It would test power efficiency and reserves. Weapons and deflectors would both be used to make certain that they could work together properly. It wouldn't be a complete test without combat maneuvers and incoming fire, but Artus thought it would be enough to know that they worked.

Artus sent his fighters to play with a merchant freighter and a couple of local patrols who were all too happy to help. He also had the pilots hopping around on drills, recon flights, patrols, and mock battles. He had even given his Marines false boarding alarms and security issues to keep them on their toes.

Space fighter combat was not the most practical endeavor for many reasons. The human body being unable to cope with the physical stresses involved was at the top of the list. Directly behind that was the fact that modern weapons could easily track small targets at great distance.

The most common weapons to reach out and touch small craft were lasers. Lasers were beams of light that fried many things including, but not limited to, computers and pilots. A fact about lasers that often escaped the knowledge of the general public was that as beams of light they traveled at light speed. Getting a space fighter close enough to a target to be effective was exceptionally hazardous.

Unmanned projects had been undertaken but did not produce any viable solutions. By removing the pilot you saved a lot of money. The problem with that was that you removed the ability to make judgment calls. Pilots conducting remote operations in a control ship seemed like a solution until it was determined that having all of your eggs in one basket was a bad idea. One also had the problem of not being able to dodge as well because of control problems. This was due to time lag experienced the further away the ship got from its controller. By the time the pilot saw something about to happen, it was too late to do anything about it.

For the modern stellar navy a fighter plane was useless, almost. They could intercept incoming conventional weapons. They could also escort and protect against lightly armed opponents. Pirates and terrorists were the usual. They were also effective at keeping shipping lanes free from debris and rogue asteroids.

This was the norm for most space fighters. They were far more efficient at such tasks than larger vessels due to maneuverability and cost. A modern space fighter may have been expensive, but it was far cheaper than even a transport or corvette.

As a strike craft the only viable solution was to set an ambush on or near an asteroid field, moon, or planetoid where their emissions were more difficult to pinpoint. They could be used in assaults if they spread out and came at their target from multiple directions, but losses would be high. If one looked at the assault problem objectively, and if success were achieved, it would still be cheaper in money, material, and loss of life.

With the advent of practical space flight, the air force found itself out of a job. It was decided that ocean navy captains made an easier transition to starship command, especially submariners who already worked well in three dimensional environments with only sensors to guide them. They also understood ship maneuvers for large objects that had a large turn radius and couldn't stop on a dime. Many of the operations, commands, and tactics used for a starship were direct evolutions from submarines. Thus, orbital and space transit defense were both contracted to the navy.

Talks of merging the air force and the navy had arisen often. The air force always managed to survive due to a fact of human nature: conflict. Space ships capable of interplanetary travel were far more expensive than fighters and bombers. The navy could never financially justify using its resources to police both the space lanes and local planetary governments.

As a result, the air force continued to excel in atmospheric and gravitational environments such as the inner planets and moons. When a conflict arose on a planet or moon's surface, the air force was sent for the long term combat and peace keeping operations. Nonetheless, the public considered the development of the Capellan Arms Joint Strike 18s and a navy lieutenant commander in charge of the test program as two steps toward an inevitable merger.[7]

However, what most didn't understand was that the fighter was initially developed for the air force. The only reason the navy was involved was due to certain advancements in propulsion, miniaturization, stealth, and physics absorption and dampening. These new advancements and others offered a probable space operations weapons platform that could go planet side if needed or vice versa. Lieutenant Commander Carmen and her team of navy and Marine pilots were testing for space operations, nothing more.

For this voyage, the JS 18s were going to be police. They would have drills and war-games both in space and planet side at Rigil Kentaurus Beta Two. It would also be a test of theatre operations and coordination between the fighters and a mother ship, the *Bismarck*.

The JS 18s were large as fighter planes went. They had a sleek, rounded, arrowhead shape with short wings toward the back end that curved downward. The plane had vertical takeoff and landing ability. In all environments, while it could maneuver like any other plane, it usually operated more like a helicopter. It could dance about the battle space quite nimbly. It excelled at being a bomber and ground attack weapons platform.

It was a strike craft, not a superiority fighter. It was not meant to dogfight. It had an internal weapons bay that could unload a large payload. For planetary operations, the payload was usually guided bombs and smaller conventional weapons for ground support. In space its payload was usually missiles and torpedoes.

A plane's crew consisted of three people; the pilot, navigator, and weapons master. All were qualified to fly the JS 18 as well as do each others' jobs. As a result of the size of the plane and the number of crew, there were not as many planes per squadron.

The JS 18s were brand new and so there were not many of them. The *Bismarck* had been issued all but two of the twenty-four planes. This was not a full wing of planes by number, but the cost, material, and personnel required the appropriate rank and authority that only came from a highly experienced pilot with a rank no lower than lieutenant commander. The traditional 'Wing Commander' title fit Carmen like a glove and she knew it.

KETHIS ARRIVAL

From an interview with Kethis Cheriatis
Iksus Armada
Admiral

Expedition 179
Operation Start: 8710 GST Month 6, Week 2, Day 5, Artex Local Time; 2314 Earth Time

Local Date: 8715 GST Week 1, Day 1, CT156 Local; October 10, 2319 Earth
Location: CT156 Binary, 2nd planet, Beta Star

Admiral Kethis would have been impressed by his arrival in star system CT156 and his landing on the second planet orbiting the Beta star if he'd been awake for it. He didn't like cold sleep or the week long thawing process, but Kengarel insisted that Iksus hibernation wasn't good enough to travel the distance from Artex Star at such low speeds. Plus, the manner of insertion was extremely dangerous. If the admiral and his contingent wanted to survive impact, they had to be encased in a special, highly secret substance.

He stopped listening to the explanation after he heard the word impact. Kengarel didn't go into any further detail and Kethis had the impression that Kengarel didn't want to talk about it, either. Admiral Kethis, his command team, and a contingent of Iksus Council Guards awoke on schedule some four years after they'd gone to sleep.

Kethis frowned as he looked at the crater he and his contingent crawled out of. It wasn't as big as he would have expected. There was plenty of rocky debris strewn about, but not enough to make a wholly convincing asteroid strike.

He didn't know how Kengarel had achieved stuffing Kethis, his contingent, their equipment, and the special shock absorbing box, in which they had spent the past four years, into an asteroid. He also didn't know how the asteroid had slowed and hit with such little force. Kethis was happy that he'd been put to sleep in cryogenic stasis before he'd been inserted into it or he would have filed the appropriate protest paperwork.

He would have gone along with the plan because he was Iksus and an Admiral. Plus doing the paperwork for a protest was all the protest that could be done. He would never fail to attempt his duty regardless of how much fear he felt or how far-fetched and ridiculous the duty was. All Iksus obeyed orders and rarely showed emotion to anyone except family. Kethis showed more than most and was often ridiculed for it. Even so, his career had been exemplary with few blemishes.

Kethis had known fear. All Iksus were fools if they had not felt such things at some point in their careers. They would be even more foolish if they ever admitted it.

Each Iksu, male or female, was brought up with strict rules. At an early age they were screened for physical and mental ability. Just because one kep, or child, appeared weak and sickly didn't mean he couldn't succeed within the Armada in some capacity. Kethis was one such weak individual, but he'd been built up by the appropriate stimulants, steroids, and drugs to help counteract this. His future as a leader was evident early, so he was given the appropriate schooling.

Fear was not tolerated. Luckily, for most kep this was never an issue, as their parents had to pass several training courses to ensure that they could raise their kep in keeping with Armada law. Parents were required to pass these classes in order to receive a kep permit. Kethis was proud that he and his mate had been able to have six, but what else could be expected from an Iksus admiral with several commendations and battles under his belt?

Pride, however, was not encouraged. It promoted overconfidence, which was decidedly deadly. He remembered a human phrase that he tried to live by. It struck him with nightmares: "If you're cocky, it's because you don't know something."

Kethis didn't fully understand the meaning of the adjective, "cocky," but the context was clear. If you thought you were going to win without difficulty then you underestimated your opponent. The human he'd heard that from was one of those known as the Cruor Prognatus, or Blood Born, in the human Latin. This human had said it to Kethis' commander when he was a fresh lieutenant.

The human raid on his outpost had been defeated easier than any had expected. Kethis' commander was feeling confident in his position. He demanded that the human give up and surrender. The rest of his team had been killed. The human made his comment and then proceeded to continue his fight to his demise. What none of the Iksus had realized was that the purpose of the human raid was to destroy the outpost. The Blood Born had snuck in undetected, planted explosives, and then proceeded to do what they called "raising Hell".

As the last human died he released a dead man's switch. The outpost was leveled. Kethis only survived because of his small frame. The large Iksus infantry that surrounded him absorbed most of the concussion. This raid had been timed flawlessly with others. Their purpose was to silence early warning stations followed by a swift strike at the Armada Second Fleet Headquarters at Kos, two star systems away. The human strike fleet was commanded by an enigma, Titus Andronicus.

That one phrase summed up the current operation. It was risky on more than one point. First, Earth was myth. Kethis had been chosen for this assignment because of his studies on humans, their languages, and their cultures. He'd learned that "where there's smoke there's fire," as the humans put it.

Earth, the fabled human home world, was generally dismissed as legend and religious nonsense. If it did exist, it was believed to be one of the planets deep within the core of the Human Nations territory. The Iksus had no credible information on the human core worlds. All that was certain was that the human core did conduct business, but with very few customers. If you weren't human, you didn't get in. The majority of humans didn't even go there. Only high ranking officials and members of the Human Legion were known to go into the core.

Some of the star ships the Legion used couldn't be built in any of the known human shipyards. These ships were few and far between, but some were newer than others and there was no information about them or where they had come from. It was believed by intelligence that there were larger and more able shipyards in the core.

It was known that there was some form of governing body within the core as well. Planetary governments sent representatives to the human core and the Legion's enigmatic commander, Titus Andronicus, went there often. If Earth existed, it was widely believed to be in the human core. Why shouldn't it be?

The binary star system of CT156 was not in any government's sphere of control and was considered by most to be unexplored. The lack of exploration was mostly due to its distance from established trade lanes and expense. This system was so far removed from the rest of the Human Nations that Earth being near to Kethis' current location, relatively speaking, just didn't make sense.

The second point of risk was that there were already facilities on the barren second planet of the CT156 Beta star. This was not unknown. A colonization attempt five hundred years ago had gotten far in its operations. The Iksus Council Archives held plenty of records.

The outpost also had Iksus armaments. They would be of older design and would not have been in use since about the time the colony failed. Kethis was happy that he and the Guard had been able to bring equipment with them. The Guard had their armor, weapons, and communication gear. Kethis had been able to procure an *E86* orbital sensor array that should serve as an excellent early warning and communications beacon.

It wasn't the most powerful or accurate, but it would likely be better than anything the outpost had. It would do until the fleet arrived.

He wasn't certain of the policies concerning colonization, but he was fairly certain the amount of military grade hardware that was supposed to be present wasn't usual. Did his government know about the Cannibal Fleet that destroyed the colony when they had started it? The evidence suggested that they certainly expected trouble.

The more Kethis thought about the situation the more things began to make sense. Kethis remembered stories his grandparents had told him about ships going missing beyond the Rytâgh Expanse. Not just ships, but an entire colony. Kethis had knowledge of scouts and other ventures past the Expanse and was told they were how Earth had been discovered as well as the location of the Cannibal Fleet, but he didn't buy it.

The third point of risk was the Cannibal Fleet. The Iksus had tried colonizing the CT156 system once before. A fleet of powerful ships had arrived a few months later and told the Iksus colony to get out. The colony complied. As the colonists were about to leave, this fleet changed its mind and told them to stay put. Why this fleet changed its mind, and why the colonists didn't comply, no one knew.

The Cannibal Fleet, as it had been called by Titus Andronicus, lived off of the destruction it caused. The Iksus had sent an escort for the colonists which attempted to break the siege. There was a record that the colonists had tried to flee before the fighting started and that the escorts had shot first. When a larger Iksus task force charged with investigating the incident had arrived, they immediately started firing on the Cannibals. The investigating task force had observed the Cannibals ripping the colony and escort ships apart, making repairs, and even producing new ships. The second encounter was well documented and it was decided that a third encounter would prove useless.

Why would a fleet of starships be in the area to begin with? There was no data on the surrounding systems. They could be automated, protecting some old supply or weapons cache from all the way back to the last Ikar'ys incursion or earlier. They could be protecting Earth, but why Earth? What made Earth so important, beyond being the fabled home of humanity?

The Human Nations were not advanced enough nor had the scale of production to produce this fleet. This meant that someone else wanted Earth protected if indeed that was its purpose.

How Titus Andronicus knew about the Cannibal Fleet, or if the mysterious individual was even referencing this fleet, Kethis didn't know. That worried him because this fleet did what Titus had described on more than one occasion. Titus' knowledge could mean only two things as far as Kethis could reckon.

First, Titus was in contact with this fleet so the knowledge of the invasion would be learned about far sooner than the Council expected. Second, there was more than one fleet with this ability and Titus knew of their existence. Kethis wasn't sure which of these theories he liked less. If Titus had control over or contact with this fleet, or any other like it, then this venture would be lost swiftly. The Armada would have spent its best and brightest in a defeat that it would not likely recover from. It would be better if Earth really was a myth and this venture was all for nothing.

Kethis was now very curious about the Council's motives. They had been loath to strike the Human home world like Titus Andronicus struck Armada Second Fleet HQ at Kos. Titus had only launched a very successful raid, but the Council wanted an invasion. This seemed to be a perfectly reasonable answer to many of the problems the Iksus faced where humans were concerned. At first, Kethis had agreed with the idea.

The plan, as explained to Kethis, was to invade and blockade Earth to force it into submission. Once accomplished, assuming of course it could be accomplished, the idea was to occupy it and hold it for ransom. The Council hoped to use Earth as a bargaining tool. The whole plan was a purely hypothetical debate until ten years ago.

Kethis was still on patrol and skirmish duties back then, but had participated in some larger engagements. He had been at the battle of Kos, as well as some others. He had heard rumors that an attack on Earth was being actively pursued. He and his fellows laughed at the gossip. Back then, the idea of attacking Earth was fanciful at best. Even if it did exist it would be at the core of the Human Nations; a place where politics, espionage, and force couldn't reach. The humans were fanatically protective of their core systems.

Spies and other assets had determined that there was little, if any, record of Earth beyond the scope of human imaginings. As Kethis rose through the ranks he learned that the higher echelons of command had many rude jokes about where humans came from. Kethis believed that all rumors, myths, and legends had a basis in truth. He believed that a place called Earth had existed at one time or, over the centuries, its name had been changed. Long story short, where ever it was, it was clear the humans had lost it. That fact was the foundation for many of the rude jokes.

Kethis never believed that Earth existed in any modern capacity. Any communications intercepted from the Human Nations core worlds never made the slightest mention of Earth's actual location. He never expected it to be discovered, at least not going by its ancestral name. He also didn't expect for it to be exposed and alone.

Either the Human Nations were conducting one of the biggest, most successful acts of subterfuge in the galaxy, or the jokers were right and they had lost it. One thing was certain: once the invasion was revealed, Titus Andronicus would act swiftly and bring much ruin to the Iksus Armada and Dominion before the situation was resolved. Kethis prayed to Atraés, Goddess of Battle, that everything was proceeding as planned.

KETHIS SURVEYS

From an interview with Kethis Cheriatis
Iksus Armada
Admiral

Expedition 179
Operation Start: 8710 GST Month 6, Week 2, Day 5, Artex Local Time; 2314 Earth

Current Date: 8715 GST Week 2, Day 3, CT156 Local; October 19, 2319 Earth
Location: CT156 Binary, 2ⁿᵈ planet, Beta Star

Kethis was happy enough with his current situation. His team had performed a record forced march from the crater to the outpost in two and half galactic standard days. They had reconnoitered the outpost. It was more than an outpost. It was a fortress built around and under a mountain. The above ground buildings could take several direct hits from almost anything except high altitude and orbital fire.

The atmosphere on the planet was not natural, that much was obvious. There was no plant life and the outer zones that kept the breathable air from floating into space were thin. The atmosphere was being circulated by a large station within the mountain. The air was not thick enough to breathe if you were doing a lot of work or if there was a ground battle.

The landscape was pockmarked with impact craters which were to be expected. There were also hills and mounds. The mounds were the oddest feature of all. They were low to the ground and looked like graves. They weren't very close together and didn't seem to form any kind of kept pattern that one would expect to find in a graveyard. He wouldn't have been surprised if they were graves, of course; there had been a conflict in the system centuries ago. The lack of a pattern didn't mean much over such an expanse of time. Asteroid impact and dust storms could easily alter the landscape so any graves could be completely covered.

The buildings were adequately sealed and the air supply was good. Kethis ordered anyone on the march back to the crater for supplies to take air with them. Anyone who felt weak should also get air.

There were ground vehicles. There were two medium tanks and two anti-air vehicles. If the Guard could power them up and get them running, they could be used to ferry supplies from the crater. There was also an old *Sonai* transport that would prove useful if Commander Tonais could get it working again. Kethis was relieved that the transport had shields.

He was surprised and impressed when he learned that the outpost had a bombardment shield which could protect against orbital bombardment. It could deflect and diffract laser based weapons. It also produced a strong magnetic field that could repel many conventional weapons. Plasma weapons could pose a problem, but the shield could siphon off most of the energy before the plasma filtered through and fell to the ground. Ion cannons would be the ideal weapon against the shields, but they would have to be big. Ion cannons used electrically charged atoms in order to overload shield systems and electronics.

Kethis feared disruptors above all. Disruptors worked by accelerating molecular bonds to the point that they could no longer hold together. Disruptors could penetrate and cause damage to anything the shields protected unless the shield was operating on the correct wavelengths. Disruptors took a lot of power to operate and only a dedicated vessel the size of a battleship could mount one. A bombardment shield could stand against a disruptor for only a few shots.

All disruptors left high levels of residual radiation. Just because you didn't take a direct hit didn't mean that you would live. If you were out of the line of fire you would need medical attention swiftly before your atoms decided to take leave of each other. Another, more painful side effect, was that the water in your body would cook out, steaming you to death. It was not uncommon to survive for a short time afterwards. Dead or not, the body would begin to shrivel up, leaving a lifeless husk.

Admiral Kethis made the transport and bombardment shield the primary focus of the techs. The Council Guard worked around the clock to get the ground vehicles working again. Those of the Guard not working on the vehicles were inspecting the defenses and building further entrenchments outside the wall.

The outpost communication systems did not take long to activate. Lieutenant Granis, the lead comms technician, had his squad busy sifting out static and interference. They quickly intercepted local transmissions. There was a space station in orbit somewhere around the Alpha star with what sounded like humans aboard. Although the language was foreign, some words could be made out. Earth was one of them.

Kethis noted that the name did not hold the same symbolic reverence to these humans as it did to even the most nefarious individuals in the Nations. It seemed to him that they used it in an everyday fashion. In the Nations, if one spoke so openly about Earth, they either drew crowds or were told to be silent out of respect.

The outpost sensors were online quickly. Lieutenant Granis wasn't a sensor tech, but he did have the skills necessary to work out most of the kinks, so he was put in charge of the sensors as well. The supposed human space station did not appear special. It was about as good as could be expected from any colony station. Its power core had plenty of extra power that was probably meant for additions and upgrades, but it was inefficient compared to modern Armada or Human Nations standards.

He saw no obvious signs of the Cannibal Fleet that should have been there, but that didn't mean that it wasn't lurking nearby. The surface colony outpost had sensors, but they were not as good as the E86 satellite he'd brought. It had better range, resolution, was omnidirectional, and could operate in near real time. The *Sonai* class transport in the hangar was to be used to put the satellite in orbit, but it wasn't up and running yet.

Kethis prayed that the Cannibal Fleet didn't exist, wasn't in the system, or was out of action. In the end, he decided it didn't matter one way or another as long they hadn't been detected. He was about to leave the sensor station when he noticed something. A single blip just entered scanner range heading toward the human colony from somewhere nearer the Alpha star.

"Lieutenant Granis," inquired Kethis, "what is that?" Kethis pointed to the new blip.

"Probably one of the colony transports," replied the lieutenant. "We'll know more once the E86 satellite is deployed."

"Commander Tonais," called Kethis.

"Sir," responded the commander.

"Make getting that *Sonai* transport running your priority. I want that sensor satellite deployed."

"We have partial power now," replied Cmdr. Tonais. "We've plugged in to the local power system for the reboot. We can use most of its systems as it sits, but orbital flight will take some hours still." Kethis grumbled in frustration. "If I may speak freely, sir?" questioned Cmdr. Tonais.

"Yes," replied Kethis.

Tonais pulled the Admiral out of earshot of the rest of the team. "A lot of things haven't made sense to me; the Cannibal Fleet, this outpost, and Kengarel most of all. My scales are tingling."

"I understand your concern, commander," replied Kethis. "There is nothing that can be done about it now. Pray that Atraés guides our fleet and that Mark'ai'Dyn will protect us."

"Yes, sir," replied Tonais. "One more thing, sir. The transport has a shield. It appears to be functional, but it needs more power. I've hooked it up to the base power supply and it is currently active. When the transport's power is full enough to reach orbit, we'll unhook. However, it will leave you unprotected until we get back."

"With the shield running, will that slow the refueling process?" asked Kethis with concern.

"No," replied Tonais. "We have the ship's shield system routed to a separate charging station. As long as it's plugged in, the outpost power supply should keep it at peak levels…"

"…As long as we don't get any orbital fire."

"Correct, sir."

"I'd rather be safe than sorry," said Kethis. "Good work."

Tonais snapped a salute and went about his business.

Commander Tonais did not disappoint in his duty to get the *Sonai* transport operational. It would be on its way to deploy the *E86* two days later if the satellite had made it in one piece, which it hadn't. It had been damaged in their arrival and would need to be repaired before it could be used. There were some spare parts, but some repairs were temporary at best and there was no clean room to do the work in. Deployment would only take about a day once the satellite was repaired.

Journal of Captain Artus
Entry #64
October 25, 2319

Lieutenant Commander Reyla Hudson is a woman of surprisingly modest appearance compared to the rumors. Her reputation, based on reliable sources, is not. I've heard of her before, but only in hushed tones like some kind of myth: Like the Boogeyman. Astaroth's warning hasn't helped my opinion.

Her team performs the part of psychologist well, but they are more obvious cover ups. Each member of her team carries himself like he'd rather be somewhere else, but they are disciplined, and, when they need to, they make an impressive presentation of themselves. The three odd men are all senior chiefs and are apparently old friends of CMC Billings.

Billings claims that they used to work together on sensitive missions. This is Billings' usual phrase for his early career that involved some sort of violent, secret action. I've done a couple of similar, if less violent, missions myself, so I know better than to ask.

They are also a motley crew of size and attitude. There is one taller than me, one about my height, and the third is proportionately shorter. When they are together, which is most of the time, they stand from tallest to shortest or vice versa. They are able mechanics and technicians along with whatever psychological training they may have.

Their questionable psychological methods involve comparing everything to some kind of mechanical or technical operation, usually some form of vehicle or engine. This seems to work better than one might think. They have attached themselves to the maintenance company of engineering and their work is impeccable.

They come across like Astaroth only with less freedom, or more. It's kind of hard to tell not knowing them. That being said, I have overheard them more than once arguing about all manner of technical and mechanical aspects. Engines and the newest commercial vehicles, usually the most expensive and luxurious, are the most common subjects.

The tallest seems to be the least useful of the group. This isn't too surprising given his size and the relative smallness of the ship's corridors and work spaces. I expect that it is difficult for him to fit, and given his apparent age, it's probably difficult for him to get up and down on his knees. That or he's lazy. Comments from his fellows would suggest the latter.

As for Lt. Cmdr. Hudson, she is a psychologist by education, a lieutenant commander by suspicious means, and by all accounts an interloping, conniving weasel who will do what it takes to accomplish her mission, whatever that is. I admire her tenacity and her results. I just don't like the way she achieves those results. I understand the political value a woman like Reyla Hudson can bring, but I'm not a politician nor do I like being used. I do realize that "being used" is a relative phrase.

Reyla Hudson is a flirt and, after only a few psych evaluations, has quickly become popular with the crew. This confuses me, for I had been under the assumption that she would cause fear, especially after hearing Ensign Heinz's story. I've thought about it and came to two conclusions.

First, being a psychologist is not like being a Lt. Cmdr. Sure you have to know your crew, but a psychologist would have a different approach. She has obtained her rank because she is effective at something; I presume psychology. The second thing I've decided is that she is here to spy on me so she would have to befriend the crew to learn how they see me. Do they like me? Do they believe I know my stuff? Do they trust me?

This makes me ill at ease around her. She is always watching me. I can feel her calculating eyes drilling holes through the back of my head, and at times I feel like I know what she's thinking. It's disturbing.

It also makes CMC Billings and Carmen upset. Billings doesn't like having to restrict someone of command level from information. He is also tired of having to fight her out of my office and quarters. I think Carmen is just jealous. Greenland is too busy studying or running the ship to notice.

Richards is glad that Hudson isn't here for him. He enjoys poking fun at me about it. I'm curious about his stories of both her and Astaroth. He refuses to tell me.

Hudson seems to suffer erratic behavior. If she isn't flirting then she is all business. If she isn't being either of those, she spends hours in her office being aloof. Her mood swings tend to be swift and aggressive.

She flirts with me no more than the rest of the men aboard. She does keep it mostly professional; only glances, smiles, and the occasional sly wink. She never gives the civilian reporters the time of day. She only speaks to them when she has to. This, as well as her personable nature, which I find difficult to resist, makes her popular among the crew.

She is occasionally observed in a confused state, pacing around as if there is something she is supposed to do, but has forgotten what it was. Greenland reported entering a lift Hudson was in. Greenland made a greeting, but Hudson didn't even realize that she was there.

Greenland said that Hudson was leaning against the wall of the lift moving her eyes like she was reading something but had nothing in her hands. When Greenland returned to the lift some time later, Hudson was still there reading nothing. Greenland asked if she was okay. No response. Greenland helped her to her quarters and sat her on the bed. Hudson hadn't made any indication of awareness, so Greenland called medical. This only happened once.

The rest of the time she is reported as not having slept. She can spend twenty-four to thirty-six hours awake. Greenland noticed in her quarters that she does have sleeping medication. Her behavior could be stress related.

Despite her quirks, she has developed a following within hours. This may be due to her physique and personable nature, but I need to put a stop to it. I've received reports of crewmembers going to her with their problems as opposed to their NCOs or COs. She does her best to be as professional as possible in those situations, but the crew needs to take their problems to their superiors, those who are responsible for the job or the trouble.

I don't like doing the paperwork for such problems as "My officer just doesn't like me" or similar issues, but the crew needs to know that I or Greenland will fix the issue if it exists. CMC Billings is more approachable. I will have him take a look at the situation after a complaint is filed. I trust his judgment. I have called Hudson to my office to express my feelings on the matter.

Lieutenant Commander Hudson entered in uniform and gave a crisp, by the book, salute and greeting. Artus let all six feet of her stand at attention for a time. He was doing his best to look busy before he acknowledged and allowed her to sit.

She had exceptional posture. Artus marveled at her physical aptitude. He realized that, although she wasn't a babe like the rumors claimed, she was very pleasing to look at. She was not heavy, not light, and no obvious muscle, but carried herself as one who could easily break things. Despite her physique, she had shown many of the Marines who was top of the pack in the gym.

She was even more clean cut and by the books than Greenland. The only persons aboard who could compare were CMC Billings or Lieutenant Cole, who looked his best most of the time. CMC Billings was built for power and it was no secret. His professionalism, physique, and combat abilities made him an excellent political buffer and body guard.

This was the second time Hudson had been to Artus' office since she had joined the voyage at Titan. She was somewhat like Astaroth had warned. She had learned from the first encounter with Artus that playing the flirt wouldn't work. She had also made the mistake of reporting for duty out of uniform. This time there was not a single hair out of place. She sat and waited for Artus to start. She had amazing posture.

"You have a reputation," Artus began. "Most of it, from what I can see, is hearsay and rumor. Some of it is good. Most of it is suspect. Until recently, I have seen no reason to be displeased. Bear in mind that, while you are only an observer and not a permanent part of this crew, you do wear the uniform – very well I might add – so make certain that you uphold its integrity and maintain the respect and responsibility of your rank. Being friendly to my crew affords their respect and loyalty to the wrong person or persons. Reports have come in that my crew is going to you for their problems and not to their officers and non-coms as they should."

"Permission to speak freely, sir?" asked Hudson.

Artus nodded his head.

"My orders are to evaluate the crew and the colonists..."

"Your orders are bull. They merely serve as an excuse and plausibility to be here."

"Might I ask how you came to that conclusion?"

"I am dubiously informed about you and your orders in particular. I also got to be captain of this ship because I am very smart and clever. I have been told that my looks help. Rumors are often founded on some sort of truth. Also, when you first came to my office it was not in a manner befitting an officer or the circumstance. All of my officers, regardless of how they got here, understand what is expected of them, especially when officially summoned."

"I had only just disembarked my transport."

"It is policy, both official and tradition, to perform a duty transfer in regulation clothing and attitude. You should have taken the time to clean yourself up. I am pleased to see that you have yourself in order this time. In fact, you are in such good order that I wonder why you were not presentable when you first arrived. You have also demonstrated good discipline since then. My initial impression, it seems, is somewhat unfounded."

He sighed. "You are not in trouble. I am merely requesting that you be more aloof around the crew. Many of the problems onboard that I've heard about, I've only heard about and that's a problem. There is policy in place for the crew to follow and it is for the benefit of all. I am aware that it often seems as though I or any other commander doesn't hear them, but if the paperwork isn't done then I can't be certain what they think the problem is and so I can't fix it if it exists. Please send the crew to their officers and NCO's even if it's of a personal nature.

"The only way this ship is going to function on the fringe of known space is if it becomes a family, within reason of course, and the only way that can happen is if the crew goes to their superiors or file a proper complaint."

"Yes, sir, excellent idea, sir," replied Hudson with one of her sly smiles. She then seemed to relax as if a weight had been lifted. Artus sat back in his chair and relaxed a bit, seeming not to notice.

"My informant suggested that you would act the way you did when we first met," continued Artus. "You're either very good at your job or very bad. I thought that you would have done your homework and found that I would not tolerate such behavior. If you really are spying on me for the Order then you should have known better. Were you misinformed about me or were you seriously expecting to get lucky? Most stories about you suggest the latter. You seem to be far too capable to have screwed up. Why are you really here?"

Artus struck a nerve. Which one he wasn't sure. Hudson went from relaxed to looking as though she was going to burst. Artus was surprised to see tears. He suspected a trap.

"You don't strike me as the crying type," said Artus.

Hudson took some deep breaths and began to speak. "First of all, I do what I have to in order to survive, just like anyone else. I have Doctorates in Psychology, Philosophy, and History. I have Masters in Diplomacy and Battle Field Ethics. I am certified for Military and Civil legal practice. I bench two-eighty-five and squat three-ninety.

"As for the Order, I don't technically work for them. I am here on their behalf, this is true, but I'm as much a slave to them at the moment as they want you to be. I requested this assignment because it gets me away from them. My original intent was vacation. This was no secret to my boss and he approved on my behalf. As for my behavior, I'm sorry. I've been under a lot of stress about my new orders. I had hopped an old classmate would have been more understanding. You don't even remember me."

Hudson started to cry outright. She stood, saluted, and just before she left she said, "Just so it's clear, I don't and have never gotten around, so to speak, ever." With that she left.

Artus sat stunned. If she was acting then she was in the wrong profession. His office bell rang.

"Yes," questioned Artus.

"It's Billings, sir. May I come in?"

"Yes."

"Permission to speak freely?" questioned Billings as he entered.

"Granted."

"I know you've had doubts about her, but she looked like she wouldn't make it back to her quarters."

"She said we were classmates. I don't know a Hudson from the academy. Get me her file and try to find out when she was there. Send her some chocolates or flowers or whatever we've got onboard with my apologies."

"Yes, sir," Billings turned to leave.

"And find Astaroth! I want him in here now."

Artus went from shock to fury when he considered the high probability of Astaroth's manipulation. He had intentionally gotten Artus worked up enough to confront Hudson. Artus couldn't see any secret information in her outburst that a man like Astaroth would not already know.

Upon entering the office Astaroth allowed Artus to give him a good, solid hit with no effect. Astaroth's lack of reaction made Artus even angrier.

"Ouch?" questioned Astaroth as he realized that he had not provided the appropriate response to being hit by the academy boxing champ. "I take it you've had a talk with the spy," he stated bluntly.

"She has orders to spy, I think, but she's not following them because she's on vacation. She feels as though she is a slave and requested this assignment because of the distance from Earth and the length of the deployment. I suspect that it's the same reason you're here; to get away and cause mischief without getting into trouble. Tavion said she was here on vacation. Perhaps you should've listened to him."

Astaroth chuckled uneasily at the mention of Tavion. "She has been overworked, but she is by no means a slave. She's tried to lord herself over me more than once. She thinks that her status in the Order gives her authority over many of their assets. If it were not for the fact that my boss, who is also her boss whether she knows it or not, punishes more severely than the Order or Tavion, I would have left them ages ago."

"So what did you do to earn this sentence?" asked Artus.

"I made some insensitive comments to an exceptional cook and a cat. This is my punishment." Artus found that more believable than anything else Astaroth had said so far. "I am not on vacation," continued Astaroth, "though I do enjoy being away from the bureaucracy. As for Hudson being on vacation, well, no more than I am. I'm on a mission and you'd better believe she is too. Her mission, whatever it is, is probably less dangerous than mine, but it might have some bearing on how I achieve my goal. I was hoping you'd find out what it is."

"Uh huh," grunted Artus with obvious skepticism. "If you have the same boss and he didn't tell you what she's doing here, then you probably don't need to know. Have you thought of that?"

"Yes, but it's unlikely. The problem comes from the manner of operation. There are, in fact, two bosses. I know this because I've met them both. The problem is that although their goals are always aligned, they often operate independently of each other and play their cards close to the chest.

"I do not think she knows that there are two different people giving orders. They don't communicate to us face to face if they can help it. In fact, now that I think about it, both bosses may not realize that she is working for the other either, and therefore don't realize there's a problem. Things make much more sense if that's the case. I had a similar problem for years until I realized they were two different people. Then I met them both and explained the situation. Then I got myself into my current punishment. One boss has refused to communicate with me until my sentence is over. It's made life somewhat more bearable." Astaroth assumed a very pathetic and depressed look. "I do miss the little girl." He stood quiet and did not continue.

"Well," returned Artus. "As for Lieutenant Commander Hudson, she may be lying, but she doesn't work for the Order. She seems to be stuck with them, though on what basis I did not find out. She hasn't been invasive or disruptive, so until then I'm going to try and make peace with her. If you want to know what she's up to, ask her yourself. She did mention something about having new orders, you might start there."

Astaroth was intrigued at the mention of new orders. "So, she does have something to do other than psychology, spying, and vacation. Given that our schedule was rushed forward and the army reequipped, I must assume the worst and so should you."

Artus thought he understood the threat. "I remember something about awakening defenses and an armada."

"If it comes up in conversation, you didn't hear it from me." He sighed. "I can only guess at what her orders are, but I think that she is testing the crew for preparedness. I also expect that she will reveal her intentions. Of course you could order her to reveal them. The bosses often work in vague enough terms that, although orders are secret, if they are challenged by the officer in command they can be revealed. One thing that has been weighing on me I think has been relieved. She does not seem to be the problem I was expecting. This means that any future operations should go unhindered."

"I don't like talking to you."

"Few people do. Are we done?"

"For now and if you ever use me like that again, it had better be for more than your curiosity. I'll have you thrown out an airlock next time. Understand!"

"Yep," chirped Astaroth.

"Get out."

HUDSON ADDITIONAL

Lieutenant Commander Hudson was an oddity indeed. There was a terrible seriousness about her. She also had a knack for sneaking and lurking, an impressive feat given the presence she exuded on most occasions. The confusion, with exception to whatever stress her orders were causing, came when she was off duty. This confusion was compounded by the fact that Artus couldn't tell when, or if, she was off duty.

When not doing anything useful, off duty or not, she was a fickle lark. She would hum to herself, dance down the corridors, be flirty, and tell jokes both clever and slapstick. During these moments she was a pleasure to be around and made one feel as if the rest of the world and its cares didn't exist. Then, like a flip of a switch, she could turn serious and back to playful again without skipping a beat. Artus had experienced this firsthand during his first encounter when she had arrived and reported in an unprofessional manner. Then there was her first encounter with the crew at large.

There was an incident in the gym with two crewmen. The crewmen had gotten into a fight outside the boxing ring. Hudson had been showing off and making eyes at some Marines when the fight started. Shortly after the fight began, Lt. Cmdr. Hudson had crossed the room and separated the two crewmen. She held them up slightly on their toes by the backs of their jerseys like cats by the scruff of the neck.

Reports indicated that Hudson got the two crewmen to shake hands without saying a word. It didn't take long for stories of her stare to become a legend. After things had settled, Hudson bounced like a bunny back to showing off and flirting.

The crew quickly learned that making her upset was a bad thing. None of them dared to say or do anything to each other with her in the room, which bothered Artus because they shouldn't have been arguing or fighting to begin with. They also learned that she was very playful when not laying the smack down. She never touched anyone, but she was very suggestive and more than one non-regulation proposition had been presented to her by both men and women.

Artus studied the incidents that involved Hudson. He viewed and listened to the security tapes and official reports. At first glance her behavior was everything the stories claimed; a tease, a flirt, or a hammer aimed at what was left of your career. When Artus added his own experiences with Hudson, he saw something different. It was subtle, but it was there.

Artus could never get a clear view on the ship's security footage to see what Hudson did with her face. The more he watched the more he decided that she was never flirting. He wasn't certain what she was doing, but it wasn't flirting.

Her expressions and body language were, in actuality, simply well balanced and graceful. She had an inviting smile. She listened intently to what one had to say. It was refreshing and made one feel cared about. It seemed as though she was responding to the emotion of the event or the individuals involved.

It was possible that she was testing the crew, but it came across as though the crew were making something of her that she was not. If this was the case, then it was evident where Hudson's naughty reputation came from; those in the fleet who were simply alone, or sick in the head. She definitely did not bounce like a bunny when she moved either. She glided across the floor with elegant discipline. She never put a foot wrong.

Hudson had taken to playing cards with some of the junior officers in the officer's mess. The reports of these games were mixed. Some thought she cheated, but she allowed all players to shuffle and deal in order to stop most suspicion. Artus finally got a moment to watch a game and learned a lot fast. It made more sense to him when he could see it for himself and in context.

The most experienced men faltered at her smile or if she batted an eye in their direction. The women didn't take long to learn that she was scamming them into error. The problem the women had that played against her was that, even with the obvious drama, they still couldn't read her. She played each person different and was acutely aware of what such deviance did to the other players at the table.

When a new player started, she would intentionally lose. That was standard procedure and an obvious tactic for anyone who had any idea how to play poker. What wasn't obvious, especially if you were sitting at the table playing the game, was that Hudson was also aware of the crowd's reactions as much as the players. More than once Artus noticed particular onlookers who were honestly enjoying the game give their own tells.

Learning the onlooker's tells was easy. Most people who weren't participating weren't concerned that they might be giving signals also. That was one reason Hudson always played with her back to a wall. All Hudson had to do was learn onlooker's tells and then pay attention to who that person in particular was watching.

She made it look easy, but to do all of that mental work in the time it took for all the cards to be dealt and through each round of betting would take a champion or a computer. A champion could and would tire quickly at the amount of work Hudson did with new players and onlookers coming and going from hand to hand. A computer could learn tells, but making the appropriate interpretations and judgment calls was something else.

One lieutenant considered herself to be an excellent poker player and probably was. She was certainly no novice and didn't fall prey to most of Hudson's tricks or taunts. If she did, she quickly learned it and practiced to counter it. The lieutenant was also onto the onlooker, over the shoulder, racket. She played her cards on the table and only raised them enough to see what she had once and rarely looked again. This forced Hudson to measure the lieutenant directly. Sadly for the lieutenant, Lt. Cmdr. Hudson was a better judge of character. Combined with slyness and endurance, Hudson was out of the lieutenant's league.

Artus enjoyed cards and liked a good poker game, but it was too easy to get caught in a lie. In his opinion it wasn't a real game of skill. True, it was a contest of wit and will in its own right, but it didn't test players like chess.

It was possible to gauge a player's intent to a degree in chess. Being nervous, jittery, or even calm and controlled didn't give the other player enough information to make a reliable judgment call unless they were playing a novice. Even then the pieces on the board could not and did not lie. No matter how someone acted or how obvious the next move was, the other player would either make a gain or be forced to sacrifice.

Artus had met many a nervous, cocky, jumpy, or calm players who were very consistent. Watching the player was often not enough. To make a proper judgment call you had to look at the pieces on the board and they never showed emotion. Every move could be seen. You had to hope that the piece you were about to lose meant that you could force the other player into a mistake.

Chess was a game of academics. You had to know where your pieces and the opponent's pieces were and how they could move. Once you understood the movement of each piece you could usually tell by its position what the other player intended to do with it, but it might cause you to lose sight of something else; a pesky pawn that just got your knight. Pawns were often underestimated and left to their own devices by even experienced players. An unguarded pawn was a dangerous pawn, especially with a move known as En Passant.

Hudson took an interest when she first saw Artus and Colonel Richards playing. Apparently she had never played before. Artus didn't buy it. Even if it was true, she learned fast. He explained the rules and special moves that many didn't know existed, including the "King's Castle" and "En Passant". He finally showed her how to win.

Hudson never looked at him once. She was quite involved. Despite her aptitude, Artus was confused by the fact that she made very poor and often foolish decisions. He considered that she was leading him to a false sense of security.

Artus finally came to the conclusion that Hudson was losing on purpose much in the same way as in poker, but something didn't seem right. After a couple of days, they had played several matches and she did not appear to have made progress. If she was trying to test him, she was taking her time. He didn't get the idea that she was learning anything about him either.

When Lt. Cmdr. Hudson wasn't lurking or playing, she was nosey, which was most of the time. She wandered the corridors making observations and taking notes. These were often followed by impromptu quizzes and bad looks. This was her primary task aboard ship, and her orders came from high up.

It was Hudson's job to constantly test the knowledge of the crew and officers, as well as gauge their mental preparedness. There were tests of equipment knowledge where the crew had to prove that they could operate their equipment and maintain it. There were basic mental tests that the crew had to perform on a regular basis. Then there were tests on policy. The correct answers to most tests varied on the test, morals, and how classified the material was. Policy tests were different. For policy tests, you'd better know and understand the policy or you'd get a lecture that was more dreaded than the punishment duty.

The equipment tests were such that every crewman should have been able to perform correctly every time. Sadly, no one was perfect. Some could not get past the idea that everything the lieutenant commander did or said was a test, a trick, or some kind of hidden truth. Artus had noticed that she almost always made her intentions clear, but it didn't matter.

This was compounded by the lieutenant commander's mode of operation. She would wink or threaten in an attempt to get information she wanted. This revealed a lot about the reputation she was infamous for. If the equipment was classified outside her clearance, and many things were, then the crewman had better say so and put their foot down against answering her questions about it, regardless of winks or threats.

If they told her what she wanted to know, then they would get a mark and have to go through a security screening. Most crewmen only made that mistake once. When the crew challenged her about classified material like they were supposed to, she would smile, make a note, and continue. Occasionally cookies were given as reward.

Morale shot sky high. The overall view of this was one that increased security and knowledge. Crewmen were now questioning each other on all non-classified knowledge they might be able to learn. This was done in hopes of getting a cookie. It often worked. Artus knew that his crew was the best in their respective fields, but some had been questionable security risks and questionable workers. Now all had fallen in line and were becoming knowledgeable about other jobs on ship.

Artus approved on the basis of being under crewed for this voyage as well as many others that were likely to come. It was always a good idea to have crew who could perform multiple jobs just in case. It also looked good on their reviews. He could now boast, and grudgingly thank Hudson, that he now had the most prepared crew in the fleet.

Hudson rarely tested the senior officers so openly. She would give performance evaluations from time to time. Most of her tests involving senior ranks were of the observational, lurking, notebook variety. She didn't look directly over shoulders. In fact, she kept her distance well, but the overall effect was there.

On the other hand, while morale had jumped and the knowledge base of individual crew members was up, tests were bad business in the navy and other branches. If a crewman failed, that meant punishment of some sort, which was being issued, but it also went on record. This is where Artus agreed with his junior officers responsible for divisions and shifts about the dislike of cookies.

If a crewman failed a test, they could be transferred or worse, reduced in rate. A ship may end up without the properly skilled personnel. This was a major concern for those crewmembers who grew up as laborers or were only schooled in a particular trade.

The cookie rewards were a great idea. However, Artus' biggest problem with them was that it was Hudson doing it. The practice could undermine one of the long standing traditions of the captain and other senior officers to reward their own crews. The long term effect of this would be a shift in loyalty. The crew, probably without realizing, would tend to favor Hudson's authority, limited though it was.

To Hudson's credit, she was keenly aware of what Artus expected of her. Such rewards were uncommon at best and punishment was organized with direct superiors. Still, Artus would have to put a stop to it even though it was providing an immediate positive effect. Also, if the crew became too used to the cookies, then what would they say and do when the cookie supply was gone?

Artus explained to Hudson his feelings on the matter. She agreed with him and was pleased that he had finally done what was expected of him, but she still had orders and her methods were the most efficient and agreeable for all involved. Artus' anger at being tested himself in such a way almost ripped a hole in space and time.

From that point on he took Astaroth's advice on Tavion's methods and told her how it was going to be on his ship. Hudson was enthusiastically cooperative in a way that surprised him. She saw no reason to pursue her orders to the letter since they brought up the very reasons that bothered Artus. She was well aware of the risks and was not happy about the situation either. They came to a compromise.

During drills Hudson would observe each division and compartment at her leisure. If she had anything or anyone she wanted to question, she would approach the officers and NCO's. Artus hoped that this would restore the proper chain of command, and it did. If Hudson wanted to test the crew in any way beyond her duties as the ships counselor she could, but not in an official capacity.

With the compromise in place, Hudson showed him her orders. Whoever was pulling her strings, Tavion most likely, had intended such a response from Artus all along. The orders were clearly stated to make any compromise necessary as long as Artus understood that he was the master and commander of the *Bismarck* regardless of rank, standing, or orders. The ship and the crew, although federal property, were his sole responsibility. Her orders were designed to force his hand. Astaroth's advice proved correct.

Once Artus understood this, he ordered her to show him the rest of her orders. As far as Hudson's orders were concerned, she had performed them flawlessly. He was even more upset by this. Hudson made her apologies and was glad that she could have more time to herself and no longer needed to second guess those whom she respected as the best. She also admitted to having a second set of orders that she was not allowed, under any circumstance, to reveal until after the *Bismarck* had crossed the Rigil Kentaurus gate.

Artus had noticed that she had been stressed. Once the compromise had been made, her physical appearance improved and she was no longer professionally difficult, for him at least. The less effort Hudson had to put into her orders, which became more vague as further compromises were made, the better she looked and acted.

She kept herself busy as the ships counselor, but she sent many of the minor, every day, worries of ship life back to their superiors. She took to only handling situations of being away from home and family or problems thereof, such as babies, children, spouses, and deaths. She only attended drills occasionally and practically stopped randomly questioning the crew.

The ships readiness did not appear to diminish any from what her previous actions had accomplished. She would still hand out cookies from time to time, but not as rewards for passing tests. She might hand someone a cookie as she passed them in a corridor. She now performed the bare minimum tasks required of her and Artus and his command crew saw no problems with that. She was quite content being the ships counselor and nothing more.

KETHIS PREPARES AND PONDERS

From an interview with Kethis Cheriatis
Iksus Armada
Admiral

Expedition 179
Operation Start: 8710 GST Month 6, Week 2, Day 5, Artex Local
Time; 2314 Earth

Current Date: 8715 GST Week 3, Day 6, CT156 Local; October 29,
2319
Location: CT156 Binary, 2nd planet, Beta Star

The outpost shield was operational. It was, however, several hundred years
old and a bit temperamental. The techs would never say such a thing, but
it was obvious that they were thinking it. Lieutenant Granis noted that
he and his techs were not shield specialists, so the power efficiency and
effectiveness would be better if they'd brought a shield tech. As it stood,
the shield drew so much power that it drained other systems.

The magnetic shield could repel much in the way of conventional
weapons. The energy deflector could deflect energy based attacks. Both
systems interfered with communication to the satellite. There was
interference from somewhere else, but the techs couldn't pinpoint it. All

they knew was that it was on the planet in the direction of the asteroid they rode in on.

Kethis ordered that the shield be kept in a low power state and ready to go full power at a moment's notice. This would protect against most small arms and lower powered lasers, but not anything orbital, airborne, or heavy ground weapons. Communication with the satellite was improved, but there were still false readings and images arrived blurred. The techs were trying to calibrate the satellite using what appeared to be a rogue asteroid.

Things were going well. If the fleet was on schedule then it would arrive within a week. Kethis and his advance team hadn't been challenged by the Cannibal Fleet or the humans. This made Kethis nervous. He was nervous about becoming relaxed. He decided to go and contemplate the events that had brought him this far. He found that such pursuits kept him calm and served as a good way to pass the time.

Kethis understood the reason why the committee system existed. The previous events at CT 156 were a prime example. Every Iksu there acted impulsively and it got them killed.

He agreed with the committees in principle, but getting out of something alive meant that you had to be able to act at a moment's notice. Sadly the reasons for the system, while noble, had changed and were now concerned more about the tax payer than achieving objectives. Like any government, the Iksus had to take taxes.

The size of the Iksus Dominion had forced it to take a different approach to the civil sector than it did in the past. For years, if a planet rebelled, then it was crushed. It was faster and often cheaper to undertake this route. This put a damper on military supply, so planets were now given citizenship and paid taxes.

This didn't solve the issue fully, especially on human worlds. Now everything had to be voted on, documented, and released to the public so that they could see where their hard earned money was being spent. Of course, the information was released after the military operation had taken place to ensure security. It was a good idea, but it was slow and full of politicking.

It was argued that the humans were chaotic and squabbled amongst themselves too much to respond to a move against their home, especially when their home was discovered beyond their reach. Even if they did rally, it would be too late. Earth would be held for ransom.

The humans could not compete technologically. Kethis admitted the Iksus had the upper hand in technology, but the humans could out produce the Iksus. In the year he spent at Artex Star preparing for the invasion, only five Iksus cruisers had been commissioned. The humans had produced twenty-three, which covered their losses and put them ahead by eight. They were only the ships that Titus and the Legion had produced. The individual Human Nations had security forces which could produce a myriad of smaller ships and also received donations of larger, outdated ships from the Legion.

Pirates and mercenaries might also get involved. The Iksus also ruled several, densely populated, human controlled planets that, for the moment, were relatively friendly. Holding Earth hostage would merely serve as a fuel for the human fireball that would result.

What the committees failed to realize about humanity was the strength of their resolve. They were easily manipulated, yet they held together. The Iksus had tried on multiple occasions to achieve some political influence over the Nations. The Ozuk'ai had tried to some extent, but had given up, claiming that, "such pursuits in regards to humanity were pointless." They had a mob mentality. You could convince one here or there. You might even succeed in getting a group to be on your side, but they were often treated as crazies or fanatics.

The Iksus had even tried to score points using the fickle human media. On the whole, this proved unsuccessful. The Iksus government believed that humans lived and breathed by their media. Kethis had noted in his studies that this was only true to a major minority.

The Iksus couldn't believe that the majority didn't believe everything they heard or saw. The media was a major source of communication, so it had a large impact on politics. The reality was closely related to the reason why the Iksus had the committee system. If an individual is paying taxes then he is critically analyzing what his money is doing. Most tax payers, regardless of race, were not ignorant of reality regardless of whatever the media tried to make it.

Humans were fiercely independent and yet they had the habit of banding together against a common foe. Those independent and critical humans were the majority. That majority had one goal even if it didn't enter into their daily life. From birth they were told stories about Earth. Those who they thought were from Earth, appearing naked on a street sometimes, were held in high honor regardless of who found them. Even pirates would count themselves lucky to find a Transplant. When word got out about the existence of Earth, the Iksus would be lucky to survive.

The humans would be led by the Great Ones. They had been around for centuries and were seen by many to be saviors of humanity. The Great Ones were supposed to be an ancient family line that passed down some kind of powerful bloodline and the centuries of knowledge it contained. They were formidable opponents in all forms of battle. The histories claimed them to be extinct until two hundred and fifty-six years ago.

Titus Andronicus was supposedly human, a member of the family, and immortal. Kethis didn't believe immortal. The Ozuk'ai were the longest lived race that Kethis knew about. They lived around two hundred years. The Iksus came in at one hundred fifty. The humans were lucky to hit eighty. The only humans known to live longer were the Transplants and the Great Ones. They never reached old age as far as Kethis could tell. They all died in combat, got sick, or disappeared. No one knew how long they could live.

Titus was the oldest on record, but no one had seen his face. He wore a protective suit and armor most of the time. It was not even known if Titus was male or female. Kethis was of the opinion that Titus was a scam to keep up human morale and security. He theorized that Titus was several humans who took up the name and position when the previous title holder retired or died. It was a very successful scam. Nonetheless, his ability to fight was in line with the family tradition.

Another rumor was that Titus had a Drac'lornai battle commander. The Iksus claimed lineage from the Drac'lornai. They were an apparently extinct lizard like race. History claimed them to be the longest lived race right after the Marna with nearly fifteen-hundred years of life. It was not impossible that some were still alive and in hiding, but the last Ikar'ys invasion had been thorough in its mission to eliminate the Drac'lornai. It was widely believed that the Ikar'ys had succeeded.

The Drac'lornai started life as a bipedal creature not unlike any of the other major races. They could grow to immense bulk and size. They would often take to a quadrapedal form in order to support this bulk. Some, it was said, could even grow wings and fly as well as breathe fire or some other elemental force. A story from the Ikar'ys invasion claimed that they could fight in the vacuum of space without assistance. Most of the races had myths and legends about the Drac'lornai that were consistent with each other enough to assume that such a race once existed. If Titus had somehow found and earned the service of a Drac'lornai, regardless of age, then much about Titus' success would be better understood.

THE WARP GATE

Arrival at Sol Gate on November 1, 2319

Upon arrival at the warp gate, the *Bismarck* was greeted by the Second Fleet of which it was a part. A lot more civilian traffic had gathered to witness the event than Artus had expected. The Fleet was busy rounding them up and sending them on their way. A sizable freighter task group was also present, for what reason Artus had not been briefed. The colony emergency must have been worse than anyone was letting on.

At this point there was no pomp or ceremony. Artus thought about trying to make a quote or come up with something memorable to say, but that had already been done by the colonists. He decided not to embarrass the moment, or the navy, and so kept his mouth shut.

The gate charged up and opened. The *Bismarck* wouldn't have long to get through before it would close. The amount of power needed could only be sustained for a brief time before the gate needed to close, cool, and recharge. It had massive capacitors that could be quickly changed with new ones if more frequent jumps were necessary. The RK gate also had this feature. Artus noted that some of the freighters had been fitted to carry these and would likely follow the *Bismarck* through the gate in order to provide the same service to the RK gate if needed.

Artus sent a query to Admiral Fleming. She simply said that they contained supplies for the colony. This made sense, but it hadn't been mentioned in any of the briefings. He didn't like it.

The travel through the gate was not noteworthy at all. Nobody died or got sick. In fact, there was almost no indication that anything extraordinary had happened unless you looked out a port hole, which the *Bismarck* had only a few of.

There was a whirl of blackness mixed with the occasional unknown light source. Artus guessed that the large red-orange light to the bottom right of the passage must have been from Proximal Centauri. The entire transit only took an hour. Upon emerging through the other side, Artus could not help feeling impressed. He smiled from ear to ear as did everyone else.

The ship's surgeon, Dr. Evaline Burns, began screening everyone on board for any problems. A few had fainted and some reported being nauseous, but there was no sign of any trauma. Hudson and her team also performed psych evaluations to make certain everyone was still thinking correctly.

Lieutenant Commander Hudson performed her evaluations under the auspices of a little believed but widely known phenomena. Warp travel being what it was, some thought that it also warped brain function and altered the perception of time and reality. Artus agreed with the basic principle of the argument due to the fact that he didn't understand the finer points of how warp travel worked either. However, he didn't believe there was any real danger, as long as the equipment worked. He'd made several journeys in warp during his tenure in the navy. Any problems were purely metaphysical or imagined.

Captain Artus sent his report back through the gate. He was preparing to begin tests as planned. Admiral Fleming acknowledged and told him to get his ship out of the way while the freighters with the gate recharge equipment went through. Then she told him to set course for the colony. She was also ordering Lt. Cmdr. Hudson to provide full disclosure.

The freighters carrying the capacitors didn't take long to make the voyage. As soon as they had arrived they began to set up shop. The gate was tested for any abnormalities.

The other freighters that Artus had seen began to arrive. As far as he could tell they were empty. Why send empty freighters to resupply the colony? Then it hit him. The colony was incapable. Incapable of what he didn't know, but the freighters were there to break it down and bring it back.

Did the colonists know what was going on? He could understand the need for secrecy. If word of this got out, it could damage reputations and many projects would be canceled. They couldn't hope to keep it a secret for long. Word would leak out and there would be hell to pay.

Then his thoughts brought him to Lt. Cmdr. Hudson and Astaroth. Hudson's presence for psychiatric evaluation of the colonists made sense given the circumstance. She had brought four large crates with her team. What were they, parts? What of her team? Astaroth had spent most of his time with the army offering his skills for martial training. One of the items of note Artus remembered from Astaroth's interrogation was that of an armada. He didn't want to deal with what such a word implied, but all of the changes to the mission so far suggested that something big was about to happen and it wouldn't be good.

The colony had not been informed of the situation. They screamed at Artus for an explanation, but he didn't have one. None had yet to be informed of the freighters purpose, but the colony had come to the same conclusion he had.

Then the colony simply went silent. That was the most ominous thing Artus had ever experienced. Artus sent a report to Admiral Fleming. She responded using the QE communicator and told him to go radio silent from that point on. He was only to use the QE communicator.

That was a bad sign. The QE, or Quantum Entanglement, communicator couldn't be read unless you had access to specific sets of paired, subatomic particles, which were often unique to each unit. The QE didn't actually send data. Such a thing, as Artus understood, was impossible.

What the QE did was vibrate a set of paired particles. This was something else that Artus didn't comprehend. It was explained to him thus:

"Think of it like Morse Code. I have a code book and you have a code book. They are identical. This series of beeps is a B, and that one is an X, and so on. You, with your code book, can read anything I wish to communicate.

With the QE it is more like a set of vibrations viewed by an electron microscope. This vibration pattern represents this letter, that vibration pattern that one, and so on. When I vibrate my atom on my end, it vibrates your atom on your end in an exact match or exact opposite of mine. As long as the patterns are consistent, all you need to do then is pull out your code book and interpret these patterns in order to understand the message.

The transmission of data, in the sense of audio or visual packets, has not taken place. I simply wiggled a particle on my end and you observed your particle's reaction. The information traveled faster than light simply because you already had the information in the form of a code book. All that is needed is a medium."

Such forms of communication, like Morse Code, had been used in the past very successfully, if not so scientifically. Unlike older systems like radio, this system was expensive, large, and so secret Artus had only been told what he needed in order use it. Its use was prohibited except in war time emergency.

Artus now wondered as to the real reason of Hudson's involvement beyond that of vacation or counseling. She would not have been sent, regardless of premise, unless there was a reason that had so far not been stated. Due to the current circumstances, Artus considered the unlikely possibility that Hudson might not know what was going on either.

While Artus sat at his table in his quarters contemplating these things, he received a meeting request from Lt. Cmdr. Hudson. He met her in his office. It seemed as though she had not slept in a day or two. She came ready to reveal her second, secret set of orders.

THE BRIEFING

November 2, 2319

The briefing room was large enough for all of the *Bismarck's* officers and then some. Artus guessed that this extra space was to accommodate any tag-a-long politicians or the press. It was built and arranged like a college classroom with several levels that rose up toward the back of the room. The desks had touch-screen terminals and data ports. Whoever sat at a desk could send data to the large display at the front of the room and interact with it from their terminal. At this briefing by Lieutenant Commander Hudson were the *Bismarck's* senior officers and NCOs, as well as Colonel Richards with his senior officers and NCOs.

Hudson had done her best to make herself more presentable. She achieved success. Only a few moments earlier in the captain's office, she looked as though she would pass out from stress and fatigue.

Artus wasn't as concerned about her wellbeing as much as he probably should have been. She had handed him a video recording of Admiral Fleming made shortly before the *Bismarck* had begun its voyage. It explained the situation and Artus wouldn't have believed it if it hadn't come from the Admiral. Attached to this was evidence taken by the colony in Rigil Kentaurus.

This additional evidence was the reason why the *Bismarck* had been launched early, its route altered, and the army refitted. The communications black out was cautionary and justified. The press didn't think so.

The reason for Hudson's involvement was made clearer by this. She had admitted to being high level within the Order. Apparently she was the only one with proper authority, in the proper place, at the proper time. It was not her job. Her physical and mental state appeared to stem from the stress involved by bearing this knowledge and forced to keep it secret.

The *Bismarck* had already put the pedal to the metal, so to speak, and was moving as fast as it could without using warp. Two members of the fighter wing were present and their planes being readied to explain the situation to the colony in person. They were the most junior in rank at the briefing.

"This briefing is top secret," said Lt. Cmdr. Hudson. "If you have not already guessed, the *Bismarck* is operating at full war time readiness. We are currently making best speed to the second planet of the Beta Star. Estimated time of arrival is three days. We have until then to plan a possible assault on this facility." She pushed a button on the lectern and images that Artus had already seen appeared on the big screen.

"What!?" was the consensus outburst from the assembly.

"I'm told that this facility is centuries old," continued Hudson. "It is a military supply base from a war that has raged for thousands of years. It is well stocked with hardware, communication systems, and a planetary defense shield capable of absorbing or deflecting most energy based weapons and conventional arms. Most of the facility is buried under…"

The assembly burst with questions and statements all at once. "Who built it? How old is it? How do you know all this? Is this first contact? This must be a joke, a shield like that is science fiction!" Lt. Cmdr. Hudson produced her hand cannon that had been concealed about her person, somehow, and placed it on the lectern. The room took the hint and fell silent.

"My primary duty is internal affairs," returned Hudson with a glare of doom. "I do not have adequate information to answer most questions. I can assure you that this is no joke and, Mr. Harris, warping space, as we do, for means of travel is just as mind bending and fanciful as this shield.

This ship is also outfitted with some sort of shield. I am not an engineer and have been given no operational technical information." Hudson took a breath and tried to relax.

"Before anyone asks," she continued, "we are using sub-light speed due to the need to insure that the planes of the assembled pilots are prepared for a long distance flight to the colony. There is also concern that any intruder may detect our approach…" Hudson was interrupted again. She slid the action of her weapon thus arming it. The room gulped. "Captain Artus, if I am interrupted again, would you please have Mr. Mitchel escort the offenders from this briefing?" Artus agreed and gave his own verbal warning.

"If there are no more interruptions, then I will continue," said Hudson, who was swiftly losing composure. Artus took notice now. As soon as the briefing was over he would see to it that she rested. "I have no idea how my superiors intended to spin the eventual discovery of this facility," she continued. "Nonetheless, as I understand it, Colonel Richards' mission to survey and construct has only been put on hold until it is determined whether or not there is any threat."

Hudson shot another glare at the crowd and went for her weapon before anyone said anything. Engineer Harris made a noise that he managed to turn into a yawn and squirmed as he tried to make himself smaller. His neighbor, an equally capable and more down to earth engineer, produced a roll of "speed tape" and slapped a piece over his mouth. Those nearest him relaxed.

Hudson relaxed and continued. "The reason for diversion from our original launch plan and the refitting of the army is thus. First, I was informed to prepare the army for war games while repairs to the colony station were made. As I have clearance and was already on Titan, it was left to me to make those arrangements. This is the story that has been fed to the Press. I was not informed further until after I arrived on the *Bismarck*. If there is no threat, the original survey and construction mission will resume and equipment sent through the gate.

"I'm told that the facility has been known of for a long time and its condition is monitored. This, by itself, is not a concern. My superiors assure me that it is no threat by itself. The perceived threat and the army refit are because of this." An image of a large object resembling an asteroid appeared on the screen.

"A little over a month ago," she continued, "the colony detected this mass hurtling at great speed toward the planet. This is not the first they have recorded and so were merely observing it. However, it became an emergency when the asteroid slowed down and moved to an atmospheric entry trajectory. At great risk, they sent a manned probe to take these pictures of the impact."

It was hardly an impact at all, considering the asteroid measured nearly a kilometer across and the atmosphere was thin. It was mostly intact. It was obvious that the asteroid had not moved like an asteroid should, nor with the speed one would expect.

"The probe, low on supplies and fuel," resumed Hudson, "could not linger for more photographs. I have been informed en route that assets in the field reported movement near this facility. The colonel's current objective is to investigate and report the threat, if any. Details of the ground operation will be discussed after this briefing."

"What assets in the field?" questioned Artus and Richards.

Hudson took a deep breath and released it slowly. "There are two in the Rigil Kentaurus system beyond that of the colony. The dreadnaught weight pirate, *Black Jack*, and its captain have reported movement on the ground. Carpathian also reports a large, distorted, warp anomaly heading for this system. He believes it to be an alien fleet on approach, but I must admit that his motives are devious and suspect even when he's not raving mad."

The energy in the room at this point was tense. Artus realized that many of his suspicions about Carpathian were probably correct. Colonel Richards went pale and took several deep breaths. The rest were fighting an urge to release their rising anxieties.

"He has," she continued, "attempted to contact and activate the second in system asset, but claims to be encountering interference from a source on the planet. He suspects that it is coming from the asteroid body. Regardless of Carpathian's mental state, my superiors trust him. Even if he were not present, the asteroids ability to retard its speed and maneuver would be reason enough to investigate.

"Due to this warp signature and the communications interference, Ensign Heinz and Astaroth, who I assume you've all seen lurking about, are prepping a transport to go to this." Another image appeared. It looked like a cloud with several larger objects mixed in. "This is both a graveyard and a dormant fleet located between the two stars. The only information I have about this fleet is that it is intended for the defense of Earth. The graveyard is what is left of the last intrusion. Astaroth and Ensign Heinz will attempt to activate this fleet manually.

"I'm told that, although dormant, the fleet should have already reacted to any foreign intrusion. The fact that it hasn't makes Carpathian's claim of an incoming fleet all the more dangerous. It means that this unknown intruder has somehow circumvented the Defense Fleet's early warning system. If there is anything to this asteroid and there is an alien fleet on approach, the *Bismarck* is the only thing in system to oppose them.

"We have been ordered to maintain radio silence. This is why Flight Lieutenants Johansen and Riggs are here. They will leave as soon as their planes are ready in order to communicate in person with the colony. This will take about a day. We will travel at sub-light speeds to a point a day's travel from the colony to drop them off. This will be the extreme range for these planes. I am informing them now that they will not come back with us. They are to leave with the colony evacuation.

"I will provide them a secure copy of this briefing. Lieutenant Commander Carmen is currently planning the details of their flight and will brief them further. I'm instructed to order them to use any means necessary to prevent the station from using its radio. The colony director is ex-navy and should be cooperative. I will also send orders to instruct him that the lieutenants are to have full unrestricted access to the colony's QE Communicator and they will be in overall command. The director should be allowed to proceed with the evacuation as he sees fit. This evacuation is a precautionary move, but it cannot, under any circumstance, go slowly.

"We will release Ensign Heinz and Astaroth for their mission at the same time. We will attempt to retrieve them at the drop off regardless of circumstance. They are both aware that they may be, God forbid, on a one way mission.

"The freighter fleet we observed should already have arrived and be moving to the colony. They will retrieve the colonists and any sensitive data or material. They do not have security forces, but will be instructed to take orders from the director or the military representatives only. Captain Artus, I suggest having some Marines ready to reinforce the lieutenants when and if possible. Any other mission operations not dictated in orders is up to the captain's discretion.

"This concludes this briefing. I will make myself available to the command for any further information if I have it. Captain, Colonel, here are your orders." Hudson handed them envelopes. Artus already knew what his orders were and Richards probably had a good idea about his. This was merely a formality.

"I have already alerted fleet to battle order 001," said Artus. "My orders to this assembly are to enforce Ship Combat Status Delta effective immediately. I will send for command crew and division heads at my earliest convenience for further instructions." He sighed. "I don't like or understand the circumstance, but these are the orders of Admiral Fleming signed by the Secretary of Defense and Joint Chiefs of Staff. I expect you all to perform your duty without question. Am I understood?"

The assembly chimed compliance. Artus looked at Hudson. "Anything else?"

"Not at this time," she replied.

"Then I will confer with you and further inform the crew as I see fit. Lieutenant Harris."

Harris jumped as his neighbor removed the tape from his mouth. "Sir," he snapped.

"Prepare the ship for silent running and wait for my order. You've got half an hour." Harris acknowledged and saluted. Both he and his team left. "Lt. Simons, I want two probes, one to update us of the situation on the planet and the other for electronic warfare and countermeasure. It only needs to be able to monitor and jam communications at this point. That may change so have more probes on standby." Simons acknowledged and left the room.

"Captain Mitchel," called Artus. The Marine commander ran over and stood at attention. "Keep the corridors clear. I don't want the civilians moving anywhere without being authorized by myself or Commander Greenland. Don't hurt them, but make them understand that this is no game. Pass out ammunition, but don't load it. The last thing we need is an accident. Don't let our crew get around either. Other than division heads everyone needs to remain at their posts. If they need to visit the head, then they need to be escorted. Shift changes should be escorted as well. Commander Greenland will work those details out with you.

"I also want you to select a squad to be ready to deploy to the colony at a moment's notice. If we can send them it will be a long trip with very little comfort. Food will be at a minimum and they may not be able to return with us. Inform them that they may need to leave with the colonists. It's going to be busy, so if you have questions then please leave them with CMC Billings, or Commander Greenland's and my stewards. If it can't wait, then CMC Billings will get our attention. Understood?"

"Yes, sir," snapped Mitchel.

"Get to it," said Artus.

"Sir!" Mitchel saluted and left to get his Marines in order.

Battle Preparations

Journal of Captain Artus
Entry #70
November 3, 2319

It has been eighteen hours since the <u>Bismarck</u> arrived in Rigil Kentaurus. I've only been in official command for little more than a month. My crew is green and of dubious experience. Thankfully, they are well schooled in their jobs.

There are two individuals aboard who make matters worse. Luckily, Astaroth is about to leave on a fool's errand. What is perhaps more odd is that I think I trust Astaroth. This realization has made me analyze my definition of trust.

I think Astaroth can be trusted because he is just like any other spook, only with more apparent power. Astaroth is in the business of getting things done. I respect anyone who gets work done and is efficient in said work.

Lieutenant Commander Hudson is a different kind of scary. She has admitted to me that she is here to keep an eye on me and the crew, at least officially. Keep an eye on me she does, especially since our compromises have given her plenty of extra time. Her constant gaze is becoming more unnerving.

I go to the mess and there she is. She sits on the bridge with her notepad chewing seductively on her pen. She is always lurking and eyeballing me in a very non-seductive way.

I've told her to stay off the bridge because her presence has caused issues.

Two-thirds of the bridge crew are young, inexperienced, junior officers or enlisted men. They are not taking the situation seriously. They've turned into high school misfits often dropping things and trying to find a reason to get a look at her.

Lt. Cmdr. Hudson admitted to playing the bimbo because it got her what she wanted. When I heard that, I recognized her watchful gaze to be one of a boss making certain that I and the crew aren't going to break the new toy. It wouldn't normally bother me, but for three reasons: her looks, her questionable performance, and her agenda or, more likely, the agenda of her superiors.

The lieutenant commander is not drop dead gorgeous. The girl I seem to have had slight acquaintance with at the academy, however, doesn't exist. Looking through the yearbooks, I've found her picture and little has changed. I don't remember her at all. She is pleasing to look at, however, and takes full advantage. Her looks are what gets others into trouble. Her way of carrying those looks, and her well-practiced poker tricks, are the basis for her naughty reputation,; which has no reality beyond rumor.

The women of the fleet consider Hudson to be a gold digger. This is probably true due to the fact that she has passed over many other women for promotion. Those that earned it consider Hudson to be loose. Others are upset that she beat them to it. Of course, the reality is that she is in charge of internal affairs and has often gone under cover in the pursuit of her duty.

The men, on the other hand, give her mixed reviews. The opinion of those I do not trust, or respect, like her mostly for the obvious reasons. Those that I do trust like her for the same reasons, but call her a "Career Black Widow". Those with that opinion never go into detail.

I had never met her until the day after arrival over Titan, but I had seen the damage done. Some officers or enlisted men, some women even, had thought they were going to get lucky or get some scam past the ditsy, amber-eyed, strawberry blonde. After her target had been court-martialed or lost and forgotten on some isolated duty, she would take over their position and sometimes get promoted.

I'm certain that her performance is just that, a performance. The sob job she had used in my office the first time we met had to be faked. Hudson exudes an exemplary deviousness. I do, however, believe her when she says that her original orders were to watch me, the crew, and evaluate the colony. She has shown me her orders and those of Admiral Fleming.

I've done my best to understand the woman. Billings told me that I'm overanalyzing her and not to worry about her too much. Because of his prior relations with her team, he may know more about her than anyone else, even Astaroth. I requested Billings for this assignment because I trust him and I should do as he suggests, but there is much I still do not understand.

I now fall upon the immortal, unofficial, motto of the military through the ages, "Keep it simple stupid." When she's happy everyone around her is happy. I should accept that, like the rest of us, she is following her orders regardless of how convoluted they may be. I also need to get my head in gear for the conflict that may be coming.

Right now the Bismarck is tracking the 150 year old pirate ship, <u>Black Jack</u>. The reputation of this ship and it's seemingly immortal captain are not to be taken lightly. Hudson claims that they are an asset, but she and everyone else agree that prior history dictates caution.

Commander Greenland snapped Artus back to reality. "What is it doing?" she asked.

The *Black Jack* was attached to a large asteroid, which matched what Artus had read about its abilities, and was moving at great speed on what appeared to be an intercept course. Lt. Collins in the wheelhouse projected the point of contact and said that it could move faster and cut the *Bismarck* off completely. She also said that something about the *Black Jack*'s trajectory seemed off.

When Artus asked her to clarify, she said it seemed as though it moved like a rogue asteroid. This explained the tumble. She then suggested that its intercept seemed coincidental.

"There's no way it's a coincidence," said Artus.

"I'm inclined to agree with you," said Commander Greenland.

"Tell Astaroth and Ensign Heinz to be ready to leave at a moment's notice," said Artus, "If the *Black Jack* so much as twitches, I'm canceling their trip."

"I got it," snapped the helm's Ensign Apprentice who was stationed in the CIC. She froze as she realized she was now the object of attention.

"Enlighten us, Ms. Landry," said Artus.

"Sorry, Captain. I think I know what's odd about the *Black Jack*'s trajectory!"

"Continue, Ensign," said the Captain.

"Yes, Well..." Ensign Landry was understandably nervous but quite certain of her theory. "Well, sir," continued the Ensign, "what did our sensors first detect when identifying the *Black Jack*?"

Artus called the sensors.

"Lieutenant Cole was stargazing and noticed a flicker," said Lieutenant Simons over the intercom. "He ordered a scan. The computer identified the asteroid. Then out of nowhere alarms began to sound and the computer confirmed with a 99% certainty that the dreadnaught *Black Jack* was stuck on like a leech."

"Does it have power?" asked Ensign Landry.

"No, not as such," replied Simons. "It's there, but minimal. We didn't even recognize the power signature until the computer identified it as a ship. We thought it was just background radiation as it tumbled from the far side of RK Beta."

"Recalculate trajectory based on gravitational force," said the Ensign, who went white with terror as she realized she'd just given an order. Simons remained quiet, waiting for instruction.

Captain Artus glared at the Ensign.

"Sorry, Captain. I... I... My terminal doesn't think..."

"She's right," said Lt. Kern who was overseeing her instruction in the CIC. "The helm computer doesn't think. It only calculates tactical information. It only takes into account what it needs to in order to keep the ship stable and can only guess at target movement. It doesn't take into account stellar forces unless it has to."

"Why not? Isn't that standard?" asked Artus.

"It's a calibration that wasn't considered to be necessary for this voyage. Lt. Cole can do the math faster than it'll take us to recalibrate."

Artus ordered Cole, Simons, and as much of the Sensor Division as necessary to figure it out and then make the necessary calibrations. A new path for the *Black Jack* emerged on the bridge view screen in moments. Cole was fast.

The *Black Jack* was moving like an asteroid. Artus' original statement about coincidence was now more evident. Instead of an intercept course with the *Bismarck,* the *Black Jack* was heading for RK Beta Two. The computer projected an impact within three to four days, but Artus didn't buy it.

"That's why he's here," said Artus.

"Who?" asked Commander Greenland.

"You have the Conn, Commander."

"Where are you going?" questioned Greenland.

"To warn Colonel Richards," replied Artus as he entered the lift. "Good work, Ensign," he called as the lift doors closed.

Ensign Landry sighed in relief and smiled uneasily.

Artus searched the ship for Colonel Richards. He didn't have to look long. Colonel Richards was on the flight deck organizing his men and equipment. Armor and survival gear were being inspected. Weapons were being cleaned. The vehicles the army had brought with them were being fueled and armed.

"We've made sensor contact with the *Black Jack*," Artus told Richards. "He is piggybacking an asteroid."

"What's Carpathian up to?" questioned Richards.

"The computer projects a collision with RK Beta Two near the facility within three to four days."

Colonel Richards frowned. "That only gives me a day on the ground before..." he took a deep breath and let it out slowly. "When they assigned me this posting, I thought I was being rewarded. Then I thought I was being thrown away. Then I read the files of my engineering battalion. One-third of them are veterans of Titan and some have been recalled to active duty. The rest are here for God knows why. Lieutenant Steiger over there is a prime example. His record is not impressive and he was due to be retired unless he got promoted. I requested him not because I thought I would be doing him a favor. I requested him because… I've got this feeling that he has to be here. I can't explain it."

"I've had a couple of moments like that recently, maybe. Boris for one," said Artus.

Richards nodded. "Exactly, why would he be here otherwise? Fleet allowed it. There's no precedent for that sort of thing." He took a deep slow breath. "Half of those recalled for this duty were with us in the Cauldron.[8] We then head to Titan and are outfitted with combat gear. I have two Panther scout cars and a Raptor assault tank. Hudson's crew has unpacked their crates to reveal the new Atlas Orbital Insertion Assault Armor and their assorted weapons. If Carpathian and the *Black Jack* are heading for the same place we are…" He sighed. "…Then we have until he arrives to complete our mission, whatever that is. Be careful around that silver-haired ▮▮▮."

"Astaroth?" inquired Artus.

"Yes and Little Miss Hudson. I did a job with them on Capellan Station. I know the truth behind the 'incident' and it has haunted me ever since. I won't talk about it. I will say that Lieutenant Commander Hudson is older than she looks, a lot older. What powers back her are beyond my reckoning. I got the idea from Astaroth that she'd been operating for some time before that. The girl you may have known at the academy never existed. I do not know why she was even there posing as a student. I can also tell you that her emotional displays are probably authentic. She has a lot of responsibility for one person and it shows. I don't know how she keeps going.

"I wasn't told what to expect when our orders changed, but when Hudson gave that briefing… I knew why I was sent here to begin with and it was never going to be survey and construction. Whoever is calling the shots expected a conflict long before Hudson was even involved. My battalion and I were assembled months in advance of our original orders."

"You may not have to go," said Artus. "I don't know a lot about the *Black Jack*, but I expect it intends to rectify the situation itself."

"Well, I do believe that," said Richards. "He'll probably drop that asteroid on the outpost, but it doesn't make me feel any better."

"Why not?" asked Artus.

"That ship, its captain, and I have a history," continued Richards. That surprised Artus. Richards continued, "Astaroth, before he came to the flight deck, made a stop by mess hall two and had a conversation with a man named Pat McEnna."[9]

"I know Pat, retired Marine Master Sergeant. What's he got to do with it?"

"You should ask him what he knows about the *Black Jack*. He was there too, on Capellan Station." Colonel Richards went back to his work. "I'll let you decide the best opportune moment to land us. I expect plenty of air support, Captain. I would prefer having Lieutenant Commander Carmen in the air to back me up, but that's your decision. She's a pretty little thing. Don't let her slip away, Captain."

"If there is an alien invasion going on, I might not be there for you," said Artus who was fighting his emotions.

"I think I've accepted that, but most of my battalion is made of children. They ought not to be sacrificed like this. Do what you can for them," Col. Richards offered Artus a hand. Artus took it, then snapped to attention and saluted. Col. Richards and his senior officers and most nearby saluted back.

Many of the men and women who returned the salute Artus recognized. He had fought with them on Titan. They at least understood something about their situation was not as it seemed. There was a stack of lock boxes with names, and addresses, and next of kin in the center of the flight deck. The moment was too much for Artus. He turned and went to check in with Carmen. He barely made it to her office before he lost it.

Carmen sat him on her couch. She gave him a drink of water. Then, she sat next to him, gave him a hug and patted his back. He was reminded of his eldest sister. His thoughts now returned to home and his family. Would he or any of those onboard ever see home again?

Bismarck on Approach

November 3-5, 2319

Captain Artus ordered a feast for the army. He also locked down the deck, preventing any goings and comings. Spirits were high, but the majority still did not know or comprehend their danger.

"How much time do we have until we reach the planet?" Colonel Richards asked Artus.

"About a day and a half," replied Artus, "I'll see what I can do to get more speed."

"Don't rush on our account."

"Lieutenant Commander Hudson has informed me that, if you succeed in time, I can recover you. The *Black Jack* will lay waste to the planet surface. You have until then to complete your mission."

"When does the *Black Jack* arrive at planet?"

"Less than three days," replied Artus.

Colonel Richards rolled his eyes. "That gives us a day at most. There isn't much room to play with."

"More speed then?"

"Yes, please."

"Except for the food, I'm going to lock down the flight deck," said Artus. "If you suggest, I will allow groups out under escort. I'll also allow some of the press in to see you off if you wish."

"Not all have prepared a last will or testament," said the Colonel. "Also, it may help morale even more if they think that they'll be on some show."

"I'll let the more trusted and conservative press in."

"Thanks."

The next few hours were uneventful. Members of the army were understandably upset at being in lock down, but the majority was well chosen for their discipline and attention to duty. Artus instructed the *Bismarck*'s crew to make their wills also. Many of the press personnel decided it would be a good idea to follow suit.

The *Bismarck* had managed to shave some time off of its travel and it appeared that the *Black Jack*'s pace had slowed. It was estimated that the army would now have a full day and half at the most to accomplish an as yet uncertain feat. Astaroth had given Colonel Richards some clue as to what he should expect.

The probes that Artus had ordered were filling in many blanks. There was indeed life on the planet that certainly should not have been there. The reptilian creatures were bipedal. Their physique was wide ranging, but it was certain the larger ones were combat oriented. They had already dug in at the facility. The *Bismarck* watched as a large transport delivered a satellite into orbit. Artus felt good about having a jamming probe already in place. There was not enough information to guess at their motivation, but they were prepared for hostility.

Hudson had made herself an open book on what the aliens were. They were known as Iksus. A race genetically bred for war. The larger ones were definitely warriors while the smaller ones were technicians and command personnel. She claimed that if the Iksus were involved then it was likely that they would shoot first and ask questions later.

She had the impression that the Iksus might not be aware of the colony, but that Galactic Law prohibited them access to this system and several others so it didn't matter if they were hostile or not. They would have to go. She did not elaborate on how she knew about "Galactic Law" or the means by which "they had to go".

Artus sent a query to fleet over the QE. The response was a code to unlock a safe in QE operations. Inside was a letter. It read, "Any information provided by Lt. Cmdr. Hudson is to be taken as though God himself were providing it. Explanations will be forthcoming in time. Until then, do as she says." The letter was nothing Artus had expected. It was signed Aetonyx.

Artus confronted Hudson with the letter. She seemed taken aback that it wasn't from Tavion. This was the first time she'd admitted to working for, or with, him. As she read the letter her face lost color and she fainted. Artus was caught so unaware that he did not move to catch her. He called medical and checked her vitals.

Lt. Cmdr. Hudson was physically fine, but Dr. Burns wasn't so certain about her mental state. She sedated Hudson and then asked what caused it. Artus showed her the letter. She didn't understand it either. The only opinion she could offer was that the letter triggered some kind of reaction. Such a trigger could have been learned or forced through a conditioning process like hypnosis. She also admitted that the best person to ask was now sedated. Artus didn't know what to make of the whole situation, but this Aetonyx was the man with the plan and he would have much to answer for.

Col. Richards, Lt. Cmdr. Carmen, and Comdr. Greenland planned the approach, landing, and air support. Colonel Richards estimated a two to three hour raid once the landings were finished and units in place. That was assuming the information was good and weapons effective. The entire battalion had been briefed and each unit, down to the squad, was given instruction.

Artus suspected that surprise would not be achieved so he launched more probes to get all the information possible as well as provide false readings. With fresh images coming in, Artus updated the plan and prepared bombardment targets. Then something no one expected happened. The *Black Jack* made contact.

Artus wasn't just surprised. He was flabbergasted. Later, Artus admitted that communication from the *Black Jack* wasn't all that surprising and after Hudson's briefing should have been expected. The form of communication was the cleverest and simplest form: light. The *Black Jack* was communicating using a series of flashes. Artus had instructed Lt. Nguyen and three others to dedicate their attention to the *Black Jack* and it paid off.

The Morse Code was recognized immediately. Artus made note to mention the ages old communication work horse to the fleet for future operations. Using the flashes of light was the clever bit. It gave no transmission. There was no possible way to intercept the message without having line of site. Light moved fast. The only catch was knowing where and when to look. What were the odds that anyone on the *Bismarck* would be looking? Then Artus remembered that Lt. Cmdr. Hudson may still have a means of communication with her superiors. He let his anger go. She was trying to help.

The *Black Jack* communicated that it would hold its bombardment as long as it could. It also said that the destruction would be total. If anything did manage to escape, or survive then the *Bismarck* should let it go and make a note. Coordinates for targets were handed over as well as a timeframe.

Whoever was on the *Black Jack* believed that having a ground presence would be enough to hamper coordination with the alien fleet. Thus, the time frame for the ground operation was extended to two full days. It might move forward drastically if the need arose.

The *Black Jack* had been watching the aliens and believed that they were not yet capable of detecting the *Bismarck* if it was rigged for silent running. The mysterious communicator, probably Carpathian, applauded Artus' jamming probes. The aliens probably believed that surprise was on their side. If things appeared to be going well, the *Black Jack* would push its time table back.

Colonel Richards was relieved.

When Ensign Heinz made her first scheduled check-in, Artus asked Astaroth's opinion on the matter. Astaroth seemed surprised at the *Black Jack*'s behavior.

"Carpathian must have received orders," he said. "It isn't like him to be so accommodating."

"Orders," questioned Artus, "from Lieutenant Commander Hudson?"

Astaroth chuckled. "Not likely. He likes her less than I do. He does operate with the Order, but he's an independent agent. I don't mean that he does what he likes. He gets his orders from higher up. As far as I know he has one standing order and that is being the last line of defense.

"The details of his assignment are broad. Mostly he fixes mistakes made by the Order, takes charge where the Order falls short, or finishes what they can't accomplish. He is also a scout and look out. He's not very nice and extremely fanatical in the pursuit of his goals. If the Order, for whatever reason, cannot get the job done, Carpathian steps in and dispenses swift and brutal action. The loss of Capellan Station by a terrorist act is a cover up for his intervention. I find it odd that Carpathian is communicating and being so accommodating. He has to have new orders, direct orders."

"Orders from who?" questioned Artus.

"With the Iksus invasion," continued Astaroth, "the big boss may have decided that there is no point in hiding any longer. This could be a good thing. We might have the aid of the *Black Jack* in this battle. However, if he thinks that there are more nefarious things going on, he may leave us high and dry at a moment's notice. Be prepared for anything."

Artus didn't like talking to Astaroth. He also forgot to ask about Aetonyx

Captain Mitchel requested a Marine detachment be sent in support of the army. Artus would have liked to send some Marines to help, but they did not have the equipment necessary for ground combat operations. All the available resources were meant for the army. Plus, there might be the possibility of defending the *Bismarck* from boarding. Artus didn't think it would happen, but it gave the anxious and idle Marine captain something to prepare for. This sat well with him, and Artus witnessed the efficient deployment of Marines and defendable check points put in place. Captain Mitchel's assignment to the *Bismarck* was now made clear to Artus. He knew how to do his job when it counted and did it well.

VALERIE AND ASTAROTH

November 3-5, 2319

Ensign Valerie Heinz and Astaroth left for the Defense Fleet, a trip that would test the extreme range of their shuttle. The *Bismarck* traveled to the drop off, sending two of her pilot friends to the colony in order to inform them of the situation. The *Bismarck* was now moving to RK Beta Two to investigate a facility on the planet.

Due to the need for speed, both wore combat flight suits. These suits could keep one alive in the vacuum of space provided there was enough air to breath. For that purpose they were fitted with military grade re-breathers. To survive the acceleration and deceleration forces involved, the suits also contained a layer of sophisticated gel with the primary purpose of combating the effects that such maneuvers had on the body. Valerie was not used to such acceleration and struggled despite the suit.

If all went well, then this would be a day and half trip to and a day and a half trip from the mysterious fleet that was her destination. If there were supply and refueling facilities available at this fleet, then the shuttles return range could be extended. Even then she may not be able to get back if there was an invading alien fleet on the way. For Valerie, all the good things she had found on the *Bismarck* might be ending.

Valerie was transporting a dark, mysterious individual called Astaroth to a sleeping fleet of star ships on the eve of an alien invasion. She didn't like Astaroth because he brought news of impending disaster to her new life. Other than that, she thought Astaroth was pretty cool. His name was cool. She didn't know if it meant anything, but she thought it fit him perfectly. He was one of the scariest people she had ever met.

Astaroth was a tough guy with a hefty dose of spooky. The navy was full of people trying to be tough and mysterious. Some had even asked her out on dates. They were posers. Astaroth was the real deal. He was tall, well built, scarred, and had silver hair. Valerie had thought it was grey, but it sparkled and reflected the light. This gave him mystery.

What made Astaroth go from mysterious to spooky Valerie wasn't sure. He commanded respect. He gave her the feeling that if you didn't respect him he didn't care, but you had better do what he said or he'd squash you.

Astaroth wore a uniform Valerie's squad-mates said was centuries out of date. He had no rank and, as cool as it was, Astaroth had to be some kind of code name. The officers, including Captain Artus and Colonel Richards, were visibly shaken with him around. He had a commanding presence more powerful than the *Bismarck* and he knew it. Perhaps what made him spooky was the fact that he could just appear and disappear. The man was quiet and you couldn't see him coming. When he decided to disappear, he was gone.

All in all, Valerie did not feel threatened by him. Lt. Cmdr. Carmen had given Valerie a gun and said that it was just in case, but Astaroth had treated Valerie with a completely different attitude than he'd been given credit for. The man was cheerful and respectful. He could sing. He'd been singing almost the whole trip. It was nice. However, she had informed him that if she couldn't be there to save Lieutenant William Steiger, if he died because she was providing taxi service instead of flying combat support, then Astaroth would have to die. Astaroth had simply said that was understandable and he would do his best to accommodate should the need arise. Although he was oddly agreeable and soothing, Valerie could not deny that she was afraid.

Valerie hadn't been truly afraid often. She could only think of three times. The first was her first solo flight. The second was her parents' death.

The third... the third was an episode with Terror Incarnate, Lt. Cmdr. Hudson.

With five and a half hours left in their flight, Valerie reported the sighting of a formation of unidentified objects. Two were maneuvering to the Defense Fleet graveyard and two more to the far side of Kentaurus Beta Two's moon. Most were moving toward the colony. They did not appear to notice the shuttle and so did not move against it. She woke him and informed him of the situation. She was nervous. He was unconcerned.

"We have five more hours," said Astaroth. "Don't worry about it until it's an issue. Besides, by the time we get there, the defense fleet should be waking up."

"I thought we were supposed to wake them up?" questioned Valerie.

"We were, but time and events change things. The Defense Fleet will have recognized the arrival of hostile alien ships in its vicinity, and it will respond. Due to the apparent time the aliens have been on the planet, however, I'm concerned as to why the Fleet is not already awake."

"Are we under threat?"

"No. The Defense Fleet should recognize us as human and will actively defend us. We only need to be concerned if the aliens threaten us before we get close. Something else bothers me more. The *Black Jack* and Carpathian should've been here and already had the fleet warmed up and tasked. I shouldn't have to do this. It means that the She Demon had him doing something else and not his job."

"Lieutenant Commander Hudson?"

Astaroth chuckled. "You catch on fast."

"We've met," replied Valerie, "on Outpost Lima."

"Oh, I've been there," said Astaroth. "So you were the extra passenger. She told me about the delay and the turn of good luck it brought. We'd been searching for a way into that bed of corruption for years. Don't worry, you weren't set up. She was there for me. Your... hmmm... adventure, was truly coincidence."

"I get sick thinking about it. I thought I'd gotten over it."

"And then she showed up on the *Bismarck*. Don't worry. She has that effect on most of its crew. The majority were hand-picked for this voyage by her. I expect your run in with her earned you your place aboard."

"Wing Commander Carmen requested me."

"Based on what? You're a good distance pilot no doubt, but you're not the only one and the others have cleaner records."

"But Wing Commander Carmen told me it was because of my record that she brought me on," insisted Valerie.

"It probably was," replied Astaroth, who sat forward in his chair. "But I'll bet your name wasn't on the commander's list until Hudson put it there. It often doesn't take much manipulation if any. Carmen..."

"...Wing Commander," interjected Valerie.

"Hmm... yes... Wing Commander Carmen" corrected Astaroth, "knows what it takes to get the job done. She had full decision on the pilots she recruited for this voyage. However, if it weren't for Hudson you probably wouldn't be here."

"How would you know?"

"She had me slip your paperwork into the Wing Commander's pile. It was a very thick, heavy pile. You also have a questionable commendation awarded to you for Conspicuous Valor during classified duty in the Kuiper Belt. Your time on the station was secured and erased. You were never there."

Valerie stared at him jaw hanging open. She slugged him hard on the leg. He began to laugh, hard.

"What about the people she killed?" demanded Valerie.

"What about them? They were scum!" He sat back in his chair. "However, if you must know, there was a prison riot which allowed for the removal of some unsavory characters from the system and saved the taxpayers some money on court and prison expenses."

Valerie hit him again. Astaroth laughed some more and resumed singing. She didn't argue how or why anyone should be able to get away with that kind of thing. She realized that those dead men had been getting away with a lot for years and got what they deserved. Astaroth's cover story explanation was good enough.

"Wait!" belted Valerie. "There's my case, but you said she hand-picked the crew. How does a lieutenant commander have that kind authority?"

"Yes, I'm not at liberty to discuss it. Let's just say that you've been more involved than most. I suppose that grants you more right to know, but not from me. As far as authority goes, it's not her making the call, if that's what you're asking. She takes orders. This is a guess, but I would imagine, as far as the crew is concerned, she read their files and submitted them for approval by the appropriate authorities. She and I are agents of a higher authority, nothing more.

"I'm staying with the Defense Fleet. She's staying on the *Bismarck*. If you want to know more, just ask. She'll probably tell you. Please, though, do not mention me or this conversation. If she catches wind that you've been talking to me about anything, she will take steps to maintain security at any cost. Understood?"

Valerie nodded. She knew full well what Hudson would do.

Astaroth sighed and started, "Hudson is not a lieutenant commander in the navy nor a major in the army or air force. She has multiple doctorates. She has been many things over the years and is far older then she looks. So am I."

"How old are you?"

"Two hundred and something. After the first century and half you stop counting."

"Two hundred and something," grunted Valerie in disbelief.

"Yes, I'm not making it up. I am an experiment in genetics. Hudson isn't, but she is at least over sixty. Well, that's how long she's been ordering me around. It's my bet that she's had many surgeries in order to keep her looks. As for her lifespan, modern medicine is far more capable than you're led to believe and, in her case, I wouldn't rule out an amount of cybernetics."

"That would explain a lot," commented Valerie as she remembered the Colt Devastator. Astaroth nodded his agreement.

"Carpathian, the pirate, is one of my brothers. He and I are all that is left of the Myrmidon Project. Despite rumors, and his shenanigans, he is quite sane. It's an age thing. I think it's a way of coping. I do it to, but not to the same degree.

"As for Hudson, she had experience when she became my boss, but not the right sort. She could best me in a fight, but she was never willing to do what was necessary to secure the Federal borders from all manner of riffraff. The mess on Titan was her first real test. She only passed it because of my brother and me. To be fair, though, I did try and do things her way. I think it would have worked, but she took too long planning it. If you want to know the details, ask Patrick McEnna."

"Pops?" questioned a perplexed Valerie.

"Yep, Pops and my brother have met; and Colonel Richards. It was on Capellan Station during the Titan rebellion. I would tell you the story, but even I have nightmares." Astaroth sighed. "My brother has only ever obeyed the orders of one man. My brother and I are the only ones who have met him for certain. Hudson only gets orders through coded messages and dark, shadowy, video conferences. I'm certain it has to do with deniability."

"So what exactly does Hudson do?"

"Well, you are already familiar with two things she does, look good and kill people. Her actual job is internal affairs in pursuit of the defense of the Sol star system. She is charged with tracking down the corruption in the government and keeping it within acceptable levels, as well as insisting on certain government and military legal actions. I don't know how she achieves it. I've watched. People just do what she asks. Many think that she is in love with them and they want to be in love with her, even women and happily married couples. I would say that is her most bizarre aspect, but I digress.

"If anything or anyone threatens Earth's safety, she eliminates the threat. It does not always involve killing people. She prefers to fight them within the bounds of law when and where possible. She'll kill without question if she thinks she has legal grounds to do so or if the threat is big enough. Trials have been held in abstention and posthumously. Sometimes the goal is to discredit. Other times, things get buried in red tape until they are lost, forgotten, or the parties involved have no further interest."

"Sounds like conspiracy nuts would have a field day," retorted Valerie.

"They would and do. Not that it does any good. First, someone would have to believe them. That means proof. If they ever get their hands on any, it would be in violation of some law. They'd be discredited and possibly sent to prison.

"Most conspiracy theorists we don't bother with. They are self-defeating. They eventually get so caught up in the confusion that they confuse themselves into a false reality. They misunderstand and misinterpret the data, and thus get completely the wrong idea behind what is actually going on. Often, the biggest conspiracy theories out there are based on little to no truth. Sometimes, we don't even try to hide it and they still get it wrong.

"It's all hearsay, conjecture, supposition, and assumption. It makes the real cover ups easier. We often have the truth published to the public, but red-tape is thick. If anyone gets through it, then they have to get through the legal language which is complex, difficult to understand, and put in broad and generalized terms.

"If anything is uncovered we can truthfully claim it was published and available to the public. This usually stops big media stories in their tracks, because the controversy they thrive on doesn't exist. It may get a big mention here or there but no one listens or cares and it dies a quiet death."

"So, what's the deal with Senator Whitney?"

"He's scum. Most politicians are. It's part of the job description. Senator Whitney, although useful in the past, had gotten above himself. Since some corruption is allowed and at times encouraged, it took some time to track down his dirty dealings and make certain that assets were secure. He was better than most at covering his tracks which is why we've used him. So good was he that we theorized he had external help; the same external help that has probably orchestrated this invasion."

"So there are alien spies back home?"

"More than likely, but they are exceptionally difficult to find. I won't bore you with details, because I don't know most of them. The bosses don't like it when we talk about matters above our pay grades either. It starts rumors and spawns uncontrolled misinformation."

The two sat for a long time in silence. Valerie contemplated what she'd heard. Astaroth seemed lost in events long past. Valerie finally decided it would be a good idea to inform Captain Artus about the probability of the Defense Fleet reinforcing the *Bismarck*.

THE BATTLE BEGINS

Journal of Captain Artus
Entry #72
November 5, 2319

*T*he time has come. Colonel Richards and his battalion have high morale despite making first contact, under arms, in a foreign land. After a fairly detailed scan of the planet surface and more information from the <u>Black Jack</u>, the odds look good. The aliens do not act as though they perceive an attack. There doesn't appear to be too many of them either. Numbers don't mean a whole lot, though, since the aliens probably have better technology and are supposed to be an elite force. An elite force bred for war if Carpathian is to be believed. Colonel Richards is counting on air support and orbital bombardment from the Bismarck to even the odds.

  The Bismarck is making its approach from the far side of the planet in order to hide as best as it is able. It is conceivable that the aliens have their sensors up and working by now. The army is currently landing over the horizon. Soon they will march with the fighter bombers providing air support.

  Two flights are set to drift in orbit over the primary target and wait. They will power up and strike as soon as surprise is lost or they are ordered to start their attack on the facility in coordination with the army. Once their first assault is finished they will return to the Bismarck to reload and then head back out for close air support. The Bismarck's guns are too big for close support, *but will follow up the first air strike on the hardest looking targets. Once the ground fight starts, I don't think the Bismarck can be much help.*

Something that probably shouldn't surprise me also happened. CMC Billings has been transferred to Lt. Cmdr. Hudson's team. He is with them now on the hangar deck preparing their Atlas Assault Armor. The armor is designed to be dropped from orbit, impact, and then unpack into heavy infantry power armor. They each have two Colt Devastator chain fed hand cannons. Although they are Lt. Cmdr. Hudson's command, I have instructed them to hold back until needed. They have agreed.

I was also correct in thinking Boris, my pilot, had more to his story than he'd told me. I have been given reactivation orders for him. He was some kind of black-ops operative in his hay-days. He has been reactivated with the code name "Thor" and, although he reports to me, he is an independent operative. He has requested launch clearance for the Phoenix and told me not to worry. He fully intends to return with the shuttle safe and sound. He and the Phoenix have begun a low and indirect approach to the planet outpost. I am anxious to know what he's up to.

I'm curious if Boris being involved is somehow Tavion's doing. It would make sense since I was on his shuttle before and after my run in with Astaroth. Still, what are the odds that I would choose him as my ride to Moon Base Armstrong to begin with or like him enough to keep him around? He probably would have just been reactivated and assigned to the Bismarck.

Everything decided to go from very good to very bad in the hours after the army had deployed. Two and a half hours into their march, Ensign Heinz sent a warning. The alien invasion had begun.

The colony station sent a distress call. Artus still didn't know if his two pilots had made it or if they were in control. It was at the extreme limit of their range and those two pilots would set a record for distance and endurance in a fighter if they made it. They had been instructed to maintain the *Bismarck's* security by not allowing the colony an attempt at contacting the *Bismarck* or alerting fleet in case unfriendly ears were listening. The pilots were authorized to use force if necessary, but Artus didn't think there would be too much trouble. However, the call of distress was against his and Admiral Fleming's orders.

The *Bismarck* sent a message via the QE system. The *Bismarck's* message informed fleet of Battle Order Zero Zero Zero and instruction not to attempt to contact the *Bismarck* upon arrival in system. Artus guessed that the alien fleet could already see him, but he didn't want to give them any help. Artus also assumed that the army's timetable was now rushed ahead by several hours.

Artus sent his transports back to the army. They were to pick up the infantry and fly them to the outpost perimeter for a combat drop. He suggested the vehicles and whatever reserve Colonel Richards wanted follow up on the ground. Richards agreed. Artus moved up the *Bismarck's* bombardment.

Artus ordered one of the lurking bomber flights down to make a flyby of the outpost. He wanted the aliens to know something was going on and hopefully leave their positions to have a look. It worked. Artus ordered them to maneuver just outside the *Bismarck's* weapons blast radius while it approached and began the assault.

The *Bismarck* started at one end of the outpost and walked its fire to the other side. The first flight moved in right behind the line of barrage hitting targets of opportunity and reporting the damage. The outer wall and many of the buildings had been flattened. The outpost shield, however, quickly became operational and further conventional attacks would be ineffective. Artus recalled the first flight to re-arm.

Artus changed his tactics to his ion cannons and pummeled the area for five minutes. The second lurking flight was sent to probe the shield for weakness and move in as soon as they saw an opening. Sadly, the *Bismarck's* ion cannons, having been meant for ship to ship actions, were not big or powerful enough to break the planetary defense shield. Colonel Richards was informed of the problem and halted his advance.

The colonel powered everything down and waited. He kept his reserve moving in hopes that they would catch up and perhaps fool the aliens into believing that the ground force was further away than it appeared. Thankfully the planet was cold enough that, when they put their survival suits in low power mode, the army's heat signatures would be minimal.

There were a multitude of hills and craters to hide behind and in. There were also a series of odd mounds that littered the landscape. One report claimed that they looked like graves.

"Conn, Comms, Ensign Heinz reports that the two contacts heading for the Defense Fleet are cruiser class ships. She says that a cruiser and a destroyer have maneuvered and are now in route to Kentaurus Beta Two's moon and may be using it to mask their approach to our flank. The rest, frigates and destroyers, are moving in formation toward the Colony."

"Conn, aye, send acknowledge," replied Artus. "What's the Ensign's ETA?"

"Ensign Heinz estimates two hours until she reaches the edge of the Fleet and the two cruisers will arrive at about the same time."

"Let me talk to Astaroth," said Artus.

"How's the colonel doing?" asked Astaroth.

Artus ignored the question. "What exactly is your plan with the fleet, Astaroth? How do you plan to activate them or change their orders? Is it something that can be done remotely?"

Astaroth ignored the captain's questions in return. "The proximity of this advance force to the fleet suggests that they are aware of its presence. The two cruisers heading to the field may be attempting what I am. It would be best not to discuss such things over the radio. There are other humans in the galaxy. Even though this is a coded frequency, it is possible that the Iksus can translate and understand us."

Artus slapped himself in the face. Even if the Iksus didn't break the code or understand, Artus shouldn't have asked those questions. The shuttle was now in more danger. The enemy would likely try to prevent the shuttle from doing whatever Astaroth had planned.

"No need to worry, Captain," said Astaroth. "Their proximity should be their undoing. The purpose of the Defense Fleet is to keep alien influence out. The fleet should be waking up now on its own to repel the invader. I had hoped to get there first and get them warmed up, but we can make this work."

Commander Greenland cleared her throat, "Captain, our bombardment is having minimal effect…" She was cut short by a man who appeared on the main view screen. His appearance matched that of Carpathian.

"Please excuse the intrusion, Captain, but I have a crazy idea with many positive vibes," said the image of Carpathian. The entire bridge crew was stunned to silence.

Carpathian continued, "I'll take your silence as a maybe then." He put his hands up, "Hold on now. Don't say no until you've heard it. If you would point your nose at the outpost, open all the way up, put on full power, start to spin and try to make yourself as big as you can, please. Then I'll put a high energy ion pulse plus disruptor on target. It will bring the shield down. It will give the Iksus a good shock. I doubt they think you've got my kind of power. It'll make you look like a hero genius, make the Iksus afraid, and keep me a secret. What do you say?" Artus stared, bemused. "Come on, Captain, it's a win, win, lose situation. I'm a good shot. It won't burn you, much."

Artus was understandably worried about the use of the rather large Planet Cracker ion cannon and disruptors of the *Black Jack* being fired so near to the *Bismarck* and the army on the ground. Lt. Cmdr. Hudson, who appeared recovered and was lurking, stepped forward and said that Carpathian's plan was a good one and that he wouldn't miss. Artus still didn't like it, but deferred to the strange authority of Aetonyx.

After a consultation with Greenland and the engineers, Artus haggled out the details with Carpathian. The *Bismarck* did what it could to look big and spun on its horizontal, central axis. The engineers managed to redirect some power to the hull, giving the *Bismarck* an apparent charge.

As the *Black Jack* hurled past in close proximity, it fired a swift burst from its Planet Cracker ion cannon and one of its disruptor cannons. The shots came perilously close to the *Bismarck* shorting out many of its systems. Thankfully, the heavily shielded life support, communications, maneuvering thrusters, and main engines remained operational. Even though the *Bismarck* could no longer directly support the army, it could maintain orbit and continued to launch and recover its fighter bombers.

With the outpost shield down, the fighter bombers moved in and renewed their attack. Their first pass didn't see much resistance or success. The second pass saw significant alien movement. A battle vehicle of some kind trundled its way out of a hangar in the mountain. It was followed by two smaller vehicles. The smaller vehicles had anti-air capabilities and they began to sow confusion in the human pilots.

The army moved into position. Their Raptor assault tank deployed its cannons and opened fire on the alien's anti-air vehicles. The shots glanced off the well rounded armor. Colonel Richards ordered the assault vehicles to focus on the weapon mounts. The next few shots showed mixed results. The missile launchers were taken out of action, but the rapid fire guns were still blazing away.

Lt. Cmdr. Carmen in flight ops informed the colonel that the alien's defense was scattered and inaccurate. After the initial shock of first time combat the fighter bombers realized that the ion and disruptor blasts had indeed caused more damage to the aliens than just bringing their shield down. The aliens were in a similar situation as the *Bismarck*. They had no computer tracking and were simply trying to fill the air with bullets. With this knowledge, Richards re-tasked his Raptor Assault tank on the larger, heavier alien combat vehicle.

The heavy alien vehicle began sending counter battery fire to the human positions. It was inaccurate, but it would eventually find its mark. Richards tasked his Panther Scout Cars to infantry support and asked if the fly boys could do anything about the alien vehicle.

Artus had Carmen outfit a transport as a heavy bomber. Some of the *Bismarck's* heavier, conventional munitions were loaded. The transport flew miles above the action, but didn't arrive fast enough to save one of the Panther Scout Cars. The alien heavy combat vehicle scored a hit.

The army took cover as the transport pushed large, heavy ship to ship armor penetrating and high explosive ordinance out the door. Luckily, with the thin atmosphere and no wind, they didn't need much guidance. To be certain, however, the transport dumped its full load of twenty projectiles. It then returned to the *Bismarck* to reload.

The ordinance fell silently toward the ground. The area was peppered with explosions. All three alien vehicles were destroyed. There appeared to be no alien movement. The army cheered.

The celebration was premature. The hangar facilities had not been hurt. Another heavy vehicle appeared and began to pulverize the human infantry. A company of heavy alien infantry accompanied it. A ship taxied out of the hangar and blasted into space. The anti-air weapons these new alien infantry had were in full working order and they quickly won back the sky.

The alien heavy vehicle quickly dispatched the Raptor assault tank. The humans fell back quickly. If it hadn't been for the hills and craters for cover, the humans would have made a run for it. Richards ordered them to rally and regroup, but it was difficult given the terrain. The fighter bombers stayed to provide what support they could but were taking losses. Artus informed the colonel that the alien ship which had left, more than likely, was the alien commander and that there was no reason to stay. The transports were coming in for pickup.

Two transports began to pick up groups of soldiers. The other two set up a rendezvous point where the soldiers would get a ride back to the *Bismarck*. The remaining Panther Scout Car carried as many soldiers as could fit. Even the fighter bombers ferried soldiers where possible. Soldiers fixed climbing gear to the weapon mounts or squeezed into the small internal bomb bays. It was cramped and crazy. Luckily they were dropped off at the rendezvous and didn't have to ride like this back to the *Bismarck*. This procedure was not planned and was purely a spur of the moment idea. Artus made note of it and planned a major tongue lashing followed by medals.

Once the shipbound transports were full they took off. The remaining soldiers that were able formed a perimeter and did their best for the wounded. Some of the fighter bombers landed and allowed the soldiers to strip their guns and rig them as heavy weapon emplacements in order to bolster their defense.

The first transport went down over the horizon. It had been shot in an engine and lost a stabilizer. Communications with it were lost and all aboard were feared dead. The second transport was blown to pieces attempting to rescue Col. Richards and his group. Soon after, Richards was hit. He relinquished ground command to the only other officer left that anyone knew was still alive. Captain Artus, however, took overall command.

KETHIS UNDER FIRE

From an interview with Kethis Cheriatis
Iksus Armada
Admiral

Expedition 179
Operation Start: 8710 GST Month 6, Week 2, Day 5, Artex Local
Time; 2314 Earth

Current Date: 8715 GST Week 4, Day 6, CT156 Local Time;
November 5, 2319 Earth
Location: CT156 Binary, 2nd planet, Beta Star

"**A**dmiral Kethis," called a communication tech. "We are receiving transponder signals arriving in system… it's the first wave of our fleet, sir."

"Excellent, they are ahead of schedule." Kethis twitched nervously, however. Early arrival meant that something had changed, which was not always a good thing.

"They are hailing us now, sir."

"Send response and welcome."

"The human colony is surprisingly calm," said another tech.

"They haven't shown any distress to us being here so it's likely they can't detect us," said Kethis. "If so, they probably can't see our fleet either. Have the first wave proceed with mission."

"Admiral," said the first tech. "First wave acknowledges us and reports the fleet will arrive momentarily. They also report that the Cannibal Fleet is present and closer than expected."

Kethis started to shake. "How close? Is it active?"

"The Cannibal Fleet is within six hours of the arrival zone. Cannibal Fleet is inactive and the Marine cruisers are moving to search it for its control center. They are approximately five and half hours away from their objective."

Kethis felt relieved. Things were going better than he had honestly expected. He began to think that the whole operation would succeed.

"Admiral," called the second tech. "The colony just sent a coded transmission to an object near the Alpha star."

"There goes their distress call," said Lieutenant Granis. "Not that it'll do them any good so far away from their home."

Kethis' gut burned with anxiety. "I want the shield at full operational power now."

At that moment Kethis heard an unmistakable sound of screeching engines overhead, an air strike.

"Take cover," he yelled as the first two explosions hit nearby. "Shields up, get the shields up!" Then the ground shook like an earthquake and everyone fell. Kethis looked at the external views of the outpost. Orbital fire had flattened the outer wall and buildings. Kethis felt sorrow for those outside, but the bulk of his people and equipment were in the mountain bunker and had survived.

The subterranean structures were taking the bombardment, but only just. Kethis' scales twitched as the shield came online. He had a flash back to the only orbital bombardment he'd ever experienced on the planet Orlan. The difference with this bombardment was that, here they at least had a shield. With the shield up the orbiting aggressor began to use ion bursts, but they were not powerful enough to affect the planetary shield. They were obviously meant for ship to ship engagements.

"Alert fleet that we are taking orbital fire from an unknown source," barked Kethis as loud as he could. He was barely heard by the communications techs. "Commander Tonais, alert the Council Guard to prepare for a ground assault. Get those armored vehicles powered up."

"Admiral," called Lieutenant Granis. "First wave acknowledges distress and reports that the Cannibal Fleet is beginning to move. The Marines are proceeding to objective, but communication with them has been lost."

Kethis cursed his premature excitement. His gut had been right about this invasion being a mistake. He could now hear small assault craft making probing attacks against the defenses. At least the bombardment had ceased.

"Admiral," called Commander Tonais' voice over the communicator, "Guard reports having observed ground movement some distance away."

"Can they engage?" asked the Admiral.

"They advise against it. They say that the shield should protect from ground fire. Until the enemy force declares itself, they believe the best decision is to let the shield do its job."

"What about a probe of our own?" questioned Kethis.

"I don't follow, sir," inquired Tonais.

"Not a scouting party. Fire a couple of shots from the vehicle guns and see if they respond."

"Will do, sir," replied Tonais.

"Lieutenant Granis, what does the E86 show?" barked Kethis.

"We've got what we can, Admiral, but we've had to take shortcuts so accuracy will be off."

"Better than nothing," replied Kethis. "What do you see?"

"There are several small craft swarming around our position. There are two large blips in orbit. The smaller object is the aggressor. The larger is the rogue asteroid we used for calibration. We can't see more than that without finishing the calibrations proper... There is a buildup of energy from the point where the colony sent its distress call."

"Is it a ship or another station?"

"We can't tell, sir. It just spiked and released. Energy matches that of a warp field."

Kethis ran to the sensor station. He watched as the power on the object began to grow again and spiked. The power levels dropped, but they did not dissipate. Another blip appeared and began moving toward the colony. The power levels on the object began to rise a third time.

"They have a warp gate," grumbled Kethis.

"It would appear so," agreed Lt. Granis.

Kethis didn't like his situation. The territory was unknown. The enemy was unknown. With the enemy in possession of a warp gate, they could have their entire fleet in system before the main power of the Iksus arrived. Then there was the Cannibal Fleet, but Kethis had never expected to secure it.

"Admiral!" cried Lt. Granis. "Vessel in orbit is experiencing a power spike… ion cannon!"

Kethis could feel the electricity in the air. This was a much larger ion burst than before. All of the equipment went dead. The shield collapsed and the air craft pressed the assault.

"Commander Tonais," called Kethis over the communicator. "What's the situation outside?" His radio didn't work. "Lieutenant Granis, go and report to me the situation outside… Lieutenant Granis?"

Granis and most of the techs were dead or unconscious. The ion cannon blast had done its damage. Those in contact with the equipment had been shocked with the power surge. They were the lucky ones. Ion cannons disrupted electrical operations in a similar fashion to an electromagnetic pulse, but without the radiation that usually came with it. Ion cannons had their own detrimental effects on living organisms. They disrupted nerve and brain function, leaving most unprotected in a vegetative state as well as causing organ failure.

Kethis then felt a sudden heat. His body started to ache. His specially modified scales protected him from the ion blast, but not from the disruptor that had just been used. The mountain and bunker absorbed the most dangerous and direct effects of the disruptor, but radiation got through. He would need treatment soon. Kethis ran to the hangar where the *Sonai* transport had been refueling in a powered down state.

As Kethis ran he could see the Council Guard in action. They were the most physically capable of the Iksus and their armor helped protect them from the disruptor, but most that were outside when it hit were suffering.

Most of the guard had retreated to the protected hangar when the ion cannon had been fired. Medics now rushed to their comrades.

The vehicles outside worked, but their computers and drive motors were out. They could be operated manually, but had no targeting assistance and were immobile. The enemy air craft were taking full advantage of the disorganized and inaccurate anti-air fire. The tank was being used for fire support against the enemy ground assault and taking everything the enemy aircraft had. The air craft weren't using anything heavy so they must have already used their munitions or were holding back. That gave Kethis a chill. It meant that another orbital bombardment was on its way.

Kethis grabbed the nearest medic inside the hangar. The medic treated him for the residual ion and disrupter damage, but he would need proper stabilization and decontamination, which wasn't available. Kethis' only option was to leave the Guards to deal with the enemy ground force and get to the fleet. Just then the ground shook and everyone collapsed. Kethis fought for breath and covered his ears, which were bleeding. The impact and explosions of orbital bombardment created a depressing mood. The Guards pushed Kethis onto the *Sonai* transport with a medic and charged out with the remaining heavy tank to continue the fight.

Kethis taxied the transport out of the hangar and took off. The enemy air craft did not pursue. As Kethis left, he observed that the last orbital strike had laid waste to everything outside of the hangars. The majority of the Guard had been in the hangar that was now crumbling. The vehicles in the hangar were still fully operational thanks to Commander Tonais' timely return with the transport, which added its shields for protection from the ion cannon and disruptor.

Regardless of how the ground battle turned out, Kethis was not happy about leaving Tonais behind. Tonais had been Kethis' trusted right hand for more than a decade. Tonais' initiative to prep and use the *Sonai* transport was something Kethis relied on. Such initiative among the Iksus Armada and its Dominion was not unheard of, but not encouraged. Kethis acknowledged Tonais' ability and often allowed him to operate independently. Kethis' rise in rank was, in part, due to Commander Tonais' direct support.

KETHIS FLEES

From an interview with Kethis Cheriatis
Iksus Armada
Admiral

Expedition 179
Operation Start: 8710 GST Month 6, Week 2, Day 5, Artex Local
Time; 2314 Earth

Current Date: 8715 GST Week 4, Day 6-7, CT156 Local Time;
November 5-6, 2319 Earth
Location: CT156 Binary, 2nd planet, Beta Star

Kethis put the transport on course to rendezvous with the cruiser *Xar* which was trying to communicate with him. He realized that he had ear damage and couldn't hear. He typed his messages. The *Xar* plus a destroyer from the first wave were nearing the planet in order to provide support and recover him. Since the coming fleet action took precedence, their ground support order was withdrawn. The *Xar* was a more advanced cruiser five years ago when the campaign had been launched. It should have had adequate medical facilities for his injuries and the latent disruptor damage.

The *Xar* reported sensor and communication interference. It appeared that the troubles Kethis and his team experienced on the planet were not localized. However, it was likely that the jamming was coming from multiple sources, which would make any anti-electronic warfare all the more difficult. The only reason the *Xar* was able to speak to Kethis was due to proximity.

During his flight Kethis contemplated on events so far. Other than his dislike of Kengarel, things had, for the most part, gone relatively well. The fleet was arriving ahead of schedule, which was good, but odd. Even though the ground force would be lost, he had gotten away, which meant the battle could continue.

What concerned him was that the fleet arrived early. It meant that someone had changed part of the plan. He was happy but concerned. Such a change could mean that success on other fronts allowed for more personnel and material sooner than expected. It could also mean that short cuts were made and the operation rushed.

The presence of an unidentified, hostile warship in the system and in orbit was unexpected and may well have ended the invasion in one swift stroke. He thanked Atraés for the outpost shield, but more importantly he praised Mar'Kai'Dyn, the Sovereign Protector of his people. Without his protection and the initiative of Commander Tonais, the operation on the ground would have failed without a chance to defend itself.

Kethis contemplated espionage. A spy was unlikely, but even if there was one, the entire operation had been planned and launched in a communication blackout. It was also unlikely, due to the systems location in the galaxy, that it had communication with the Human Nations. If Earth was as isolated as was supposed, then the Iksus should be their first contact and it was expected that the Earth humans would not react violently until it was too late. However, the presence of this hostile ship and a ground force suggested that they had prior knowledge of the Iksus arrival and knowledge of Iksus intent.

The presence of a warp gate changed things. Kengarel had not mentioned anything about it. The lack of such information didn't surprised Kethis. Kengarel's knowledge of the situation was suspect in his mind. The warp gate could explain a swift response of local authority. A ship could have already been in the system on patrol and moved to investigate. It was, however, too coincidental for Kethis. Kengarel aside, this situation screamed with the meddling influence of Lok'Im'Bagh, the Trickster, who was present in every aspect of an operation, as well as life in general.

Kethis did not believe that the vessel conducting the bombardment was a member of the Cannibal Fleet. If it was, then the Cannibals should have been awake already. It could have considered the Iksus advance team to be pirates and didn't think a mobilization necessary until the Iksus Navy arrived. However, that didn't explain the ground force.

Kethis' medic doctored his ears and fixed a hearing aid. Kethis then scanned the communications frequencies. The Council Guard on the planet must have secured some working communication equipment. Kethis listened entranced by what he could hear.

The Council Guard was busy coordinating efforts with their remaining tank. They appeared to be doing some good and had destroyed all of the enemy vehicles. The enemy was definitely human and, if they were part of the Human Nations or the Legion, they must have been overdue for an upgrade in weaponry. The human weapons were not penetrating the Guard body armor and those that got lucky didn't penetrate their thick scales underneath. Kethis decided that the humans were definitely not part of the Human Nations or the Legion. Legion troops would have given the Council Guard a proper fight and even the backwater colonies of the Nations would have had something partially effective at the least.

The human ground vehicles were destroyed and their infantry was scattered. Despite their predicament, the humans fought on. They were using their landing craft to recover the infantry and move them to a more distant location. The Guards could see more transports heading for orbit. The humans were leaving. They had probably spotted Kethis' transport leaving and assumed that there was no need to continue the fight on the ground.

It was standard procedure for the Iksus to eliminate the enemy chain of command when possible. With the enemy scattered this was proving difficult. The human ground force was using a verbal code that the Iksus had never encountered, which was complicated by the fact that they were also using what sounded like a language that had never been recorded. The ground commanders were speaking through designated communications personnel who made spotting specific command targets a bit more tricky, but explosives usually got the job done. The Guard had taken out many of the communication personnel, but others took their place. Even though the humans had scattered they were still mounting a reasonable resistance.

The Guard began to whittle down the communications and finally started pinpointing officers. They had also started targeting the human landing craft. The Guard commander was certain that the loss of transports and officers would start to break the humans. The human will did not falter and they seemed to become more aggressive. Kethis knew that the human ground force must be reaching its limit. When backed into a corner, a tame animal will become a monster as feral as its wild brothers. Kethis was impressed.

The Guard commander finally tracked down his human counterpart. The Guardsman was certain the human commander was in a crater next to him. The Guard had been hitting it hard. There was no movement, but somebody was still giving orders to the squad in the adjacent crater. The Guard commander's lieutenant requested the honor of killing the human commander and his superior allowed it.

The Guard lieutenant and his team charged the enemy crater and were claimed by a large explosion. Kethis had already realized that the Guard's enemy were determined and would rather "go out with a bang," as the humans put it. Kethis considered the practice of claiming honor and trophies a crude and dangerous practice.

Such practice was in violation of the Armada's rules on pride. The infantry, and especially the Council Guard, tolerated this because their life expectancy was measured in months at best so they rarely had opportunity to show off for the females. Thankfully, Kethis' mate was more impressed with one who did not lower himself to such ill-fated posturing.

It helped that he and his mate had known each other since they were kep and she knew well what he was capable of. Still, he did his best to bring her "sparkles" and "shines" whenever he could. He had, more than once, found her admiring these treasures despite her claiming that they were only social convention. It made his heart sing that she was pleased.

The loss of their commander caused a surge among the humans that Kethis was not surprised to see. The humans were obviously elite troops and free to act independently. They learned that the Iksus battle rifles were effective against the Iksus body armor as the Guard commander, thinking the battle was his, exposed himself.

The human's use of Iksus weapons resulted in a chaotic counter attack that the Iksus were not ready for. The Iksus had thought the humans were beaten only to find that they had not taken as much loss as was guessed. The humans, in their scattering, had succeeded in thinning the Iksus line and took advantage of it. Also, a new, smaller force had joined the counter attack. These new combatants had powered armor and carried small, chain fed weapons that were piercing the Guards armor easily.

An airstrike disabled the Iksus tank. Some humans had retrieved some Iksus anti-air missiles and tried using them against the tank. Due to not understanding how to operate the weapon, they killed a squad of Guardsmen who were taunting them. Such an occurrence was the fate of those who did not heed the wisdom of Atraés, Goddess of Battle, and Kethis felt no pity for his foolish brothers. The Iksus tank responded and the offending humans were silenced.

With the human commander dead, whatever it was that was encoding their communications failed. Even the strange language ended, for that was indeed what it was. Those left were now broadcasting using what must have been their real language. Kethis could even recognize some of the words. Whoever was in command in orbit was still encoded and he couldn't understand the return messages. Then all human communication ceased. The orbital entity still spoke on occasion, but the ground force was silent. It was eerie and the Guard agreed.

VALERIE ON COLOSSUS

November 5-6

Ensign Heinz reported in once she and Astaroth arrived at the Defense Fleet. It was indeed waking up. Valerie flew straight ahead and almost ran into a leviathan of a ship that had just turned its lights on. Captain Artus ordered her to record everything possible.

The derelict Earth Defense Fleet was massive. It contained many ships of different shapes and sizes. Astaroth told Valerie the fleet was in a constant state of automated refit in order to keep it up to date and in full repair. It was also tied into the Federal Defense Network.

Many of the ships names were recognized from Earth legend. Some were gods like *Athena*, *Apollo*, and *Thor*. Others were people and places. The list went on. Some ships appeared to have their names painted in more than one language.

There were enormous stations and platforms as well. Most were octagonal obelisks that tapered toward each end. Valerie had to acknowledge their resemblance to the *Bismarck*.

Astaroth said that most were defensive in nature. There were shipwrights, foundries, armories and greenhouses. They would provide everything needed to survive a war of attrition and siege. There were two that stood out from the rest. These were their destination.

The *Tower of Babel* was the primary communications hub. Valerie was going to drop Astaroth off there. He would then proceed to the command center and complete his mission. He finally explained that the whole fleet would interpret his orders how it saw fit. If it thought it necessary, then it might move to Earth and redeploy. He didn't explain how the fleet could think for itself. Once he'd been dropped off, Valerie was to leave Astaroth behind in case his bosses had other plans.

Upon approach to the *Tower of Babel*, something took over control of the shuttle. Valerie instinctively began to shut down the power in order to prevent unauthorized access to the computers and prevent any further loss of control. Astaroth told her to stop. The *Tower of Babel* was bringing the ship in remotely.

After Astaroth disembarked the shuttle, he told Valerie to go to the *Colossus*, another station. He would instruct the *Tower of Babel* to upload directions to the shuttle. He gave her a disk that had blueprints and build orders. Valerie was to take it to the control room and plug it in. Then she would have to sit and hope that the fleet could keep her alive until the *Bismarck* managed to retrieve her or stay on the *Colossus* until it returned to Earth. He apologized for putting her in the situation.

"How will I know where to go when I get aboard?" asked Valerie.

"If you get lost, just ask it, the station that is. It may or may not talk back. It probably won't like this shuttle either."

"What do you mean, won't like the shuttle?"

Valerie didn't get an answer. Astaroth left the shuttle and hurried his way out of the hangar.

Valerie lifted off from the *Tower of Babel* and headed for the *Colossus*. Valerie started her approach and something took control of the shuttle as had happened on approach to the *Tower of Babel*. Instead of the large main hangar, the shuttle proceeded to a smaller bay directly to its left.

A perky feminine voice spoke over the shuttle's communication system. "Welcome to *Colossus* shipwright. Please remain seated until your ship has come to a complete stop. Do not leave your ship until the bay has been pressurized and the all clear given. Once you have disembarked please proceed to quarantine for processing. Remember to pick up a brochure to browse all of our upgrades, extras, and sweet rides. Thank you for choosing *Colossus*."

Valerie sat confused. "Not what I expected."

A minute or so after the bay doors had sealed and the shuttle had landed, the voice said it was safe to disembark.

Once Valerie left the shuttle, the voice chimed over the bay speaker system, "Please follow the guide lights in the floor to quarantine. There is a window in quarantine for both this bay and the primary hangar. This is so that you can view the action while you wait. It is designed to help with morale during the long and often boring days in quarantine. This is in keeping with paragraph four, section three, of the Galactic War and Peace Health Code Regulation. Please enjoy your stay. Don't forget to pick up a brochure of all our upgrades, extras, and sweet rides."

As Valerie walked up the gantry to the bulkhead door in the front of the bay, she noticed a kiosk with several video brochures. She was stunned at the offers. The *Colossus* could design, fabricate, and produce anything from single fighter craft to battleships. Valerie picked up the data pad brochure for transports.

Valerie sat in quarantine and watched the brochure. The same female voice narrated and described all the *Colossus* had to offer in transports, upgrades, and extras. When it had finished Valerie couldn't hold back a giggle.

"Awesome," she exclaimed.

The female voice returned over the speakers, "While you wait, would you like to design your own ship?"

"No harm, I suppose. It's a shame I didn't understand most of the brochure.

"Was the brochure unsatisfactory?" questioned the voice politely.

"No. It was awesome. Very nice..." The voice made a noise that Valerie could only describe as a contented purr. Valerie couldn't help being disturbed. "...I don't understand what all the things do."

"In that case, try our new, patent pending, job evaluation design program. You will be asked several questions about your line of work and *Colossus* will design a ship for your needs."

"That could work."

The voice began asking questions. "What is your job? Please be descriptive."

"Ensign Valerie Heinz, Earth Federal Navy. I am a qualified fighter pilot, but I have a long history in distance transporting. I mostly do long distance supply runs. I'm currently assigned to the E.F.N. battle cruiser *Bismarck* for supply, army, or V.I.P. transport."

"The *Bismarck* is one of our finest productions," said the voice. "Do you like it?"

"Oh, yes!" Another purr of contentment lilted over the speaker. "Wait... the *Bismarck* wasn't built at the Ganymede Naval Armory?"

"Final assembly took place at the Ganymede orbital shipwright, but design and fabrication of most of the superstructure and advanced components were done here... This just in, the ground battle on the second planet of Kentaurus Two does not go well. All but one transport remains. A lieutenant called William Steiger is now in command."

"... William," gasped Valerie.

"Do you know this William?"

"Not well enough."

"Then allow us to speed you on your way with a readymade assault transport suited for the task at hand. Have you ever performed combat evacuation before?"

"Only drills."

"Do you have aerial bombing experience?"

"Not much. We did two runs in a simulator in flight school."

"Would you like to go fast?"

"Yes please."

Red lights began to flash and sirens came from the landing bay. Valerie whirled around and looked through the quarantine window into the bay. The gravity switched off and the bay doors opened. This sucked the shuttle out into space.

"Hey! What's going on?" screamed Valerie in terror. How was she going to get back? How was she going to explain it? She let the voice have a piece of her mind.

"Your vessel has been determined to be inadequate for your needs and will be scrapped for parts..."

A rough, hearty, mechanical, masculine voice boomed over the speaker. "Not worthy!" A beam of light surrounded the shuttle which then fell apart. The bay doors closed.

"...Do not worry about transportation," continued the feminine voice. "A brand new Harrier Seven Assault Carrier Super is on its way up to the primary hangar from the production floor. It has capacity for an entire company, a heavy vehicle and crew, or anything in-between. It has medium armor, a laser deflection and diffraction system, point defense turrets, a full array of counter measures; both electronic and physical; two heavy bombardment cannons, two anti-aircraft turrets that can be used on infantry and an Aries, forward firing, hyper-velocity mass driver. It is powered by a vastly scaled down version of the *Bismarck's* Horizon reactor and is warp capable. Bear in mind that this is a heavy assault craft not a superiority fighter."

Valerie watched in awe as her new transport rose up into the primary hangar. It was big and looked dangerous.

"How do I fly it? I mean, I'm by myself. I'm not familiar with the controls and I don't know the weapons."

"Not to worry," said the voice. "There is a basic AI aboard that can handle the weapons. All you have to do is select targets. Be aware that it is not a substitute for a full crew, but it should suffice for the immediate term. It can also inform you of maintenance tasks. On your way back to the fight, I recommend you ask it for the inflight tutorial. Congratulations on becoming the new owner of a Harrier Seven Super. Have fun with your sweet ride!"

"Oh..." Valerie jumped. "I have to deliver these work orders to the control room!" Valerie pulled the disk from her pocket. A beam of light engulfed her hand and the disk.

"Data received. Production will commence immediately. Please leave the disk on the counter and someone will be around to collect it eventually. Now run along and have fun with your new fragin' wagon."

Valerie didn't wait. As soon as the quarantine door to the primary hangar opened, she rushed aboard the new ship. It was already warmed up and ready to go. The transport closed all its doors and took off before Valerie found her seat in the cockpit.

As the transport left the bay, Valerie could see fighting nearby. The two alien cruisers she'd spotted on the way in had penetrated into the Defense Fleet and were near the *Colossus*. Most of the Defense Fleet ships were ignoring them or still asleep. One of the two alien ships had been engaged by a nearby station and didn't fight back for long. Before it was done kicking, a swarm of small craft began to rip it apart and carry the pieces back to the station.

The second alien ship came too close to the *Colossus*. A swarm of the small craft flew past Valerie and headed for the alien. Valerie couldn't tell if the blue lance of light fired from the *Colossus* was some form of laser or hyper-velocity gun. What she could tell was that it lit the cockpit with a pleasing glow. The alien cruiser suffered a massive internal explosion and then broke in half.

Not long after Valerie's new transport had turned toward Kentaurus Beta Two, another voice began speaking from the onboard speakers.

"Welcome aboard the Harrier Seven Assault Carrier Super. I am the newest in a long line of Invasion Support Carriers. My designation is ISC 198F. Please enter your identification."

"What identification, where?"

"Your naval serial number will be sufficient. You may recite it."

"Earth Federal Navy, 1768903, Ensign, Valerie Heinz."

"Authenticated. Friend or Foe Identifiers reprogramed. I am now E.F.N 198 India Sierra Charlie. Please follow the inflight tutorial on the heads-up display. You may pause and request further details at your leisure."

Valerie followed as the transport's computer explained how everything worked. It was very similar to every other transport she had flown, but with key differences. It was the biggest she'd ever flown, so many of the flight characteristics and stress loads were different. Since the computer had an

AI Valerie could communicate what she wanted to do and the AI would do its best to oblige.

The AI could do everything on the ship, but it was a strain to keep up with a fluid combat environment. It performed better if it had a full flight crew. The AI could cover any open flight position if there was no one available. In the fight to come, it would handle all of the counter measure systems and point defenses. Valerie would have to aim the forward hyper-velocity gun and the bombardment cannons.

The computer had automated sub-routines to aid in fire support. It was a simple point and click interface. Valerie chose the weapon and the target area. The ships sub-routine would plot a course and auto-pilot to the target area. All Valerie had to do then was take manual fire command of the guns, which she could do from a control stick in the cockpit. The auto-pilot subroutines were on a separate, dedicated, computer and did not use the AI's runtime.

If manpower existed to operate weapons, but not fly, the AI could escape and evade with priority to return to the nearest friendly entity or position. The AI preferred to have all flight positions manned so that it could focus on countermeasures, flight stability, and in-flight maintenance. All systems had manual controls and access for primary operation and backup.

The ISC was much faster than any of the transports Valerie had flown. It would only take twelve hours to reach the planet. It did have warp capabilities, but could only use it two or three times before it needed servicing.

Valerie asked why they couldn't warp to the planet. The AI said that warp navigation required its full runtime and would need to recalibrate for weapons control upon arrival. The AI was under the impression that Valerie wanted to go in guns blazing. She agreed, and they began planning their counter attack.

"First," Valerie said to herself forgetting the AI "I need to know where our people on the ground are. I don't want any friendly fire. I also need to report my situation to the *Bismarck*."

"Opening channel with E.F.N. *Bismarck*," said the smooth masculine

AI "Proceed with communication when ready. I will begin download of combat data from the *Bismarck* central computer."

"So I have an open channel to the *Bismarck*?" questioned Valerie.

"Yes," replied the AI

The bridge of the *Bismarck* sat in silence as a woman's voice rang out over the speakers.

"So I don't even have to push any buttons or find frequencies?" questioned the amazed voice of the unidentified woman.

"Correct," said an unidentified male. "You provide a communication target and I can make contact depending on the depth of encryption. Since the *Bismarck* has multiple channels open for ground and air combat operations, it was not difficult. The *Colossus* also provided me with access codes to the *Bismarck* mainframe."

"Cool," said the woman.

"We can hear you," said Captain Artus. "Identify."

There was definite change of mood from the woman. There was a tense silence on her side.

"Captain, this is computer control," said another voice over the speakers. "Someone is downloading infantry and air I.F.F. data and synchronizing with our tactical protocols."

"Stop them," ordered Artus.

"We can't," replied computer control, "they have command access. The only way to keep them out is to perform an emergency shutdown."

"Conn, sensors, inbound infiltrator has identified itself and is on an assault course to the planet surface. It is the source of the computer intrusion and communication."

"To unidentified man or woman on the unidentified inbound: respond and identify yourself or we will kill you," ordered Artus.

"Sorry, Captain," said the woman's voice. "Ensign Valerie Heinz returning from delivery. Don't shut down the computer. The AI in this thing is preparing a close ground support run based on the *Bismarck's* latest data. I don't suppose we could get the army locator beacons and communication channels too? It's just that it would be easier to avoid friendly fire if we could pinpoint everyone down there."

Artus began to talk back like a superior officer and demanded explanations.

"I'm sorry, sir," replied Valerie. "I'm having a hard time keeping up with events. The AI has me doing the work of four people while it calculates assault vectors. The short version is that Astaroth is doing whatever he is supposed to. He sent me to a neighboring space station with production orders. The *Colossus* it's called. It's a ginormous, automated shipwright with an attitude. It had me in quarantine while it gave me a sales pitch. When it realized I was from the *Bismarck,* it blew up the shuttle claiming it was unworthy of the job at hand. It took the production data from me and then gave me this. It has heavy ground support fire capability and room for a whole company. I don't have time for details so you'll have to wait for my report. Now, could we please get the army's information?"

Artus smiled and complied. "I expect a full report when you get back." He was happy that there might be a way out for those on the ground.

"Yes, sir," replied Ensign Valerie.

WILLIAM STEIGER

November 6, 2319 Early Morning

William Steiger wasn't liked much in his old command because he was old for an army lieutenant. His men didn't trust him because they thought that someone of his age and experience should have been promoted already. When Colonel Richards had approached him with an engineering position with the Rigil Kentaurus expedition, William jumped at the chance. If he didn't get promoted soon, then the army would retire him.

This mission would look good on his record. If not, he planned to retire his commission voluntarily. William didn't pay much attention to Colonel Richards' words of warning until it was too late for him to back out. He now realized that he should have known something was up when the battalion was outfitted with heavy combat gear instead of survey and construction equipment.

Now, with Colonel Richards cut off in the next crater, William Steiger found himself in command of a remnant battalion, on an alien world, fighting for life during first contact with extraterrestrials.

"All squads check in," ordered William.

He tried forming a visual map in his head of the locations of squads. He realized that the colonel had special equipment for that if he could get his hands on it. He also had the Command Linguistic Encoder. This device encoded all radio traffic and could even translate one language to another. The usual favorite was that of a dead Native American language. If the Encoder was lost or destroyed, their communications would no longer be secure.

"How are you holding up, Colonel?" asked William.

"Not well," replied Colonel Richards. "It's just me and Simmons. I think they've identified me as the ground commander. Stay put. We've talked it over and we're both going to die from wounds. We've got some satchel charges. When they come for us, they'll get more than they bargained for. Sorry for putting you in this mess. Do what you can. Captain Artus will help you…" Colonel Richards coughed violently and went silent.

William peered over the edge of his crater and looked towards the colonel's crater. The bulky, alien, infantry scrambled up its outer walls.

"Look, Simmons," said Colonel Richards in an awestruck voice. "They're beautiful."

Seconds later the aliens poured into the crater. There was a powerful explosion. An alien arm landed in front of William. They didn't look beautiful to him. Surely the colonel didn't mean the aliens.

The alien arm still held its assault rifle. William decided to see how effective it was against its masters. He chose the largest target that presented itself. He was well satisfied with the effectiveness of his new toy.

An odd sensation came over him. He began to chuckle and then laugh. "To hell with these boys," he called to those with him. He threw his rifle on the ground. "I like theirs better. Let's say we go appropriate some more to our cause."

The soldiers with William had witnessed the alien rifle's effectiveness against its creators, followed William out of the crater, and rearmed themselves as he covered them. The aliens were taken aback by this sudden counterattack. The aliens took cover as William's squad began moving to help the next squad.

With renewed hope, the army began to scavenge what alien equipment and arms they could. William told the other two transports to continue the evacuation. He was more confident now than he'd ever been. He even felt different. He felt taller, stronger, and he could see more clearly what he should do. He could swear he heard a voice, but kept that to himself. It was a soothing woman's voice. He didn't know where it was coming from and every time he tried to focus on it, it went quiet. He decided that he'd worry about his sanity later. Right now, the voice was guiding him and he listened.

William called the *Bismarck*. "Captain, Lieutenant Steiger. The alien weapons are far more effective than ours. My squad is rearmed and moving up the enemy flank to the next group. We've got the aliens by surprise now, but I don't know for how long. What help can you send?"

Thankfully, the *Bismarck's* Encoder system was still functional. This only helped in that it secured all communication from the *Bismarck,* which meant that Captain Artus could still communicate freely. "The close air support is out of action and we're down to one transport. I've got two bombers on the way for that tank thing. Wait..." paused Captain Artus. "...it sounds like your surprise has worn off. Reports are coming in that the aliens are falling back and reforming. Our visual is out. I can't see what's going on, but it sounds like they are about to counter. I suggest you find cover."

"Thanks for the heads up, Captain." William addressed his squad and Captain Artus relayed it to the rest. "Take cover. If there's time after the bombers make their run, try and form two man fire-teams. If the aliens come first then I want everyone to scatter and take cover. Make every shot count. It looks like we've taken the pressure off the evacuation, so I want to keep it off as long as possible. If we spread out, we may be able to envelope their flanks and get them in a cross fire. Don't stay in one place too long. Shoot and scoot."

Those with him saluted and shook each other's hands. They dispersed taking as much alien equipment as they could. He was glad they didn't know him from his old command or they would have argued. He wouldn't have blamed them if they had.

What he was asking of them was crazy, suicidal, and against

procedure. He should have them rally to concentrate their fire. He hoped, by spreading out and cutting off radio traffic, to deceive the enemy and provide communication security. The more men, or whatever, the aliens used in the counterattack would mean the rest of the army had more time to evacuate. If he was real lucky, the rest of the cut off squads would be doing the same.

He sent one last message to Captain Artus, who relayed it to the rest of those cut off and alone. "If the rest of you cut off squads can get your hands on some alien weapons, use them and try to hit them in the back as they advance. The longer we hold the enemy the more time that last transport has to evacuate the rest."

Someone started singing. He identified them as the three odd fellows of CMC Billings serving under Lt. Cmdr. Hudson. He'd seen them unpack the Atlas Assault Armor from their crates before he and his platoon boarded the transports for landing. When had they arrived? They would be a major help, but there were only four and the alien weapons might take them out. Nonetheless, their singing of an old war song, "March of the Men of Harlech", was inspiring. Most of the army, including William, joined in.

William didn't know how long it had been since he landed on the planet or since he'd taken command. The last transport estimated that it could get everyone out of the rendezvous in four more trips. Captain Artus was using the transport's visuals for reference and had determined that all the remaining holdout squads had stayed but hadn't seen much movement in the past ten minutes.

The bomber attack succeeded in disabling the enemy vehicle. A squad had gotten their hands on some alien heavy weapons and tried to finish it off, but only succeeded in killing an enemy squad before they were killed by the vehicle. There was sporadic firing. There weren't many of the holdouts left, but they had managed to keep the aliens pinned down. The alien force may have decided there was no reason in attacking the rendezvous point without their heavy armor. The aliens were busy regrouping and patrolling for the rest of the human holdouts. William thought about trying to work his way to the rendezvous.

Then all hope failed him. An enemy squad had snuck away and shot down the last transport on its approach. William decided that was enough. He ignored the voice in his head and picked up a fresh alien weapon and explosives.

William observed the regrouped alien force moving toward the rendezvous point. William was about to open fire when one of the bigger aliens tackled him. It was red and scaly, with small horns and a stub of a tale. William had seen the bigger aliens and guessed them to be the ones in charge.

This one was big and heavy, and appeared to be naked. It charged again. All William could do was to grab the nearest rock. The rock didn't budge. William rolled up and over one of the lumps that littered the landscape. The big alien thudded uselessly on the lump. It looked wounded.

"Fighting bare handed in the nude must be some kind of death ritual or something," William thought.

The alien stood and began to move toward William again but tripped over one of the odd mounds. It gave what could only be described as a surprised expression and started to roar or scream. William scrambled backward on the ground from what he thought was an attack and ran into something hard. Dust fell on William. Whatever he'd run into was moving.

The alien had its feet pulled out from under it. It fell, then rose into the air and smacked down hard as some large arm and hand picked it up and swung it like a sack down into the ground. William panicked and tried scrambling back again. He couldn't.

William turned and looked up into the haunting red eyes of a large, metal humanoid with a long, expressionless, metal head and long, pointed ears. William froze. Alien weapons fire erupted and their screams began to echo across the battlefield.

"Oh great, first aliens and now dog men," William managed to say. Then he wished he'd said something better as it was likely to be his last words.

"Jackal," growled the metal man standing over William. William stared up at it, confused. Then something else he had never expected happened.

"Hang on boys, your chariot of fire is on its way," said the transport pilot who had gone with Astaroth. Her name was Valerie and William had a powerful crush on her. He wished to see the cute, young Ensign again.

Then the dog headed humanoid brought him back to reality.

"Get down," it said as it pushed William to the ground. A large explosion erupted directly behind the thing and the concussion knocked the wind out of William.

"I actually like 'dog men'," said another mechanical voice. It was the last thing William heard before he blacked out.

VALERIE'S FURY

The AI explained its plan of attack to Valerie. It was simple. It was very similar to the ground support role provided by the twentieth and twenty-first century C-130 Gunship. The ISC would fly a circle pattern around the target areas and the AI would operate the side mounted cannons based on Valerie's targeting input. For the purposes of the engagement, it was enough to simply tell the computer to target all Iksus. Valerie would still have to push the button and could select specific targets if necessary.

All of this could be done a fair distance away from enemy ground forces, which would allow the ISC to stay clear of the majority of infantry anti-air weapons. For the larger, armored threats, the AI painted them as priority and suggested using the forward firing hyper-velocity gun. It could take out most heavy vehicles from several miles away.

Some of the I.S.C anti-air munitions were advanced versions of old flak rounds that contained a complex dust, which had an adverse effect on sensors as well as a spray of shrapnel intended to destroy. They could also be used in missile defense to lay down a wall of fire or could be used quite effectively against infantry. There were automated point defense lasers all over the hull. There were even pods that contained directional jamming equipment.

The AI on the *Colossus* had been monitoring the battle and tuned the

ISC in before it took off. The AI had also been granted access to as much of the streaming battlefield data the *Bismarck* could provide. Valerie asked about William Steiger. His beacon classified him as alive with no injuries. He was on his own. Colonel Richards had died, taking many Iksus with him.

The AI insisted that, in order to maintain clear communication, proper identifiers should be used. The term 'alien' was not specific and could lead to confusion. Valerie said that it didn't matter what they were called to everyone else and made up a name of her own. The AI disapproved of the crude name and refused to use it.

Valerie and the ISC entered the planet's atmosphere just in time to see the last transport take a hit, burn, and break apart on impact. It was on approach to pick up another load of army personnel. Valerie had been friends with the other transport pilots all of whom, as far as Valerie could tell, were now dead.

The only Iksus ground vehicle left on the field could not move but was still deadly. Valerie made it her first target. The hyper-velocity gun screamed a heavy slug down range. It penetrated the vehicle and the concussion of the hyper-velocity round at impact rang out and put many of the Iksus on the ground. The vehicle's ammunition magazine erupted killing nearby Iksus infantry. The Iksus were noticeably shaken and confused.

Valerie let out a blood curdling war cry over an open channel. She didn't even realize it. The AI applauded her zeal and let out a screech of its own over the external loud speakers as it swooped over the battlefield and moved into position. Then, the AI had to remind her of what she was doing.

Sometime later, the event of Valerie's arrival over that battlefield was described by the survivors in many ways. Some said that her war cry was that of a banshee and the ISC's that of an eagle. The surviving Iksus were later interviewed and, although they were veterans of many battles, had never been so afraid.

Captain Artus later said this in his report, "… her avenging wrath was like the Erinnÿes of ancient Greece. It was as if a Fury had arrived onto the battlefield."

The ISC flew around the Iksus that were assaulting the army at their recovery zone. Even though the two heavy guns were quieter than expected, they still shook the ship. Valerie could feel the air pulse against her. The ring of spent shell casings hitting the ship's deck made a pleasing high tone accompanying the heavy bass of the guns. She decided she liked heavy artillery.

The Iksus scattered. Some launched ground to air missiles. Valerie watched as the point defense lasers did their job. One missile got close. Valerie punched the countermeasure button. Some flares shot out. The flares did more than flare. Each had a beacon and transmitted decoy signatures, which effectively confused the missile. It flew off and exploded a safe distance away.

"Ensign Heinz," said the AI, "bring us around to two-one-five degrees. A group of Iksus are making a run on the Landing Zone. Communicate to friendly personnel to prepare for close support, high explosive."

"Hey army boys," yelled Valerie over the radio. "Take cover."

The ISC poured high explosives onto the Iksus advance. Some rounds impacted close to the lip of the crater the army was taking cover in. Once the immediate threat was taken care of, the AI instructed Valerie to move into close range so that it could pick off the scattering Iksus. Valerie could barely hear the anti-aircraft guns, but they and their spent casings added another chorus to the heavy guns which still fired at the occasional group.

A few minutes later, the AI said that the Iksus were broken. All of those still able were returning to their outpost. It suggested that all of the army stragglers and holdouts should rendezvous at the landing zone. Valerie communicated this to the army over radio and loudspeaker as she flew over. There weren't many left.

Valerie found William's beacon. He was near the Iksus vehicle when it was destroyed. His life signs were faint, but he wasn't in danger of dying. His beacon didn't show any major injuries. The AI said that he was probably unconscious. There were other blips on the sensors that were not classified as Iksus or human. She didn't know what they were, but the AI said they were no concern and proceeded to remove the blips from the sensors.

Valerie wanted to go find William, but the AI and Captain Artus told her to pick up the critically wounded first. She would have to return to the ship to retrieve the Emergency Medical Pressure Pods first. The ISC was too big to land in the hangar, so crews in spacesuits waited to load them out on the deck with the pressure doors at the front open. The ISC opened its main door in the back and extended a ramp to the deck as it maintained its position outside. Navy corpsmen and Dr. Briggs accompanied Valerie back to the planet.

Upon return to the ship with the wounded, the unloading procedure would also have to be done on the unpressurized flight deck. Once the pods full of wounded were unloaded they would be taken to the flight surgeon in a medical bay just off the deck. Thankfully, the undamaged or repaired survival suits of the army could handle the vacuum of space and they could simply disembark.

Valerie called to the army to clear a landing in the crater. There didn't seem to be many left in the crater either. She saw life signs on sensors, but no bodies. After the ISC touched down, it opened its doors and lowered a ramp. Valerie rushed down the ramp and looked around. She saw the wounded lying in the back of the crater. She ran to them.

Finally, Valerie saw movement along the crater walls. The army was indeed alive. They had been covered by the dust and debris from the ISC's bombardment. They had stayed down until they saw Valerie run to the wounded.

Some soldiers limped up to her. "I'm Ensign Heinz," she said. "Who is in charge?"

One of the men tried to stand at attention and salute.

"I'm First Sergeant Chen," he said. "Baker Company. You're in charge here, ma'am."

"What about Steiger?" asked Valerie.

"He and the rest out there went radio silent some time ago. We haven't heard from him since. There are some officers, but they're in no shape to lead. There are some NCO's still able."

Valerie looked around at the battle weary soldiers gathering around. She fought back the tears. "Sergeant..." Valerie choked, "...let's get the wounded on first. Captain Artus wants all those who can to stay back until the critical are secured. He's going to send some Marines back with me to relieve you. The *Bismarck* has some systems back on and will keep an eye on you. They are also sending back two of the fighters for cover." Valerie turned back to the ISC.

"Ma'am," called Sergeant Chen.

Valerie turned back to him. He stood at attention the best he could and saluted. The rest of the soldiers followed his lead. Valerie snapped to attention and returned the salute. Valerie lost it. She dropped the salute and ran back to the ISC. She could hear Sergeant Chen barking orders as she left.

KETHIS OBSERVES

From an interview with Kethis Cheriatis
Iksus Armada
Admiral

Expedition 179
Operation Start: 8710 GST Month 6, Week 2, Day 5, Artex Local Time; 2314 Earth

Current Date: 8715 GST Week 4, Day 7, CT156 Local Time; November 6, 2319
Location: CT156 Binary, 2nd planet, Beta Star

Kethis turned his attention to the fleet arriving. They had communicated that they had just spotted a small vessel heading for the planet. They said it looked like a large transport, but they were being jammed and they couldn't be certain how fast it was moving or how long it had been in transit. It did not take proper sensor readings to realize that the transport was moving very quickly. Fleet estimated that it would arrive at the planet in less than three hours. They plotted its origin. It had come from the Cannibal Fleet. Kethis figured that it started its flight to the planet about the time the human ground commander set his crater ablaze.

The Council Guard commander was down but not out. After the humans went radio silent, they initiated a chaotic assault which was initially successful, but eventually was repelled. He rallied his force and the majority began a march to the human evacuation zone. This infuriated the humans.

The humans began another attack, but not one the Guard commander fully understood. Kethis drew a picture in his mind. The humans still away from the evacuation zone spread themselves out further and took careful aim. The result was what the humans referred to as guerrilla warfare. There was apparently a human on the ground still with command authority. The Guard could not find him. This forced the Guard commander to return his attention to the few humans that remained on his flanks. After sometime, the Guard commander considered the threat to his flanks manageable and again moved toward the human evacuation zone.

Kethis began feeling the effects of his radiated body. For the treatment of radiation, there wasn't much the medic could do and there were no proper facilities on board the *Sonai* transport. Kethis wiped himself with all the medical gels he could find in an attempt to clean the surface radiation from his skin and scales. He took some pain killers. Luckily, the cruiser *Xar* was on its way to retrieve him. He did not look forward to the radiation treatment ahead. He would need to go through a premature molt to remove his radiated scales.

As Kethis waited, he returned to the ground battle. The Guard commander was now using the damaged tank to destroy the transports. The humans were down to one transport. The humans had also broken radio silence and appeared to be singing. It was a sign of a foe that would not be taken alive. Then the last human transport went down. Kethis was nervous, on the edge of his seat.

The Guard began its final assault on the human evacuation zone located in a large crater. Then, there was the voice of a female war cry over the radio. The Guard reported hearing the cry of some aerial beast echo over the landscape. A human woman said something over the radio and then human comms traffic went crazy. The Guard seemed undaunted and commented respectfully of their human opponents' tenacity and the war cry. Kethis now remembered the transport traveling to the planet.

Kethis listened as the Iksus tank coordinated with the Guard infantry as artillery support. It suddenly fell silent and the Guard went nuts. Something nasty had destroyed the tank and the screech over the landscape came again as a ship flew over. As the Guard commander tried to figure out what was going on, the rest of the Guard began to receive direct heavy fire from what was now revealed as a gunship. They tried to bring it down with anti-air missiles, but it had a point defense system. The Guard commander was killed early and the rest of the Council Guard that had begun making their assault on the human evacuation zone disintegrated under the direct fire of the gunship.

The Guard left behind to deal with the guerrillas had a different problem that Kethis couldn't understand. All he heard were reports about the dead rising and something about large, mechanical bipeds ripping guardsmen in half with their bare hands. He immediately thought back to the mounds they noticed littering the area near the outpost. Someone managed to get a more complete description of this new enemy out, and Kethis immediately thought of Titus Andronicus. Could there be more than one?

Kethis shivered as realizations began to dawn on him about the leader of the Human Nations. These new enemies must have been lying in wait long before Kethis and his team had arrived. This meant that, if they were anything like Titus, then Titus was likely as old as legend claimed and far more dangerous than he or anyone else in the Armada or on the Council had previously realized. Kethis decided that it was a toss-up about what scared him more; the fact that Titus was fact or that there was more than one such being in existence.

He was certain that the odds were now stacked thoroughly against him and that winning this fight would require a miracle.

THE BATTLE UNFOLDS

Now that the remnants of Colonel Richards' battalion on Kentaurus Beta Two were relatively safe, thanks to Ensign Heinz's timely arrival, Artus turned his attention to the arriving alien fleet. Recovery of the army and repairs to the *Bismarck* would take some time. He went to his office to be alone. He had all incoming data of the alien fleet routed to his office. CMC Billings had also returned and resumed his previous duties.

"Something to eat sir?" questioned Billings.

"Don't you sleep?" asked Artus.

"When it suits me," replied Billings.

"When does it suit you?"

"When you're not looking," said Billings matter-of-factly.

Artus rolled his eyes and ordered a meal.

"Oh," returned Billings, "we've heard from Boris. He's on his way back as we speak. He requests Marines and medical personnel on standby."

"What for?"

"He claims to have, 'recovered enemy data.' His words, not mine. If he wants Marines and medical, it could be a prisoner."

"I want the flight deck cleared before he gets back. If it can't be done, send him to one of the utility bays. Inform Commander Greenland and Captain Mitchel." Artus sighed. "Lieutenant Commander Hudson may be the appropriate person to question a prisoner, if any. If she is feeling up to it, I want her to conduct the interrogation."

"So you've decided she's a friend then?"

"The jury is still out, but she has more information on what may actually be going on. Plus, her psychological background gives her experience at judging people's intent, or whatever 'they' are."

"Sounds reasonable enough. If that's all, sir?"

Artus nodded and Billings left.

Thanks to the AI on the new ship Ensign Heinz was flying, the *Bismarck* had been patched into the Defense Fleet sensors, but that was it. He could not tell what it was up to. Artus watched a blip on his screen. The blip was that of the ship that blasted off of Kentaurus Beta Two, presumably with the alien commander. It proceeded swiftly to rendezvous with the first elements of the main force.

The Defense Fleet was jamming the Iksus transmissions and so they seemed to be unaware of what happened to their fellows on the ground. The *Black Jack* resumed its rogue asteroid tumble along a new trajectory toward the arriving alien fleet. The two alien cruisers that had gone into the Defense Fleet had been ripped to pieces.

The *Hood* and *Agincourt* exited the warp gate and immediately proceeded to the colony. The two ships were considered the most capable warships in the navy except for the *Bismarck*. The *Hood* was a battleship and the *Agincourt* was a cruiser, but only just. Both were old, heavily modified, colony ships. Two destroyers and another freighter arrived to assist the *Bismarck* with repairs, transfer personnel, and receive most of the press corps.

Two frigates arrived and immediately released a cloud of remote activated homing mines along the route of egress that the evacuation freighters were taking. Once near a target they would be activated, fire rocket motors, and home in on the enemy. This was done to force any enemy ship down a corridor that the Second Fleet would fill as it fell back to cover the evacuation. With their payload launched, the two frigates began to patrol around the warp gate.

Artus was impressed at the speed with the response of the Second Fleet.

They were on alert, but he hadn't been certain they had taken the situation seriously. Battle orders were always supposed to be serious, but Artus had never seen or heard of their use since Titan. He wasn't sure Fleet knew what to do. Then again, if Hudson was to be believed, the Federal Military brass had been constantly drilled and prepared for this possibility.

Lt. Cmdr. Hudson had appeared to recover from her fainting spell and was declared fit for duty. Artus was still concerned about her for a multitude of reasons. She requested to help Dr. Burns with whatever needed doing. Dr. Burns gave her a good report. She was most helpful and, in the doctor's opinion, a very capable nurse. She was doing a good job coordinating with the doctor and her crew.

Once the majority of the casualties had been secured, Hudson made rounds and helped where she could. There was more than once when a screaming or weeping patient had been soothed, as if by magic. Dr. Burns said that Hudson did not use any pain medication to achieve this. All she did was hold a hand and whisper in an ear. Dr. Burns didn't know what to make of it, but didn't dare argue. She requested that Hudson have leave to visit the wounded whenever possible. Artus allowed it.

The first ship the Defense Fleet moved against the Iksus had a long, unarmored engine section. The front of the ship, however, branched out into three equally spaced, heavily armored prongs. If one looked at the ship from the front, the prongs formed an open, equilateral triangle. The ship was fast. The *Colossus* identified it as a Talon Ram Destroyer, or TRD

The TRD approached the Iksus on their left flank. As a result, it denied the Iksus a clean shot at its unarmored section. It launched a salvo of torpedoes at the nearest Iksus ship. The Iksus ship took two hits and blew apart. The remaining torpedoes searched for more targets as the Iksus tried to respond. Artus was curious why the Iksus had not tried to respond sooner and redeploy to counter the TRD on its approach before it launched torpedoes. It was not hiding its intent.

As the TRD neared another Iksus ship, something spectacular happened that caught everyone, including Artus by surprise. A blast of energy from the open maw at its front pierced the Iksus ship, which split in two, and the TRD flew through the debris. The *Bismarck's* sensors were frantic trying to comprehend the amount of energy emitted. The TRD continued through the debris, firing bow guns at targets as it passed. The TRD then rammed head first into a ship a bit smaller than itself. The Iksus ship was ripped apart as easy as tissue paper. Artus decided that with a designation like ram destroyer, he shouldn't have been that surprised.

Like the flip of a switch, the second Iksus wave arrived and immediately opened fire on the TRD. It responded with fire from its bow guns, but the Iksus made their shots count and the TRD lost half of its engine section. The remaining torpedoes found targets. The bow guns fired a few more shots and then fell silent.

Two more TRDs were moving in to engage. The Iksus did not move to intercept. They didn't even prepare to meet the TRDs. The Iksus rallied, reformed, and proceeded to the colony. The TRDs did not pursue the Iksus. Artus sent warnings to the *Hood* and *Agincourt*.

Artus had a difficult time understanding the actions of either side. Artus relayed all incoming combat data to Admiral Fleming aboard the *Hood*. Artus suggested that the Iksus commander understood that he now had a deadline to retrieve any information he could from the colony and so ignored the Defense Fleet attack. The alien commander probably had intended to capture the colony and was now hoping to get whatever he could. Admiral Fleming agreed.

The Iksus commander would have had plenty of time to secure the colony if it were not for the *Bismarck*. Artus guessed that with the navy dismantling the colony, the Iksus commander would take what he could get. The Admiral didn't see a boarding to be likely, but ordered that all ships were to self-destruct if the need arose. With the *Bismarck* in its current state, Artus wondered why it wasn't a target. Perhaps they thought the *Black Jack* was the culprit behind the land battle and didn't know the *Bismarck* existed. Then again, if the enemy had a deadline, he might not have the resources to spare and might ignore the *Bismarck* unless absolutely necessary.

Artus now brought his thoughts to the reason why the TRDs did not pursue the Iksus. That question was answered when a third Iksus wave arrived. These Iksus ships were bigger than the ones before and rivaled cruisers. The Iksus attempted to respond to the TRDs that were already amongst them. Due to the nature of space, the mass of the Iksus ships, and the mind-bending effects of physics, the Iksus could not maneuver or escape the TRDs.

The TRDs launched torpedoes at point blank range. They fired their energy cannons into the Iksus and followed those blasts into the bowels of the enemy, leaving gaping holes in the enemy ships. With damage done to four more ships, the TRDs were put down.

The Iksus ships would have looked like a collection of randomly designed ships to the untrained eye due to the oblique angles of their hull. Artus was certain this was to aid in deflection of conventional weapons. They also glistened in a manner that suggested they were coated in a reflective surface, probably to protect against laser and other energy based attacks.

The hulls of the ships were somewhat thin and elongated. Their engines were spread out along the hulls. The smaller ships were faster, and their engines were only armored in the front. This suggested a design for swift assault. The larger ships were of similar shape, better armored, and by far slower than their smaller cousins. These seemed to be designed on an old fashioned Earth mentality from the First World War leading into the Second: bigger is better.

After watching their performance, Artus was fairly certain that the *Bismarck* could cause some serious damage if it could defeat the alien armor. This, of course, was wishful thinking. The *Bismarck* was in no condition to fight. It was also the only ship of its kind. The overwhelming numbers would finish the *Bismarck* quickly. He put all thought of the *Bismarck* aiding in the battle out of his mind until he was ordered to join in.

Artus became confused. The Federal Navy could communicate to ships traveling at warp speeds. Surely the Iksus could also. If they could, then why were they not giving their follow up waves a proper warning? Course correction at those speeds was difficult, but possible. It would also be simple to exit warp sooner.

Artus decided that he was pleased when he'd rightly guessed that the Iksus should, and did, alter their arrival. The Iksus started to exit warp further back along their line of approach. The TRDs followed suit. The Iksus continually moved their arrival back with each wave in an attempt to form a battle-line before the TRDs could wreak havoc. It wasn't long before the larger ships of the Iksus were not able to stop fast enough and friendly collisions were now a concern. The few TRDs that remained took full advantage.

The Iksus seemed to have a plan and were unwilling to change it regardless of circumstance. The Iksus commander couldn't be that foolish. Then again, he might not have a choice in the matter.

Earth history was full of battles and campaigns where the commander was not allowed to use his own initiative. The Greeks and Romans had a bad habit of allowing the use of two commanders. Often times one would be a trained military leader and the other a politician who fancied himself the same or better. The one who was in charge could change from day to day.

Adolf Hitler was another prime example. He often redirected, intervened, or changed the orders of his commanders in the field. Although he intended, due to paranoia, to force his military to rely on him as the supreme commander, all that achieved was failure on all fronts. Of course, Artus did not argue with the way World War II turned out.

During the early days of the United States Civil War, the Army of the Potomac had its share of commanding generals. Whenever they were on the verge of a success, the President, some senator, or other influential person would come along and decide that the job wasn't getting done fast enough or could be done better. There were also profiteers in the Union Army who used any new supply to get rich, thereby leaving the army without.

The Iksus commander was likely hampered by the former issue of politics. An invasion of this magnitude had to be expensive. The Iksus commander was likely under a microscope and the influential were waiting in hunger to pounce upon him.

Admiral Fleming suggested that the Iksus commander could be making his decisions based on what he perceived the Defense Fleet was trying to accomplish. She surmised that the Iksus believed the Defense Fleet was trying to draw them away from their goal and force a confrontation for which they were not yet prepared. Artus agreed with the Admiral, but only in reference to the Iksus being slowed and drawn out.

Regardless of what the Iksus commander was thinking, the Defense Fleet was under a similar situation in that it was still waking up and was not ready for a fight. The sensor information Artus was reading verified that. This being the case, the Defense Fleet certainly seemed to be achieving its goal of slowing and confusing the Iksus.

Admiral Fleming told him that it was all guess work at this point and there was nothing either of them could do about it. She ordered him to get some sleep. Further analysis could be done when he'd been refreshed and events had unfolded. This was a smart idea and Artus signed off without argument. However, the army had organized an impromptu celebration of their survival and their savior, Ensign Heinz. Artus was requested to attend.

SURVIVAL PARTY

The ISC was too big to land in the primary hangar. It opened its doors and lowered its gantry while maintaining position off and to the front of the deck. Medical teams rushed the wounded off and Marines rushed on.

Lt. Cmdr. Carmen and two of the fighter crew joined Valerie in the ISC cockpit.

"Welcome aboard, lieutenant commander," said the AI. "Crewmen."

Valerie had fallen asleep in her chair. She jumped from her seat and almost fell over as she whirled around to salute.

"As you were, Ensign," said Carmen. "Take your seat. Jensen, Ramirez," she pointed to the other two stations. Jensen was a Red Shirt Petty Officer and Ramirez was a Brown Shirt Lieutenant not much older than Valerie. Both were mouthy but superb deck crew, so it was tolerated. They took their seats and the AI began giving them a walkthrough of their stations. Carmen sat in the co-pilot seat. "I hear that there is an artificial intelligence on this beast," she said. "Was that it or him or whatever?"

"Yes ma'am," said Valerie. "The voice that welcomed you aboard. Say hello, Compy."

"Hello, lieutenant commander," said the AI.

"Compy...," remarked the Carmen. "That's a bit campy." The two lieutenants laughed.

"Clever pun, lieutenant commander," said the AI in its usual flatness.

"I know it's not a clever name," said Valerie, "but I had to call him something, and I haven't had a lot of time to give it a think. I couldn't keep calling him Computer, AI, or ISC."

"ISC?" questioned Carmen.

"Invasion Support Carrier," said the AI. Valerie noticed that the AI was having multiple conversations with Jensen, Ramirez, the Marines, and with her and the lieutenant commander. "If I may suggest," continued Compy, "you should not concern yourself with monikers for the time being. If it is necessary to give me a name beyond my serial number and designation, then I suggest a drawing later."

"Sounds good," said Carmen.

A Marine lieutenant stuck his head in. "We're all set back here. Ready when you are."

"Thank you, Lieutenant," said Lt. Cmdr. Carmen, who saluted. The Marine returned it and went back to the bay. "Ok, Valerie," continued the lieutenant commander, "it's your ship. Let's bring'em home."

Valerie hesitated. "My ship?"

"Naval tradition, Valerie," said Carmen. "I am unfamiliar with the vessel. You are the most experienced with it, in the entire navy. Regardless of rank, the one responsible is captain and you're doing well so far. I see no reason to alter the current situation."

"Can I name a delegate or a second in command?" asked Valerie.

"I don't see why not," replied Carmen.

"Then I name you as my second, Lieutenant Commander," stated Valerie. "I need some shut eye. Take over, will you?"

Carmen laughed. "I'll do my best. Is there an instruction book or something?"

"I have a detailed tutorial I can put through in flight, Lieutenant Commander," said Compy. "With combat operation over I can handle flight operations until a full crew has been trained."

"Nice," commented Carmen. "Let's get this show on the road." The ISC took off and began its flight to the planet.

Valerie jumped out of her chair.

"What's wrong?" asked Carmen in surprise.

"Nothing," said Valerie, who eased herself back into her chair. "The massaging chair caught me off guard."

"These chairs have a massage option," blurted P.O. Jensen.

"Where's ours?" asked Ramirez.

"You haven't earned it," said Carmen. "A little faster on mine please Compy. I don't want to fall asleep."

"How come you've got yours?" argued Jensen. "You haven't been flying, around blowing things up." He gulped and tried to make himself small as he realized he'd gone too far. The lieutenant commander gave him a look of death.

"Privilege of rank," both she and Compy said at the same time. "Wow," she said, "I think I like you, Compy."

Valerie would have laughed, but she had fallen asleep.

As the ISC returned planet-side, the AI instructed the others in the operation of its systems. Valerie slept. She slipped in and out of consciousness for a while. She came to and found out that they had been back to the *Bismarck* twice. Now they were collecting the dead and stragglers.

The ISC homed in on William Steiger's position. Valerie and Carmen gasped. The AI said that he was the only soldier nearby, living or dead, and the ISC had not lent him support during the fight. The Marines and soldiers stood at the edge of the ramp and couldn't believe their eyes.

There were dozens of Iksus bodies. Many mangled and mutilated. A figure sat amongst them on a boulder. Lieutenant William Steiger was covered in alien blood and tissue. His back was to the ship and he didn't seem to notice as the others approached. An assortment of alien items lay next to him along with two heads. He appeared to be eating a ration pack.

Valerie ran out to him. He calmly turned his head as she approached. He looked up at her.

"I've had a terrible a day," he said as he stood to face her. His chest armor had three large cuts across it. One still had a claw in it. His visor was smashed, and his nose had been bleeding. A third head hung from his belt. There were alien scales arrayed on his arms, legs, helmet, and chest. He didn't look real. He threw his food down.

"God, you're beautiful," he said to Valerie. He poked her with a finger. "Just checking." He passed out. Valerie caught him.

With the final flight done, Valerie and the flight crew got some sleep while the ISC maneuvered into the *Bismarck's* belly, the only place big enough to hold it. It docked with a compartment module and was compatible with the power supply. This did mean, however, that in order to get back inside the *Bismarck,* everyone would need to take a walk inside the unpressurized bowels of the ship to an access hatch at the nearest compartment.

Lt. Cmdr. Carmen reminded Valerie of their conversation about careers. Carmen told her that she would likely be set for life now if she kept her nose clean. Regardless of the fleet's take on events, Valerie was certain to have a home with every soldier she rescued. Lt. Cmdr. Carmen put a hand on Valerie's shoulder and looked her in the eye. "Well done. Now then, about your report..." Carmen assisted Valerie in putting her report of the events together.

After several hours of flight, reports, and the alien fleet arriving, the ISC finally landed and shut down. The crew went through post-flight check lists with the computer. When that was done, Carmen and her flight crew left, taking Valerie's report with them.

Lt. Cmdr. Carmen returned shortly. "Valerie, come on. Get cleaned up and get some proper food. The captain says that reinforcements are arriving. The *Bismarck* is still out of action, and we won't have flight operations for some time. I'm giving you time off. Enjoy it while you can."

A few moments later, Valerie left the cockpit. She walked down the ISC gantry where the others were still standing. She looked up with them and couldn't believe what she saw. The maw of the *Bismarck's* interior was impressive. She had seen it from windows in other compartments, but to stand in it was something else. She could see the spinning rings that provided gravity as well as many of the large stabilizing gyroscopes. Through its shielded compartment, the light from the ship's fusion core at the back gave everything an eerie, light purple hue, casting long shadows. She stood there in awe until Lt. Cmdr. Carmen took her hand and lead her to the hatch.

Carmen didn't take her to the mess or her bunk. Instead, Valerie was led to the secondary flight deck where the army was doing its best to recover. What Valerie saw upon arriving on deck was just as impressive, if not more so, than the ships interior. Those of the army who were able, and some of those who weren't, cleaned themselves up and were now standing in parade formation on the flight deck. As Valerie stood in awe, First Sergeant Chen called them to attention and saluted her.

Valerie collapsed to her knees, unable to cope with the flood of emotions. People had died. She had killed. The world in Valerie's eyes was distorted and blurred. Maybe it was tears. She realized Carmen was right. One thing was certain: they may not have been her family, but they were as good as.

An unseen arm helped her to her feet. It escorted Valerie through the ranks, which parted in silent reverence. Valerie noticed that many of the soldiers, while at attention, couldn't hold back their tears either. The hand that escorted Valerie was that of Boris.

He sat her down at a table next to the *Phoenix*. William Steiger sat across from her. He looked lost until his eyes settled on hers. Valerie blushed.

"Lieutenant Steiger, sir," said Sergeant Chen. "Shall we commence with the pleasantries?"

"Yeah, do the thing," muttered William, whose gaze upon Valerie never faltered.

Sergeant Chen let out a whoop that was echoed by the rest of the army. A party commenced. The music blared over the speakers, and someone had rigged the deck lighting to flash with the music.

Valerie finally spoke to William. "Are you ok?"

William responded. "The doctors want me to take it easy on account of a brain thing."

Valerie retold her story. It was obvious William wasn't functioning properly. He had a hard time using his fork, and Valerie had to repeat herself a lot.

Captain Artus arrived, told them both to stay seated, and asked to join them. Boris prepared a plate of his signature gumbo. Everyone thought it was an odd dish for a Russian to make, but it was excellent, so no one argued.

"Give your man a break, Lieutenant Heinz," said the captain. "He's had a knock on the head, and I'm certain he's under the influence of medication and battle shock. You can talk his ears off some other time. Let him rest."

"Lieutenant?" questioned a stunned Valerie.

"Yes," replied the captain. "The army was not the only one fighting and dying today. The battle has only just started. With the flight crews under strength and the space battle about to begin, the chain of command needs to be as intact as possible. I've also gone over your record with Lieutenant Commander Carmen, and we both agree that you have not been shown appreciation as befits your experience or ability. The lieutenant commander also suggests that, since you have the most experience with our newest piece of equipment and member of the crew, they are your responsibility. That amount of hardware, according to regulations, also requires the responsibility of one with rank no lower than a full lieutenant. Carmen put your name forward, and I approved. The appropriate schooling and review are still necessary though. Carmen will go over that with you. This is a battlefield promotion, so it may not last once we get home, but I don't see why it shouldn't. Here are your papers and orders." The Captain handed her a stuffed, sealed envelope.

Valerie took it amazed. "Thank you, captain. Where is Lieutenant Commander…?"

"Lieutenant Commander Carmen is securing operations on the primary hangar. Give her your thanks when you report for duty. If she makes it to this shin-dig, you can give a more informal appreciation then."

"Yes, sir," said an elated Valerie, who was holding the envelope in awe.

"Now then, Mr. Steiger," said Artus. "Did you follow all that?"

"She's been promoted," said William with a look that suggested he wasn't sure of the words he'd heard or said.

"Yes," replied Artus. "You, Mr. Steiger, are in a more delicate position. Your battalion is on life support. Its colonel is dead, and its major is in critical condition. The other officers are either dead, dying, missing limbs, or have worse head injuries than you. I've been told that you can return to active duty in a few days with the condition that you report for a full physical, psychological screening, and a daily check up with Lt. Cmdr. Hudson."

"Ok," responded William. The captain produced another sealed envelope.

"When you return to duty, you will be in effective command of what remains of the battalion. I have not been in contact with the army yet, but I am brevetting you captain. The army may decide to take it away, allow you to keep it, or jump you up another rank. I can't spare any of my officers, what with a space battle coming, to see to the needs of your battalion. For the time being I am your commanding officer. Once the party is over, I need your medics to go to the infirmary and give the surgeons whatever help they require."

"The medics are already there," said William.

"Good," replied Artus. "Until you return to active duty, First Sergeant Chen will see to things. I've already discussed it with him. He has a handle on the situation. He'll bring you up to speed. I'll leave the details of things up to you and him, but don't hesitate to ask me for assistance.

"Now I know you've both just gotten relaxed, but I've been going over both of your reports. There's a lot I wouldn't normally believe, especially in yours, Captain Steiger. I wouldn't worry about putting certain details in. It would send the wrong message to those in charge of your future well-being."

"I'm not going to lie about what happened," said William.

"I'm not asking you to," replied Artus. "You can report what you want, but the army would take you more seriously if you left out the voices in your head and the dog men. I don't know about the army, but the navy would investigate your well-being and shove you into a closet to be forgotten. You may or may not get recognition for what you did. In my opinion, it would be best to keep it simple and allow them to think you're awesome and not nuts. I don't think that you're crazy, but the army will if they read your report as is. You've just been through a traumatic experience, and you will need help through the coming days. It's best to let the army assume it's trauma and that you are recovering, for your sake. Lieutenant Commander Hudson will help you deal with that."

"Help?" asked William in confusion.

"Flashbacks," stated Artus, "second guessing yourself, wondering if you should have done things differently. You should have, by the way, so expect some flak from the brass about it. However, if you had done things differently, you and the rest of the battalion would likely have died. I probably would have fought a similar holding action, but by the book. I would have concentrated and tried to fall back in good order. What you did was probably a panic reaction, but it confused the aliens. I am certain that they were hunting officers via the radio traffic. Spreading out, going radio silent, and having your men go rogue was ballsy and furthered their confusion."

"Well, sir," said William, "she told me they were killing officers."

"She? Is that one of the voices you heard?"

"A voice, sir," replied William. "She, it, told me that the aliens were targeting officers. It made sense that they were listening to our transmissions. As far as the holding action goes I didn't have any input. I remember thinking, 'well, we're screwed, so let's slow them down, and give the transports more time'. Going rogue felt like the right thing to do. The voice may have been someone cutting into our communication, and it may have been in my head, but I didn't make it up. It was not a product of shock or any other psyllichos... psychos..."

"Psychosis," interjected Valerie, who caught herself.

"Yes, that," returned William. "Whatever the voice was or is, I heard it clear as day and it sounded familiar."

"You see, that's what I'm talking about," said Artus. "It's excellent. It makes perfect sense, but don't put this "voice" in your report. If you heard a voice, fine. If you saw giant armored dog men, fine. I'm not going to argue, but the army will. You'll fight them about it until you do go crazy, or they make you believe you're crazy, or convince everyone else you're crazy."

"Captain Artus," a Petty Officer walked up and saluted. The captain acknowledged. "Captain, Commander Greenland would like to speak to you, sir."

The captain excused himself and walked over to a terminal.

"Did the voice sound like me?" asked Valerie with a hopeful glance.

"No, sorry," replied William. "This voice had something about it. It was an older voice with an air of absolute author… authorit…"

"Authority?" interjected Valerie.

"Yeah," agreed William with a look of hard fought puzzlement. "But it almost came across as playful. Now that I think about it, it is crazy."

Valerie froze. She couldn't be certain, but she had an idea of what he meant. What worried her was that she might have a name to put with the voice.

"He's right, William," said Valerie, "it would be best to keep that secret."

Captain Artus returned to his seat. "Commander Greenland has been going over the records of the ground battle to analyze their tactics. It would seem that the targeting of officers was definitely taking place. The battalion didn't take as many deaths as we thought. There are still many in critical condition, and it looks like you're the only officer who came out walking. Captain Smith and Lieutenant Hanson may not survive. The commander checked what video was available, and it's still too soon to be certain, but the aliens' random attacks weren't all that random. They used our confusion against us to track down our command structure. We don't know if they defeated the encoder or even understand our language. It took them a while, but once they had pinpointed our officers, they hit them all at the same time. It appears that they didn't even know you existed."

William looked down, "That's probably because I didn't say much."

"I know. I've read your file. Colonel Richards put a note on it. His note said that he added you to the roster as a late addition on a hunch. I don't know what you army guys put in your food to become psychic, but I could use some." Artus sighed.

"I still don't think it's wise to mention the voice or the dog men. Especially since you claim that they told you to keep them a secret. If you must mention those things, I'll make out that your concussion is worse than it actually is. It should lesson any fallout. I will try and make myself available if you need help with your report or need to talk. I'm also ordering you to go to a counselor. The only one aboard who's qualified and not knee deep in combat wounds and surgery is Lieutenant Commander Hudson. I'll tell her to be expecting you"

Artus turned to Valerie. "Your report would earn you the brig and court-martial if you didn't have proof. Compy, or whatever we'll call him, even provided audio and video logs to prove your case. He also claims that his program is designed to imprint itself on the first person to fly him. That's you. The navy will investigate the case since one of its transports was destroyed for no other reason than being 'unworthy'. I'll back you up, but it may not be enough…"

"…I want Lieutenant Commander Hudson to be my legal counsel," blurted Valerie.

"There's a story behind that," said Artus. "I look forward to hearing it. I'm ordering you to counseling too. On a side note, the both of you may be interested to know that Boris here has been reactivated. While you were fighting and flying, he broke into that outpost down there and stole us a prisoner." Both William and Valerie were stunned. They sat in silence as Artus excused himself. He passed Hudson on the way.

Hudson was on the secondary deck officially to screen the army for post-traumatic stress. This could take a lot longer to set in and may never in some cases, but it was an excellent excuse to come to the party. The party had, however, quickly mellowed out and was now spiraling into an emotional hole from which there was little escaping. Hudson went from group to group consoling, singing as she went. As soon as her voice produced the first few notes, life was restored to the assembled mass.

33
ARTUS CONTEMPLATES

November 9, 2319

Artus awoke twelve hours after the army's party. He found Master Chief Billings asleep on a pallet behind his desk. Artus let him be. Artus was relieved to see Commander Greenland, who was dozing in the command chair. He went to the log and ordered a shift change for all those who'd been at their posts for eight hours or more.

Artus reviewed the log for anything interesting. The Iksus fleet appeared to have arrived in full. Their casualties caused by the ram destroyers seemed light. They were now moving in force toward the colony. The *Black Jack* was engaging the Iksus ships that had gone ahead.

Carpathian had gone to war and the *Hood* and *Agincourt* were on their way to assist, not that the *Black Jack* needed any help. With its disruptors, heavy guns, and torpedoes, the *Black Jack* was multitasking with the best. It was currently giving two Iksus frigates a proper beat down and forcing any other ship that wanted to pass, to take the long way around. A destroyer strayed too close and even managed to get by. It was then ripped down the long axis from behind by a mammoth hyper-velocity round. The round went clean through stern to bow.

Artus couldn't help but give a chuckle. It reminded him of a comment he'd heard a gunners mate make to a reporter while they were still in the Sol system. The reporter asked the woman how easy it was to operate the weapon systems of the *Bismarck* compared to other ships. The gunner, without revealing any classified information, kept it simple. "The math involved with shooting any object, moving or otherwise, in space from another object, moving or otherwise, is beyond me. Our computers, however, make it as easy as clubbing baby seals."

Artus later learned that the gunners mate had made the comment on a dare. Artus gave her a meal from the Captain's Mess. He also expressed his disappointment that the men of the gun crew didn't have the guts to say it themselves. He'd later learned that the gun crew in question had obtained a contraband picture of a seal, with a pacifier, being hit on the head with one of their rounds. They affixed it to the bulkhead above their gun.

The colonists had been evacuated with much fuss onto one of the freighters. The other freighter crews were busy stripping the colony of all sensitive data and valuable materials. Artus ordered his two pilots to go back with the freighters. They objected but followed orders.

The freighter and two escorts with the spare parts for the *Bismarck* were still a day out, but the estimated time to rendezvous had been shortened significantly. The *Bismarck's* engineers, with the assistance of Compy the AI, had restored many of the computer systems affected by the *Black Jack's* ion blast. Commander Greenland had ordered a course to rendezvous with the freighter.

Artus ordered that the dead and wounded were to be the priority transfer instead of members of the Press. There were a few of them he wanted gone regardless. As much as he deplored the practice, he'd already requested Lieutenant Commander Hudson to investigate legal proceedings for impressment, which would make the rest hate him.

Lt. Cmdr. Hudson again proved her value in coordinating with the other three ships and the *Bismarck's* medical teams. Sadly, the other three ships did not have adequate facilities so some of the wounded would stay aboard the *Bismarck*. Hudson also responded quickly to the legal issue, by contacting Admiral Fleming and Fleet in record time. She already knew that Captain Artus would impress the Press regardless of law and had informed him that, given the circumstances it was within his right. She did, however, make certain that all the proper persons had been informed and paperwork done.

Hudson entered into an attitude of absolute power. She did follow Capt. Artus and Cmdr. Greenland's orders. However, since she was the only ranking officer not doing anything, she was given the overall command of coordinating the wounded and the Press Corps. She had become half of the myth that surrounded her, the mean half. Artus had seen her flirtatiousness and her ailing stress. Now he witnessed firsthand the terror she could bring to bear.

Hudson explained to those of the Press Corps who were resistant to being forced into service that the captain was well within his wartime emergency rights and read to them the appropriate laws. As of that moment, all who were not going to be sent back were in the Federal Navy whether they liked it or not. As such, they could be tried for cowardice, dereliction of duty, and treason, all of which, during times of war, carried the death penalty. She also explained that a trial need not be held to pronounce sentence. There wasn't time for it and even if there were the number of witnesses would ensure a guilty verdict.

Captain Mitchel now revealed another promising aspect of himself. Artus allowed the Press Corps, in small groups, out of isolation to stretch their legs and recover some of their personal belongings. This calmed many down. Some who were being sent back pulled out their cameras and started to film the wounded men and women of the battle. Captain Mitchel snatched the first camera he saw, smashed it on the ground, and said, "You will not dishonor these people or their sacrifice!" He ordered his Marines to do the same with any camera they could find. Although this was a blatant violation of free speech, Artus patted Mitchel on the back. This was a ship of war, at war, during an extreme situation. Mitchel's care of wounded finally earned Artus' respect.

One of the more obstinate reporters tried to push past the Marine. Out of nowhere, Hudson put her .75 caliber Colt Devastator in the man's face. "I could kill you now and any subsequent inquiry or trial would rule in my favor," she said. "You would also be branded a traitor and not given rights granted under Federal law. Your family would be arrested, interrogated, and always viewed with suspicion." The man wet himself. "Get back in line," Hudson ordered. Artus was bothered by the realization that he liked Hudson more every day.

A flirt and a terror were not the only qualities Hudson exhibited. Not only were her words and very presence soothing to the wounded, but she could sing. Artus overheard her singing to herself as she changed a man's bandage and checked his IV. Artus stood a fair distance behind her and listened intently. The soldier she was tending had half of his face burned and couldn't see out of his left eye, but his right eye gazed at her as if he'd never known pain. Even the surrounding soldiers watched, listened, or relaxed.

Artus was aware that the entire flight deck where the wounded were being prepared for transfer was in an oddly pleasant mood. Everyone seemed to be moving to a beat, Hudson's beat. Only those around her seemed to be aware of her presence and none gave any hint of knowledge about the phenomenon. When Hudson was finished with the bandage, she kissed the man on the forehead, whispered something in his ear, and moved to the next patient.

Artus had difficulty rationalizing the melodious episode. He decided that any pleasant voice would have had roughly the same effect on the battle weary. Hudson had the advantage of being a beautiful, classically trained soprano coupled with what must have been the touch of an angel. This was everything contrary to what Artus had expected or had decided based on rumor, credible information, and his own experience.

At one point Hudson went to Captain Artus and asked if there was anything more she could do. He mentioned her singing and suggested that she perform a concert on the flight deck for the wounded. She didn't think anything of her singing and said so. Artus argued and told her that, with her apparent knowledge of the crew, she could find someone else to sing or accompany her. He ordered her to sing at least one song. She agreed.

As soon as the replacement parts had been unloaded and the wounded and nefarious press elements transferred, the freighter and its destroyer escorts set course for the warp gate. With the repairs under full swing, the *Bismarck* was in no condition to fight and made best speed for the warp gate. This made it difficult for Hudson to find anyone available for the concert.

Artus learned that Admiral Fleming had been in contact with Carpathian, much to her surprise. He'd ordered her under some obscure jurisdiction to keep the *Hood* and the *Agincourt* in position to support the colony. The Federal ships were now tied into the Defense Fleet sensors and were receiving the same information as Artus, which gave them excellent battlefield awareness. Although Admiral Fleming could strategize with the best, Artus had not been impressed with her tactical ability. Carpathian had not explained his intent, and Artus could only wonder what the Iksus or Defense Fleet were up to. Carpathian, on the other hand, was easier to read.

Artus explained to Admiral Fleming as best he could. The *Black Jack* was the most powerful, direct fire, asset they had. Carpathian was probably the most experienced, if not trustworthy, commander in the system excluding the Iksus. Artus suggested that the Admiral defer to Carpathian. He also believed it would be a good idea that the Admiral pull back, because Carpathian's history showed that he might attack her as easily and readily as any other, in this case the Iksus. Admiral Fleming didn't like it, but she couldn't argue Artus' logic. She began to pull back, but kept the *Hood* and *Agincourt* in battle formation.

The *Agincourt* moved ahead of the *Hood* on the way back to the station. This created a staggered formation that was intended to keep any enemy that decided to make a run for the colony engaged. Any enemy ship would have to run a gauntlet in order to reach their target. Artus had not seen anything special in the smaller Iksus ships to suggest that the *Hood* and *Agincourt* should not be able to cause harm.

Later than Artus expected, some of the small Iksus ships disengaged from the *Black Jack* and set course for the colony. They must have noticed that the colony was unprotected and were going to try their luck. They were no better than their fellows. Their course indicated that they would come close enough for the *Hood* and *Agincourt* to engage.

With whatever the Iksus had learned from the earlier ground battle, they probably didn't think much of Earth technology. Even with the Defense Fleet's electronic interference, the Iksus should be able to see the Earth ships. Were they unafraid or were they a probe? Artus alerted Admiral Fleming, but she was not totally ignorant of the battle at hand and fully recognized the weakly armored engine sections of the smaller Iksus ships.

Admiral Fleming intended to be prudent and then did something that Artus applauded. The *Hood* and *Agincourt* released what mines they had in the path of the approaching Iksus. The mines were no secret, but it was possible the Iksus did not, or could not, see them, or they simply didn't care. The Iksus destroyers soon found that being blind or not caring was bad.

There were two types of mines deployed. The first was an electronic overload mine. It attached to a ship and used two large capacitors to shunt gigawatts of electricity into the ship's systems. This effectively disabled the Iksus. The second type of mine was the stereotypical, big bang kind. It would home in on a target, tear an entrance into the ship's hull, and then explode. The two Iksus destroyers were no longer a threat. Artus congratulated the Admiral with the first two Federal Navy kills.

The Iksus that were heading for the colony were stopped. The larger, main body of Iksus warships had been harassed for some time by the smaller ships of the Defense Fleet. When Artus saw that the vast majority of the Defense Fleet was mobilized, he looked forward to watching them trounce the Iksus. The Defense Fleet, however, had other plans. Artus watched in dismay as the bulk of the force entered warp and left the system. All that remained were those that were currently engaged with the Iksus and some sensor and jamming vessels.

Artus did not need anyone to explain the Defense Fleet's actions and suggested that the colonists step lively and finish the evacuation. Four ships, the size of which must have cost several star systems the bulk of their resources, arrived. They were not identical in size, but it was plain to see that they must have been designed together. They appeared to be space stations, but they were a foreign design and so might be combat vessels.

Either way, a mobile station or a leviathan combat ship was impressive. Access to four meant that the Iksus would be able to operate with relatively unlimited ease. The Defense Fleet did not look as though it had the power to fight these new opponents. The Defense Fleet was leaving while it had the opportunity. Admiral Fleming ordered that Artus was in charge of the evacuation while the *Hood, Agincourt,* the cruiser Halsey, and two destroyers would provide a screen and commit to battle if needed.

THE FIELD IS LOST

November 9-11, 2319

Carpathian sent a message. "The field is lost. Admiral Fleming, you have five hours to get everyone off the colony. At zero-three-thirty hours I will commence Federal War Directive Six of the Emergency War Powers Act, section Omega. God speed." This would allow Carpathian to perform what was commonly known as scorched earth.

Artus knew what that meant. So did Admiral Fleming. She ordered all navy ships in the system to take up escort positions for the evacuation. All navy ships were to release mines as they headed for the warp gate. The evacuation crews and freighters were told to drop what they were doing and set the colony reactor to overload and then make a run for the gate. Admiral Fleming's task force moved to set up a battle line across the evacuation line of egress.

Artus was glad that Admiral Fleming was cooperating. He'd worked with her before and she had a habit of doing things her way, and hers was the only way. She was not impossible to work with if she was in charge and she had people she knew she could count on, like Captain Artus. Taking guesses and suggestions from Artus was one thing. It was her opinion, in no certain terms, that he was the better tactician. Taking orders from the pirate Carpathian, however, had to be hard for her. Still, she was no fool and recognized that Section Omega was the only sensible course of action.

If the colony had been built like a navy ship, there would be a series of containers in strategic places all throughout the hull. These containers would hold a combination of high explosive gases that, when triggered, would vent the gas into every nook and cranny. The low temperature combustible gas, heated by the radiation from the reactor or a remote detonator, would then ignite, thus incinerating the ship's interior. This could be done manually, but the navy frowned upon losing crew in such a way unless there was no hope of escape.

The *Bismarck* had a similar system, only it was more detailed. Certain sections would have their computers saturated with acid and hard drives wiped with magnets before the reactor went critical. In the event that the crew was still aboard, a colorless, odorless, neurotoxin would flood all compartments. The details of this were known only to the captain and probably his second in command. Lt. Cmdr. Hudson probably knew also. If anyone else knew, they rightfully kept their mouths shut.

All that should be left of the *Bismarck* afterwards would be an empty husk. As an added insurance, after the incineration, a series of explosives would go off to leave nothing of the internal superstructure but heaps of twisted metal. The engine section would receive an extra-large dose of explosives in order to secure the drive technology from any interested parties. The *Bismarck's* outer hull and armored sections would then drift through space as a pile of junk. Artus doubted that the colony had anything that effective.

Hudson reported having a difficult time getting any talent to come forward from the ship's crew. Artus suggested that she lead by example. Artus knew that some of his junior officers had been members of the Naval Academy choir and glee club. A small chorus could be formed. Artus was concerned about his crew's morale after the Defense Fleet ran. He told Hudson to make their performance a personal request from him.

Lieutenant Valerie Heinz came forward to take the ISC and help in the evacuation. The vessel was fast and large. It would prove useful. However,

Artus was under the impression that speed and performance came with drawbacks. He went for a chat with the ISC to get its opinion on the matter.

"Hello?" said Artus in an inquisitive tone as he entered the ISC cargo bay.

"Welcome, Captain Artus," said Compy. "How may I be of assistance?"

"What is the operational limit of your warp drive?"

"With fuel and energy at peak, I have enough power to transit for twelve hours. If I must stop and start multiple times, there is a thirty minute recharge and recalibration procedure. After entering warp the number and distance of any subsequent jumps depend on fuel and weight. Clever piloting around gravity wells can give a boost in efficiency."

"If you were to assist in the evacuation of the colony, could you get back?"

"That depends on the nature of the assistance."

"The primary objective is the retrieval of personnel and ferrying them to their ships or to return with them here."

"Safe return should be no difficulty. If equipment and materials are to be ferried, then it will depend on their nature. If a detailed manifest can be provided, then I can calculate probabilities and a course for myself and the *Bismarck*."

"Can you make those calculations in flight?"

"Yes, but I will require a full flight crew in order to free my runtime."

"Right then, power up and be ready to leave as soon as possible."

"Very well, Captain."

Artus sent a message to Admiral Fleming and the colony that help was on the way. Admiral Fleming reported that those aboard the colony were dragging their feet. The admiral had declared a military emergency, but the deconstruction crews weren't getting the idea. Commander Greenland volunteered to go to oversee the operation, but Artus had another idea.

He postponed the entertainment until the entire situation had been resolved. Some of the crew was genuinely upset. Lt. Cmdr. Hudson, after being cleared for duty, bore a disturbing grin when he restored her authority and ordered her to take charge of the colony. She had proven her command and coordination skills with the army evacuation. He also believed Lieutenant Heinz's story and the situation warranted a heavy, unshakable hand.

Artus wasn't happy that Lieutenant Commander Carmen was going as part of the flight crew. He liked her the moment he met her, and they had gotten to know each other when duties allowed. He wasn't sure he was falling in love, but he decided he would like to give it a chance.

Captain Mitchel and a detachment of his Marines were going as well. Hudson had operational command, and Mitchel was to follow her orders to the letter. Deadly force was not authorized unless it was absolutely necessary, but there was no problem with pushing or shoving.

When the group was assembled, the ISC took off and made record time in covering the distance between the *Bismarck* and the colony. Admiral Fleming had not been aware of the ISC's existence until then. She was surprised and had many questions.

The civilians on the colony gave Hudson and the Marines a hard time for about a minute. Once an upstart had been shot in the foot, the rest got moving. The Marines added their bodies to the effort and the remaining sensitive materials were secured swiftly. The colony's experimental and highly secret communication system was the last thing to go, and it was ordered to the *Bismarck* for safekeeping.

After three hours, Hudson ordered a stop to the equipment transfer and ordered all personnel off the colony. The freighter wrecking crews had already left, and most of the colony was empty. Only navy and colony command personnel were left. The two pilots who had taken word of the situation in person were glad to get back to the *Bismarck*. Hudson activated the colony's reactor to overload, and the ISC returned to the *Bismarck* with an hour and half of power to spare.

Time to Run

November 11, 2319

Artus watched in horror as the *Black Jack* set about devouring the remains of the first two Iksus waves. After the initial shock, Artus was impressed that the cannibalization of the Iksus ships provided the *Black Jack* with power and a lot of it. He could only guess at how the process worked and decided he didn't really want to know.

A cloud of something was ejected by the *Black Jack* when its feast was over. Sensors reported the cloud to be mostly organic in nature. It took a moment for that to sink in. Everyone moaned in disgust. After this terrifying display, it turned and set course for the colony.

The Iksus slowed their advance and came to a full stop. They redeployed their line on a new heading, the warp gate. The freighters might make it to the gate, but it would be close. Admiral Fleming ordered all navy ships that were able to form a battle line and prepare to cover the fleeing freighters. She ordered those ships guarding the gate to follow Artus' command and join the *Bismarck* in aiding any freighter that couldn't get through in time. Artus didn't see any way for the Admiral to avoid a fight this time. The *Black Jack* wouldn't be able to eat the colony and support the Admiral.

Artus received a call from the Admiral on his office terminal. He was with the Admiral for some time. When he returned to the bridge, everyone looked at him and waited. It was obvious his conversation with the admiral had been heated and he hadn't yet composed himself.

"Shall we set course to rendezvous with the Admiral in battle formation," inquired the helm.

"No," said the captain. "Continue heading for the warp gate at maximum possible speed. Alert me when we are in weapons range."

"Captain," started Commander Greenland. The room fell silent. "What about the evacuation ships?"

"Anyone who can't make it by then is to set course for home and pray. Send word to fleet that we need as many supplies sent through the gate as possible." Artus left the bridge.

He sat in his office and stared into the distance. He did not watch the *Black Jack* eat the colony. He read the Fleet report that said supplies could not reach the gate in time. He sat back in his chair without thought for some time.

"Captain," Billings voice cracked the silence. Artus looked at his intercom.

"What is it, Master Chief?" inquired Artus.

"We are in weapons range of the warp gate."

"Very well, I'm on my way."

The mood on the bridge was grim. Weapons reported forward batteries were locked on the warp gate and ready to fire. Artus waited for one last transport that was less than ten minutes away.

"Alert Fleet," ordered Artus

"Fleet acknowledges," said Lt. Nguyen. "They are sending authorization… Red, Six, Delta, Nine, Omega."

"Challenge," said Artus. "Omega, Six, One, Two, Atlantis."

"Stand by for final confirmation," replied Lt. Nguyen. "Response coming now… 'Over the hills and through the vale, be safe, be true, be heaven bound… Awaiting final challenge."

Artus gulped. "...From darkened shores, through wind and gale, be swift, be sure, be homeward bound."

"We have authorization to destroy the warp gate."

Artus went to the weapons station and relieved Lieutenant Carver. He took a deep breath and flipped the manual fire switch. Streaks of blue shot forth from the *Bismarck's* hypervelocity guns. The superheated plasma burned away. Four large spheres slipped through space, without a trace, into their mark, without much grace.

"Contact with Fleet lost, Captain."

"Helm," said Artus, "make your course one, seven, five, ninety degree down angle. Keep this heading for twelve hours from this mark. Rig the ship for silent running."

"Aye, sir. Course one, seven, five relative. Ninety degree down angle. Rig the ship for silent running," echoed Mr. Whitfield.

"Alert me if the enemy makes contact or moves against the freighters. Crew stand down to eight hour shifts. Lieutenant Commander Whitfield, you have the conn."

Mr. Whitfield acknowledged with a smart salute. Artus returned it and left.

Artus sat in his office and watched the battle unfold. Then, without prompting, Hudson entered. She had a solemn appearance, wearing a simple, dark blue ball gown. Artus was impressed and now saw in full the beauty the rumors claimed.

"Captain," said Hudson. "I have decided to follow your advice and lead by example. I request that all wounded, who are able, be given leave to assemble in the gym. I have a few songs that could boost morale, at least if I can pronounce the words correctly. I would also like permission to broadcast to the entire ship."

Artus certainly liked the idea. He sent a message to Admiral Fleming.

"I'm busy, Captain," was the admiral's reply.

"My apologies Admiral, but there is a request from one of my crew to sing for the ship. I thought it might be a good idea to broadcast to the other ships in the area."

"Not a bad idea at all," replied Admiral Fleming. "What kind of songs are on the play list?"

Artus looked to Hudson. "I currently have some anthems and hymns available," said Hudson.

"Is that Hudson?" barked the Admiral.

"Yes ma'am," replied Hudson.

"Hmmm…" grumbled the Admiral. "I don't suppose you have a choir to back you up?"

"No."

"Well then, make it something lively. If you don't have that, then make it something inspirational. It may help to do something we all know so we can sing along. Go ahead and broadcast on an open channel. Maybe we'll get lucky and scare the enemy some." The Admiral signed off.

"No time to gather the wounded," said Artus. "Sing from the bridge."

Artus went to his quarters. He fixed himself a drink and sat in a chair. He listened as Hudson's sweet soprano voice massaged the air. With his drink finished, he laid himself down on the bed and let Hudson's melodies wash over him and lull him to sleep.

KETHIS VICTORIOUS

From an interview with Kethis Cheriatis
Iksus Armada
Admiral

Expedition 179
Operation Start: 8710 GST Month 6, Week 2, Day 5, Artex Local
Time; 2314 Earth

Current Date: 8715 GST Week 4, Day 7 -- Week 5, Day 6, CT156
Local Time; November 6-12, 2319 Earth
Location: CT156 Binary, 2nd planet, Beta Star

Kethis was retrieved by the cruiser *Xar* fourteen hours after he fled the planet. The situation in space looked bad. His subordinates did not agree. In their opinion everything was proceeding better than expected.

The fleet was early. The Cannibal Fleet only had four destroyer class ships engaging. The first two waves had taken losses, but were proceeding with their objectives on schedule. The Admiral was safe. Kethis' subordinates considered things to be going quite well and saw no need to alter course or activate a plan change.

It didn't take long for the third wave to see their error. The third enemy destroyer landed a barrage of torpedoes on the extreme left of the wave's line. A frigate disintegrated. The destroyer continued its assault by ramming the next Iksus ship in line and firing its few weapons with deadly precision.

Kethis ordered the third wave to finish the destroyer quickly and move up before the fourth wave arrived. This was done. Kethis tried to alert subsequent waves, but he had to perform security checks before each message. Such security on the field of battle was time consuming to a dangerous degree.

"Admiral," called the *Xar*'s captain. "The rogue asteroid will cross close to the first and second waves moving against the colony station."

"Asteroid?" questioned Kethis. "Put its path on the viewer."

The asteroid would cross the path of advance and come unacceptably close to the first two waves. Kethis decided that there was something not quite right with that asteroid. He asked for its path to be retraced. It was the same asteroid that passed the planet. He didn't like the asteroid.

"Have the first and second waves slow and watch for any movement by the asteroid," ordered Kethis.

"It is an asteroid, Admiral," said the captain, confused.

"That is the same asteroid we detected on the planet. It passed close to the orbiting aggressor. Do you believe in coincidence Captain?"

The captain rolled his eyes. "Relay the Admiral's orders to the skirmish line. Continue your tracking of the asteroid." The captain's attitude concerned Kethis.

The asteroid showed no noticeable signs of movement. However, when the skirmish line of the first two waves slowed, the asteroid made a slight alteration to keep its intercept course. The captain thought that was very peculiar and requested a visual.

"That's no asteroid," admitted the captain. What they were looking at was an asteroid, but it was being pushed and guided by some kind of ship or thing.

Kethis ran to the comms terminal and immediately tried to warn the skirmish line.

"It's no good, Admiral," said the comms tech. "They are being jammed by a local source."

Kethis watched in horror as the thing released the asteroid at speed. It slammed into the skirmish line. It obliterated three ships and caused severe damage to others that barely avoided the same fate as their fellows.

The thing that had pushed the asteroid unfolded and stretched. It sprouted long, fingerlike appendages from its bow. The elongated dreadnaught weight ship used these appendages to grasp and pull in the remains of the ships the asteroid slammed into while firing all manner of weapons on the rest of the skirmish line. Ion cannons and disrupters were its primary energy weapons, and it finished the job with assorted conventional munitions.

The debris was drawn down into a gaping maw, pulverized, and then vanished into the dreadnaught's core. Refuse was ejected out of ports on its sides and aft. The skirmish line needed no prompting to fight back. Two human ships moved to engage also but were still a good distance away. Kethis couldn't tell whose side the Horror Dreadnaught was on when it fired some shots toward the humans, who immediately backed off.

The Horror Dreadnaught was something that Kethis had never seen. He remembered childhood stories about astral leviathans that could eat moons and planets. This ship was not that big, but it fit the description in every other way. The Cannibal Fleet was a remnant of ages past and records of its existence, though rare, did remain. The dreadnaught, however, was an ancient evil from legends long past. What was it, and what was it doing here?"

Two destroyers broke off from the fight and ran for the colony station. Were they running scared? It did not matter. The human ships had assumed a column formation parallel to the destroyer's advance and deployed mines directly in the way. The two destroyers did not live to see whatever success or dishonor they'd hoped to achieve by fleeing the field of battle. The human ships turned toward the Alpha star to follow their comrades who were evacuating the colony station.

The situation at the Iksus point of arrival was not going well. The arriving ships were backed up. There were some collisions. The Cannibal Fleet ram destroyers were still making a mess of things. Kethis had a difficult time untangling the mess and could not get the captains to redeploy in order to keep the Cannibal Fleet at bay. He did succeed in convincing subsequent waves to leave warp sooner in order to prevent any more collisions.

Kethis did not believe his fleet would achieve capture of the human colony or prevent its deconstruction. The evacuation had started slow but now took on new life. The warp transport observed earlier was now aiding, and it sped up the process considerably.

Kethis sent a flash transmission back to the Council. He also reported the presence of a warp gate. Kethis now wanted to move as swiftly as possible in hopes of cutting off the human retreat. Sadly, only the Council could authorize such a deviation in plan, and they had not been aware of a gate. He had to continue as planned until the Council gave him new orders.

Strangely, the Cannibal Fleet did not move to engage with its full strength. This confused Kethis. Even in its weakened state at the battle's beginning, the Cannibals could be doing far more damage. Now they were leaving. Why were they leaving and abandoning their post? Kethis did not have to wait long to understand why.

Four massive ships arrived. Kethis' jaw dropped. The ships were relics of wars long passed. There were only a few known to exist. They surpassed anything the Iksus had ever built and could cause significant difficulties for the Cannibals. Kethis did not know that the Iksus had any. He now understood why the Council was so certain of success.

These vessels went by many names. The one Kethis liked most was Triton Foundry. Legend said that the Triton Foundries could fight, devour, and build entire star-fleets. Then Kethis realized that the Horror Dreadnaught that attacked the Iksus skirmish line, although physically different, was operating in much the same way.

Kethis soon received orders to secure the warp gate. He turned his fleet away from the now evacuated colony. He might catch the stragglers.

"Admiral," called the *Xar*'s captain. "There is a new ship on sensors. It is heading away from the second planet of the Beta star following two destroyers and what appears to be a freighter."

"What destroyers?" bellowed Kethis who was beginning to embarrass Iksus discipline. "What freighter?"

"Sorry, Admiral," replied the captain. "You were non-responsive after the cleansing and fatigued. I thought it prudent to allow your rest. You've been over busy and suffering radiation poisoning. I had the doctor check on you. You were doing well so I let you sleep."

"Yes… Well… Let's see this ship that almost killed me."

Kethis wasn't sure what he was looking at. It was not like any ship he'd seen before. The Human Nations didn't have anything like it. The preliminary data of the Cannibal Fleet hadn't given any suggestions either. It wasn't until a proper scan was performed by the Marines, who'd never left their ships, that Kethis could tell this aggressor matched the configuration of the largest ships in the Cannibal Fleet. It was smaller, however, about the size of a cruiser.

The human fleet was communicating to it, and the warp transport boarded it. It seemed to be limping along. Kethis had formed an idea that this ship was not responsible for the ion cannon or the disruptor attack on the planet and was correct. It had been damaged too. The Horror Dreadnaught and this ship must have been working together in order to achieve such a ruse.

Kethis now looked to where the Horror Dreadnaught was heading. The colony station was its next victim. Kethis watched as the dreadnaught performed its grisly task on the colony station. It must have been working with the humans.

Kethis wasn't surprised by what happened next. The human fleet formed a battle line in front of the Iksus advance to the warp gate. They were preparing a fighting withdrawal, falling back as the freighters fled. They could not expect to win, but they stood anyway. It was something Kethis admired about humans. A few hours later the humans did something else that Kethis applauded. They destroyed the warp gate.

"Why did they cut off their only means of escape?" inquired the ship's captain.

"To prevent us from claiming it," replied Kethis.

"It's a long way home," returned the captain.

"Yes, but we won't have ready access to their star system either. A strategic move."

Hours later the Iksus engaged the humans. They were inferior in technology. However, they scored many good hits. A destroyer was lost and two more put out of action. A frigate was also disabled.

As for the humans, there was an open transmission from the fleeing cruiser. A female was singing. It was moving, and Kethis thought he recognized the tune.

The humans lost all warships in the battle. The biggest ship broke apart. As its aft section drifted away, a lone gun kept firing until it ran out of power, or its crew died. It was an act of defiance Kethis had not seen even among the Nations. It moved him to tears. The entirety of the *Xar*'s command deck was awed to silence.

All of the human freighters that had not escaped fled the system for the long flight home. They were accompanied by the only definitively human warship that appeared to pose a real threat, and a few smaller warships. Kethis ordered scouts to follow, but not to get close enough to provoke the human cruiser. He felt no need to pursue. The freighters would be slow, and they had no way home. If he felt the need or was ordered to go after them, he could catch them easily. He only needed to keep track of them.

The scouts quickly lost sight of the human cruiser, which disappointed him. Kethis was pleased, however, that the disaster he'd feared hadn't happened. The element of surprise for further operations was questionable. The Cannibal Fleet was still on the loose. Kethis gave the order to stand down.

He desperately wanted to visit the outpost battlefield on the second planet to find his friend Commander Tonais. The Horror Dreadnaught had other plans. It returned to the second planet and destroyed the atmospheric generator and all external structures. It also collapsed the hanger to the mountain facility. Any hope of recovering survivors was low. After this the Horror Dreadnaught disappeared.

Admiral Kethis tasked his fleet to secure the area and begin construction of their Command Station. After this, Kethis made his way to the outpost in order to recover any Iksus assets and anything human for study. Thankfully, the Horror Dreadnaught had not completely destroyed the mountain facility. There were survivors buried beneath the rubble, Commander Tonais was one of them.

The survivors had been corralled in the lower reaches of the facility. They had been given food and medical supplies, by what they would not say. Fear of what had happened to them at the end of the fight still held their tongues. It was uncharacteristic for Iksus. Kethis remembered cries about the dead rising from the grave; and if anything would put such fear into him, it would be that. On the bright side, Commander Tonais survived but still needed critical care.

Like the rest, Tonais would not report on what had happened. He did report that a single human breached the outpost. This human had abducted a wounded and radiated female communications tech. The human used a powerful projectile weapon he did not recognize. A few of the wounded Guards got close, and those he did not shoot were smashed by a large hammer. The strength and power this human displayed in wielding the hammer was more than Tonais thought humans were capable of. The description reminded Kethis of the Cruor Prognatus.

A female communication tech was missing. This could be very bad. It would only be a matter of time until they could translate her speech. When that happened, they would be able to find out all manner of secret codes and frequencies. This human could not have gotten so lucky in his choice of prisoners. He had to have known what and who to look for.

Commander Tonais was suffering from the effects of the disruptor. His left arm would need to be amputated and most of his scales had disintegrated, leaving raw skin and muscle. He was to be evacuated for treatment and then would be discharged, receiving all benefits. He was of a weaker breed than Kethis, but he would survive. Kethis asked Tonais to investigate the Triton Foundries, but to be careful.

Kethis had a deep foreboding. The Triton Foundries were marvels of war from ages past. Plenty of reliable records of their existence and ability remained, but no one had seen one for the better part of fifteen-hundred years. At the end of the last invasion by the Ikar'ys, all of the Foundries had disappeared. It was believed that they were hidden away to keep them safe. Kethis knew about them from his academy days, but had never given them a serious study.

The presence of these Leviathans among the stars sent chills down Kethis' spine and drove visions of the terror that would come from their use into his waking eyes. This conflict was more than a quarrel between the Iksus and humanity. Its roots went deep into the annals of time long forgotten. Weapons of war against the Ikar'ys, the Fallen, were a sign of their return and Kethis had a good idea of the description of one, Kengarel. The Iksus Council was foolish if they believed this could end well. Any investigations would require extreme caution.

KETHIS CONCLUSION

Kethis pondered events thus far. The invasion of the CT156 binary star system had succeeded, but only just. The Cannibal Fleet leaving was an unexpected boon. The Council would have been happier had the Cannibals been captured, but Kethis had always viewed that as an unrealistic objective from the start. With the Cannibals still at large, however, the overall success the Council expected was uncertain.

The humans had been more of a threat than expected. The actual damage they had inflicted was minimal compared with the Cannibals. They had shown a moderate effectiveness and were more willing to fight than anticipated, as this was supposed to be a probable first contact event for them. The Council had reasoned, with Kengarel's input, that the Iksus arrival had a high likelihood of being met with no resistance and a possible peace. The Council majority would have preferred this.

Putting faith into a peaceful hello would have been easier if the Iksus hadn't sent a fleet instead. With such a show of force, peace was a fool's gamble. Regardless, the humans had obviously been ready. Warp gate aside, their response was swift and suggested that their force had been lying in wait just on the other side. This of course did not speak to the total size of their military might. There could be ancient power beyond his reckoning awaiting the Iksus. If Kethis was lucky, then they would have spent their force in this one fight, but it was too early to make an educated guess. Proper scouting would be necessary before any further offensives were launched.

The Triton War Foundries would be a major asset to operational readiness. Kethis could have his fleet repaired and rebuilt in far less time than previously estimated. He'd already sent scouts to the planets in system, surrounding asteroids, and anomalies for resources. The nearest star was also a target for resources.

The Tritons could destroy most of his fleet without help. The Cannibals were better armed and armored, plain and simple. They could take the Tritons, though it wouldn't have been easy. They could have also annihilated his fleet as it arrived, but they chose not to. Even with the Tritons in the field, the Cannibals could have stood a chance and caused considerable damage to his fleet. Why did they leave?

That thought gave Kethis pause. What could have scared the Cannibals from their post? Perhaps it was not as operational as it appeared. That would be asking a lot. Since the Cannibals had escaped, however, they would have plenty of time to conduct what repairs and readiness they needed. They may also have been simply caught off guard and fled only to properly deploy. If that were the case, then he would be attacked soon.

There was also the added problem of mines. The humans had littered the battle space with them. The majority were located leading up to and surrounding where the warp gate had been. Warp gate recovery was planned, but the mines had to be cleared first. Even so, there wasn't much to recover.

What concerned Kethis the most was that he'd received a letter. This letter was from none other than Titus Andronicus, the Human Nations war leader. It was handwritten and signed. It was dated during his absence and travel to CT156. Titus had not known who he was, but the ability to send a handwritten letter this far under Armada blackout conditions suggested that Titus knew now for certain. If the letter's content was to be believed, and there was no reason it wasn't, then he hoped the messenger might offer assistance in contacting Titus in reply. Kethis was beyond doubt that Titus had already signed his death warrant.

This letter was short and to the point. Kethis approved. It warned the Admiral of the Iksus Expeditionary Force 179 that the Council had been influenced by an outsider. The letter did not give names or point fingers, but it suggested an origin. The Ikar'ys were an ancient and supposedly immortal foe to all the races. They had many abilities; high among them was shape shifting.

The Chronicle of the Armada, a database of stories and legends long past, claimed the Iksus were bred to fight the Ikar'ys. With the aid of the other races, they had beaten them into the vast nothingness that surrounded the known universe in blackness. This blackness was collectively known as the Void. Even the vast expanses between galaxies were part of the Void's domain. Few who dared venture into it rarely came back and those that did went crazy and claimed to have seen horrors beyond imagining.

...The letter advised the Admiral, whoever he may be, to watch his back. It also advised him to seek the friendship of Titus quickly or Titus would hunt down everything he held dear and burn Iksu. Kethis knew immediately to whom the letter referred.

With Kengarel's arrival at his operations base, Kethis knew his time was short. He would sink the operation in as much bureaucratic red tape as he could. That shouldn't be too difficult or send up any red flags. Procedure was part of what made one Iksus. It would be beyond the Council to rush what he had in mind. It also might buy his friend, Commander Tonais, time to meet with a particular Council member or speak to Titus on his behalf.

Not all of the Council agreed so readily with those who sided with Kengarel. Officers and civil servants had been replaced by eager young fools with no experience or proper job qualifications. The Council was slowly becoming a puppet. The process was so slow and Kengarel so careful that few or none of the Council was aware of it.

Kethis didn't much care for the attitude of Councilor Markensis. He was fairly neutral on most counts. He favored charm and charisma over overt action unlike most of the Council. This wasn't all bad. He had power and could sway a good third of the vote. Kethis might like him personally, but he was notorious for bogging things down far beyond their already slow pace. He would often raise arguments that had already been thought decided.

He was not under the influence of Kengarel as far Kethis could remember, but he did vote that way at times. Kethis now realized that Councilor Markensis was probably fighting Kengarel and the others in a far more dubious and clever fashion than any knew. If he kept the peace of both sides and maintained his neutrality it could aid in keeping things from getting further out of hand. In fact, what Kethis had planned, Markensis might already be attempting.

Kethis sent an additional message with Tonais for his family. He wished them well and asked for prayers, but not from whom. This was a simple code alerting his mate to take the kep and go into hiding. It was a simple enough message that wouldn't raise any flags with security.

Kethis began to formulate his plan. It was audacious and involved many risks and relied on many uncertain loyalties. Markensis might join him or already be ahead. If Kengarel's nature was exposed, then the Armada would overthrow the Council if necessary in order to remove him. The key to all of this wasn't Councilor Markensis. Councilors came and went and Markensis might already be out of the picture. Titus would be Kethis' ticket to survival at least.

Titus Andronicus always seemed to know what the Armada was up to. The Council and internal affairs had never been able to completely remove the human spies. This letter's arrival meant that the human spy network was vast and very able. If Kethis could make contact with Titus, then a coordinated counteroffensive to whatever Kengarel was up to could be put together.

Exposing Kengarel could be tricky, but not impossible. Kengarel was not especially tall or short, for a human. He had few distinguishing features and was, now that Kethis thought about it, very average. He is so average that it seemed too good to be true. Kethis couldn't help thinking it was some kind of disguise, a very clever disguise. If it were only his looks and his scent, which was not altogether right either, then he would have passed Kengarel's attitude off as a servant who'd been too successful and forgotten his place.

Kengarel, despite his charm, exuded an air of disgust and distaste to all he came across. The Council was either oblivious, threatened, or simply didn't care. Kengarel's attitude could only be described in full as hate. Kengarel hated something and it would be the death of anyone who got in his way. Despite the obvious dangers, every time Kethis was near him he had to fight an urge to rip Kengarel apart.

With all of his messages sent and Tonais safely evacuated, Kethis prayed to all of the Kala he could name. Atraés, Lady of Battle, was always in his thoughts, but chief among them now was his people's patron. Mar'Kai'Dyn was the acknowledged creator of the Iksus and his strength would be necessary for the long days to come.

ARTUS CONCLUSION

Captain Artus, his command officers, and a portion of the crew sat for a show in the primary hangar. Lt. Cmdr. Hudson had succeeded in convincing some of the ship's crew and Press Corps to try their hand at singing, dancing, and telling jokes. Artus only half listened to the acts and only clapped out of habit.

It wasn't as though he was ignoring the show or that the acts were bad. Many were not very good, but that could be attributed to battle shock. The crowd wasn't very enthusiastic either. Artus was busy with probabilities and logistics. He would have liked to pay better attention, but was admittedly there only for the benefit of the crew.

He was in command of a meager task group made up of the *Bismarck*, two frigates, and a destroyer that had returned after unloading wounded and Press Corps back home. They were escorting four freighters that hadn't made it through the warp gate. It was a long way home and the *Bismarck* was the only one with a warp drive. It drew a lot of power, was fickle, and didn't have the range to get home.

Artus made frequent updates using the ingenious QE communication system. The Navy Brass wasn't happy that he'd stayed behind. The *Bismarck* was the most advanced ship in the fleet and therefore a strategic asset.

Artus argued that he wouldn't leave the freighters or the other navy vessels alone without means of communicating with HQ. He also wouldn't leave them to face a more powerful enemy. The *Black Jack* had finally shown its true colors and was friendly, sort of, but there was no guarantee that it would protect them. There was the Defense Fleet that Artus considered to be far more strategically important. Finally, he argued that the *Bismarck's* advanced systems were ideal for scouting and spying on the enemy. The Brass, with what he thought might be a powerful nudge from the Order, finally agreed and backed down. Besides, with the warp gate destroyed there was nothing to do about it now.

Artus realized that the *Bismarck* was now in a position to do exactly the job for which it was designed. He wanted to believe it was a coincidence, but Astaroth, Lt. Cmdr. Hudson, Tavion, and the unknown Aetonyx made such a belief a fool's hope. It was obvious to him that the very existence of the *Bismarck* was intended for this very event, or at least one like it. Such prediction, foreknowledge, and preparedness revealed a metaphysical power beyond what he could comprehend.

There was also the matter of the Iksus prisoner that Boris had somehow gotten his hands on. He claimed that it was indeed a female, which could hardly be argued. Her physical appearance was not too dissimilar from that of humans. Boris also claimed that she was a communications technician and would be a valuable asset if she would cooperate. However, her health was more pressing. She'd been on the edge of the disrupter blast, and this was the only reason she'd survived. That being said, her health was failing.

She was currently sedated while Dr. Burns and Dr. Briggs did their best to decontaminate her and heal any wounds. They both admitted surprise that her anatomy resembled humans enough that many of the same treatments were working quite well. Regardless of her condition, Captain Mitchel had a squad of Marines on watch at all hours. The Navy Brass was very interested in her and wanted constant updates.

Fleet had informed him that supplies were being sent their direction with the fastest ships available. Artus knew that even if the *Bismarck* could reach the supplies and ferry them back to the task force the trip would take a month at best. Starvation and mutiny would set in long before that.

Parts for the Rigil Kentaurus warp gate were aboard, but they were only meant as spares. There wasn't a full system. The egg-heads back home were taking inventory of everything the task group and freighters had to work with and were trying to come up with a solution. If a functioning gate could be jury rigged, then Proximal Centauri was a close enough power source. The *Bismarck* could ferry all of the personnel to the gate where some kind of transfer could be made.

The other ships might not last that long. Thankfully the freighter crews were small and wouldn't stress the food stores if a plan involving Proximal Centauri was put into action. Fuel would be an issue sooner than food in that case.

Artus had already formulated a plan for the inevitable. Crews and all necessary supplies and materials would be transferred to another ship. The destroyer had a small payload of nuclear weapons aboard. A weapon would be left on the derelict ship, and the *Bismarck* would linger nearby to see if anything took the bait. If not, then the weapon would be recovered and the ship scuttled.

Supply and morale were not the only things that concerned him. Carpathian, who wasn't a pirate after all, had sent a message and data packet before the *Bismarck* had gone too far. The data packet had navigational charts and locations for supply caches he had put in place. He could not confirm that the caches were still in place or the food still any good.

One particular cache was on an ice ball not too distant from the *Bismarck's* current location. It would be a valuable source of fresh water. Both Artus and Fleet didn't like to count on the word of such a suspicious individual. Supply wasn't a problem for the time being if Carpathian could be trusted.

The message that Carpathian had sent with the data was a concern. For the most part the message appeared to be the ramblings of a lunatic. He had moments of clarity. Commander Greenland noticed a pattern to his madness. He spoke a fairly simple form of code. She had deciphered a fair portion.

Carpathian warned that he was not the only thing lurking in the blackness of space. He had made intermittent contact with something after the *Bismarck* had started for home and before the Iksus moved in to recover what they could on the planet. This contact appeared to be following the *Bismarck*. He was certain that it was not Iksus. He had a hunch that this contact could prove useful to Captain Artus and so did not pursue. Artus didn't fully believe this, but the situation was dire enough not to be ignored.

Carpathian had also mentioned and given coordinates to the last known location of Cmdr, Greenland's father and his ship. Cmdr. Greenland was nervous about decoding the rest of the message. Artus sympathized and didn't force her. She could teach someone else the code and allow them to finish. Lt. Cmdr. Hudson might be able to do it without training. In fact, she might know a lot about what had happened to Commander Greenland the Elder.

Artus had gone to speak with Patrick McEnna as Colonel Richards had suggested and confirmed his story with Hudson. Neither of them could shed any light as to why Carpathian did not drop his asteroid on the planet during the battle. His involvement in the Capellan Station Incident was covered up by claiming that the station's destruction was the fault of the rebels. Although Hudson had not told him to, he decided that the truth should be kept secret and did not record it.

Among his thoughts, and not least of them, was Colonel Richards last words, "Look Simmons, they're beautiful." Although the Iksus prisoner was not unpleasant to look at, she was hardly beautiful, at least from Artus' perspective. The doctors and his senior officers were in agreement. Captain Steiger's report didn't seem to fit either. What had Colonel Richards seen?

Artus finally slumped in his chair with fatigue. Lt. Cmdr. Carmen sat to his right. She put a hand on his shoulder. It brought a smile to his face. He reached up and took it. She allowed him to hold it. It didn't mean there was a relationship, but it gave him hope for the future.

They sat hand in hand as Hudson took the stage. She was in full dress uniform, an impressive figure. She was not the final act. A choral performance by CMC Billings and the three odd Chiefs that Hudson had brought with her were the finale. He looked forward to that.

Hudson sang a solo. The power of her voice flowed over the audience like a healing spring. All of their worries and anxieties were washed away.

EPILOGUE

Letter to Commanding Admiral of Expedition 179

From:
Titus Andronicus
Legate of the Eagle's 10ᵗʰ Legion

Admiral Iksu,

I do not know you, but you have assuredly heard of me. Our peoples have been at odds for centuries due to a misunderstanding of blood. I ask that you put aside any prejudice and hear me. The fate of the galaxy and Unarem are at stake.

Your ruling Council has been compromised and a good portion is now subject to a will most dangerous. Take care in your friends and watch your back. If my suspicions are proved correct, then you will not be safe regardless of your allegiance. Joining with me may be the key to your own survival. If you side with this entity, I will destroy you along with your family and any who follow you to the last.

I do not yet know your objective, but if you cross the Krosan Expanse, I will take it as a sign of your intentions and will act accordingly. I have already dispatched a call for aid to the other Legions in the galaxy. Though it will take them some time to arrive, they will burn Iksu and decimate the Armada, which once was a most powerful ally.

If this message reaches you late and you have yet to realize your danger, then act swiftly to contact me and protect what you hold dear. If this is the case, then I will endeavor to be lenient with you. I can defend you where others fail or betray. Do not be a fool and ignore this warning.

Beware, Admiral Iksu, for the Ikar'ys have returned.

My messenger will be in touch.

Titus Andronicus
Legate, Legion X

Appendix

Contents:

1 CHARACTERS:

The following is a list of characters as of November 22, 2319. They are in order by rank and commission starting with the Earth Federal Navy followed by the Corps of Marines, the Earth Federal Army, Iksus Armada, and other persons or entities of note. The individuals name is presented first, followed by rank, then duty status, duty station, and finally any awards earned during the Alpha Centauri Combat Action. In the cases of the three Senior Chiefs who accompanied Lieutenant Commander Hudson, they are referred to as FLNU or First and Last Name Unknown.

Iksus names are similar to Asian names in that the family name comes first and the personal name comes second. The Vietnamese Lt. Nguyen Yuan is an example of this. Pronunciation of names is difficult if one is not Iksu due to physical vocal mechanics. When speaking the languages of others, humans in particular, the Iksus have a moderate to heavy lisp, a sound similar to that of snakes. Their own language includes clicks and clacks of both the tongue and jaw which are often heard in other languages. Many Iksus can communicate clearly enough in other languages to be understood. For everyone else, the accepted pronunciation of Iksus words and names follow an Ancient to Classical Greek pattern. It is believed this is partially because, when dealing with others, they favor use of the Greek and Latin that was carried out to the galaxy by transplanted humans. There are, however, inconsistencies that would take a linguist and entomologist a couple of lifetimes to understand.

Roll of Active Characters:

EFN

Sarah M. Fleming, Rear Admiral Lower Half – KIA; Medal of Honor pending, Navy Cross pending

Virgil Artus, CAPT – Active

Melanie Greenland, CDR – Active

Jorgina Carmen, LCDR – Active; Wg. Cmdr.

Reyla Hudson, LCDR – Medical Reduced Duty; Counselor

Chester Whitfield, LCDR – Active; CIC

Dr. Evaline Burns, LCDR – Active; Chief Surgeon

Michelle Collins, LT – Active; Helm

Samuel Cole, LT – Active; Sensor Battery; Navy Achievement Medal

Gregory Simons, LT – Active; Sensor Battery

Nguyen Yuan, LT – Active; Communications

Jenna Carver, LT – Active; Chief Fire Control Officer

Ishmael Amari, LT – Active; Fire Control Officer

James Harris, LT – Active; Engineering; NAM

Richard Johansen, LT – Active; Pilot; Distinguished Flying Cross pending

Janis Riggs, LT – Active; Pilot; Distinguished Flying Cross pending

Valerie Heinz, LT – Active; Pilot; MH pending, Navy Cross pending, DFC pending, CAR

Dr. Thomas Briggs, LT – Active; General Practitioner

Patrick O'Hara, LTJG – Active; Communications

Timothy Kern, LTJG – Active; Helm

Rachelle Landry, ENS – Active; Helm; NAM

Benjamin Billings, CMC – Active; Command Master Chief of the Ship; CAR

Astaroth – Status unknown; Order Spook, and all around scary guy; last known whereabouts: Aboard the Tower of Babel within the Earth Defense Fleet.

Borislav "Thor" – Reactivated; Cab Driver, Attached under Naval Special Warfare Command

FLNU, SCPO – Active; Attached under NSWC

FLNU, SCPO – Active; Attached under NSWC

FLNU, SCPO – Active; Attached under NSWC

Compy AI, E.F.N 198 India Sierra Charlie – Active; Invasion Support Carrier; Status as Crewman under Debate

EFNMC

Samuel Mitchel, Capt. – Active; *EFN Bismarck* Commandant of Marines; NAM

Jeff "Pops" McEnna, MSgt. – Reactivated; Marine

Frank Sims, SA – Impressed; Corpsman Apprentice, reporter Haven Tower

EFA

Allen Richards, COL – KIA; Army Engineering Corps, 1st Colony Support Battalion; MH Pending

William Steiger, Brevet CPT – W, Reduced Duty; 1st Colony Support Battalion, Acting Command; MH Pending, DSC Pending, CAB

All ships of the Second Fleet participating in the Alpha Centauri Combat Action are awarded the Navy & Marine Corps Presidential Unit Citation. The 1st Colony Support Battalion is awarded the Army Presidential Unit Citation. A Fleet Combat Award is being voted on by Congress for the Second Fleet and all those attached to it for the Alpha Centauri Combat Action.

Iksus Armada:

Kethis Cheriatis, Admiral – Active; Commander of Armada Expedition 179

Tonais Xerane, Commander – W; Evacuated; Legion of Valor with House Honors for actions with Expedition 179, Blood Mark with talons for wounds sustained in the line of duty.

Granis Chalchas, Lieutenant – KIA; posthumously awarded Legion of Valor without Honors.

Persons of Note:

Titus Andronicus – Name of the main character of the Shakespeare play *Titus Andronicus (~1590-1594)*. Name used by the enigmatic leader human navies and icon of the Human Nations. Status as human is questionable.

Kengarel – An enigma operating within the Iksus Armada. He is believed to be one of an ancient foe to all races of Unarem.

Ozuk'ai – One of the races of Unarem.

Marna – An ancient and powerful race believed to be extinct.

Ikar'ys – An ancient race and enemy to all of the known races of Unarem.

NOTES:

Chapter 2

1. Phrase made popular by a 20th-21st century television show called *Star Trek*. There are multiple series and movies beginning in 1966.

Chapter 3

2. This is a comment that I was instructed to research. I was told that I would enjoy what I found and I have. It is an oft made remark by one Sergeant Schulz from an old television show called *Hogan's Heroes (1965-1971)*. This was usually said when the character had seen or heard something he wished he hadn't or to stop someone beforehand.

Chapter 4

3. Ship's Wheel – Modern Earth Federal Navy vessels do not use actual wheels for maneuver. The stations which control maneuvering are computer terminal interfaces that are still called wheels. The navy likes tradition. Both the wheelhouse and the bridge have wheel stations. The Bismarck does have an actual wheel on the bridge just in front of the captain's chair between the two bridge stations, but it is purely for show.

Chapter 6

4. Mr. Artus wished me to note that Ms. Heinz was and is nobody's 'bit of fluff'. After having met her, I agree.

Chapter 10

5. The problem with traveling at the speed of light, as I understand it, is a problem of infinite mass and infinite fuel. In order to go that fast you need to have a powerful engine. You need fuel for that engine. You need a vessel for both the fuel and the engine. This enters into an upward spiral of size and weight for all factors that is never ending. To carry all that mass you need a big engine. Your engine is using its power to move the fuel and the vessel. To go faster you now need a bigger engine, and so more fuel, and more space, bigger engine, more fuel, more space, etc...∞. You can't have one without the others. Warping space circumvents the issue by creating a gravity bubble, or something, thus putting you in a state of constant free fall. This still takes whopping great amounts of power which is the reason for the anti-matter power core. A tea-spoon of anti-matter will get a vessel the size of the Saturn V rocket to the moon. I'm only an author, not a scientist and by no means an authority on the subject. There are better and more correct descriptions out there and my understanding of how it works is very limited. If I have not done it justice, very likely, go look it up.

Chapter 12

6. I was extremely thrilled to be allowed on the bridge during launch. I'm not entirely certain how this happened. I originally thought I was just lucky or had won some kind of lottery. Then I thought it was due to the amazing assistance of one Patrick "Pops" McKenna. He's a retired Marine gone correspondent. He aided me from the very beginning of journey. I was only a small time reporter for my home town of Haven and had zero experience on the outside world beyond college. He helped me get a good ride to Olympus Space Port orbiting Earth. From there he got me a ride to *Alameda* with

a man named Boris. I later found out was Captain Artus' personal pilot, but I digress. Pops was helpful all through voyage and kept an eye on me. We have become fast friends. It was not until the Bismarck returned home from parts unknown that my placement on the bridge was by design, but that is part of another story.

Chapter 13

7. FS-18 CA – The official designation of the Capellan Armaments Joint Strike 18. The 'F' stands for fighter. The 'S' stands for space. 18 is the design number. 'CA' is the manufacturer code. The reason for calling them by their colloquial designation – Joint Strike 18 – is because the Mission Design Series protocols are not understood by the majority of the public. The FS-18's primary purpose is a strike mission. It can be easily rearmed for interception or space superiority missions, so the 'F' code is used. I had originally used the official designation, but early readings by others showed that they simply didn't get it. I have included the official designation here as a proper reference.

Chapter 21

8. The Cauldron was the largest land battle on Titan during the Capellan Station Incident.

9. I was present for this meeting between Astaroth and Patrick "Pops" McKenna. The mysterious Astaroth, whom I had not met before this day, knew my name. He was and still is very scary. Imagine how I felt when this man called me by name. The heated discussion between these two men revealed what really happened on Capellan Station to the world at large; in a manner of speaking since many of Earths media correspondents were present. The resulting reaction from everyone else was a feeling of denial, betrayal, and sorrow. I had originally planned to discuss this meeting and the Capellan Station Incident at length in this volume, but it slowed things down considerably since it is only loosely associated with this event. It's telling isn't necessary at this time. Perhaps an anthology.

TIMELINE:

2039 – Cataclysm

January 18, 2169 – Carpathian steals the *Sol Defensor*

April 16, 2308 – Capellan Armaments employees mount an armed revolt against their employer's sparking the Capellan Station Incident.

November, 2318 – Ensign Valerie Heinz stationed at Far Reach Gamma for supply duty to *Outpost Lima*. There is a riot on *Outpost Lima* with some deaths. Senator Whitney is arrested soon after.

May, 2319 – Ensign Heinz is transferred to the EFN *CC6 Bismarck*. All records of her previous assignment are non-existent.

July 11, 2319 – Journal of Commander Artus, entry #1.

July 25, 2319 – Cmdr. Artus is arrested in a bar at Moon Base Armstrong. No charges are made and no legal liberties are granted.

August 1, 2319 – After being released from custody, Cmdr. Artus sees and sets foot on *CC6 Bismarck* for the first time. He meets his senior officers.

October 4, 2319 – An emergency is reported on the Rigil Kentaurus colony. *Bismarck's* schedule is rushed forward and emergency supplies are given. The *Bismarck* sets sail on its maiden voyage. Commander Artus is promoted to Captain during pre-launch ceremonies.

October 10, 2319 – Admiral Kethis, his command team, and a contingent of elite Iksus Council Guards wake after spending four years in cryogenic stasis. The Admiral begins a march to an outpost and begins to prepare for the arrival of his people's invasion fleet.

October 25, 2319 – Artus' first meeting with Lieutenant Commander Reyla Hudson does not go well. They quickly make compromises to her orders, which are revealed to be more like commands than orders.

November 1-2, 2319 – *Bismarck* transits the warp gate system and arrives in Rigil Kentaurus. Lt. Cmdr. Hudson gives a briefing that reveals that Humanity is not alone in the universe and will shortly be under invasion from an aggressive alien race.

November 3, 2319 – The *Black Jack* is spotted pushing a sizable space rock toward the second planet of Kentaurus Beta Two.

November 5, 2319 – The Iksus invasion begins to arrive. The Kentaurus Beta Two ground battle begins.

November 5-6, 2319 – Admiral Kethis flees the planet. Ensign Heinz arrives at the Earth Defense Fleet and is provided with a newer, faster, heavily armed transport. Colonel Richards is killed.

November 6, 2319 – Lieutenant William Steiger is the last capable officer and takes effective command of the 1st Colony Support Battalion. Ensign Heinz arrives in the super-awesome *Invasion Support Carrier*. With the help of Compy the AI she saves the day.

November 9, 2319 – The *Black Jack*, commanded by the very old and much alive Carpathian, goes to war.

November 11, 2319 – Under the orders of Admiral Fleming the warp gate back home to Earth is destroyed.

November 12, 2319 – Admiral Fleming and a third of the Second Fleet are killed protecting the fleeing civilian ships. Captain Artus is left in command of a meager task group and civilian freighters attempting to reach Proximal Centauri. Admiral Kethis analyzes his victory and begins to build his base of operations.

TERMS:

Brevet/Brevetting/Frocking – A promotion to higher rank without the associated pay rise. Most often seen in combat situations where a ranking individual is no longer able to perform their duty, so the next able person takes their place. One who is brevetted is of rank, but in name and authority only. It is usually temporary. If the powers that be decide to allow the rank to stay in place, the concerned individual must take the necessary classes and appear before a review board. All personnel are treated as being brevetted upon their next regular increase in rank or rate. In the navy this is traditionally known as "frocking". They wear their next insignia and device, and have the authority that comes with it, but do not get paid for that rank/rate until a grace period of approximately six months has passed. The grace period is to insure that the individual in question is able to perform their greater responsibilities.

Conn – Location of control of the ship, usually from the bridge. Whoever has the conn is the one responsible for the ship.

Iksus/Iksu – Iksu is the singular form of Iksus. Iksu is also the name of the Iksus ancestral home. There is debate as to whether the planet is named after the people or vice versa. Also of debate is use of the singular for both an individual and the planet.

Unarem – A word from the ancient and dying language of the Marna. The closest translation is universe. I'm told there is more to it than just a word, but it used as the galactic term for the universe at large.

ABBREVIATIONS:

APA – Articulated Power Arm

CAB – Combat Action Badge

CAPT/Capt. – Captain, Navy

Capt. – Captain, Marines

CAR – Combat Action Ribbon

CDR – Commander, Navy

CIC – Combat Information Center

CMC – Command Master Chief

Cmdr. – Commander, Navy

COL – Colonel, Army

CPT – Captain, Army

DFC – Distinguished Flying Cross

DSC – Distinguished Service Cross

EFA – Earth Federal Army

EFN – Earth Federal Navy

EFNMC – Earth Federal Navy Marine Corps

ENS – Ensign, Navy

FLNU – First Last Name Unknown

KIA – Killed in Action

LCDR – Lieutenant Commander

LT – Lieutenant

Lt. Cmdr. – Lieutenant Commander

LTJG – Lieutenant junior grade

MH – Medal of Honor

MSgt. – Master Sergeant, Marines

NAM – Navy Achievement Medal

NSWC – Naval Special Warfare Command

SA – Seaman Apprentice

SCPO – Senior Chief Petty Officer

W – Wounded in Action

Acknowledgements

I would first like thank my family and friends for putting up with me in this endeavor. I have not always been the easiest of people to live with and while writing this I got worse. I want them to know that any proceeds earned from this venture will be spent to make me and, by extension, them happy. Of particular note are my grandmother, mother, and two aunts – all teachers – who helped in the editing process.

My brother has been a tremendous help and vast source of knowledge, both factual and mundane. His service in the United States Navy has provided insight and context to information that, while public, isn't the easiest to find or understand without knowing the right questions to ask or the language.

To that end I would also like to thank the U.S. Navy for doing such a swell job. I must add that I find the use of both the sound powered phone and the bureaucratic, yet simple, means of communicating on a ship to be most impressive. I would also like to give all members of the United States armed forces a pat on the back and a cookie, but that would far exceed my finances and poor physical endurance. So, I'll pat my brother on the back and give myself the cookie. I would like to point out that I didn't go into detail about the sound powered phones in this book, but they're there.

Not least amongst this list of persons and entities to which I owe thanks is Emily Rollen. She provided a traditional edit of my work. If it weren't for her I would have had to go into debt just to break even.

Last and sadly least is my oldest friend of twenty-five plus years, Joe.

If it were not for his tiresome sarcasm about my labors being finished; or not as the case often was; then I likely would have suffered less stress. Well to him I say, "It is done... It really it is this time, honest." To which he'll reply, "But this is a series, isn't it?"